P...

Breath...

"Karyn Henley spins a lyrical young-adult tale of mythical and legendary beings, of reimagined angels and terrifying malevolents, in a small kingdom where the world's fate rests on a young priestess's shoulders."

—KATHY TYERS, author of *Shivering World* and the Firebird series

"Karyn Henley's novel starts with a jolt, grabs the reader by the collar, and doesn't slow down one minute. This author infuses her text with imagery, suspense, and a cast that will appeal to all ages. In addition, it has a feeling that I can only describe as "folklorish," with all the best elements that come with that—music, magic, and mystery. I think it's destined to become a classic."

—KATHI APPELT, author of *The Underneath,* National Book Award finalist, Newbery Honor Book, PEN USA Award

"This lusciously written fantasy has it all: epic battles, earthbound angels, immortal humans, and a bright, engaging heroine. Henley's young priestess-turned-warrior is forced to put her past together like a jigsaw puzzle with pieces so sharp they cut. Her story is nearly impossible to forget, so readers will be eager for more!"

—LOUISE HAWES, author of *Black Pearls: a Faerie Strand,* AAUW Juvenile Literature Award nominee; Gold Award, Hall of Fame, teensreadtoo.com

YA FIC Henle

Henley, K.
Breath of angel.

PRICE: $10.99 (3559/he   )

BREATH OF ANGEL

ANGELAEON CIRCLE
BOOK ONE

BREATH OF ANGEL

A NOVEL

KARYN HENLEY

WATERBROOK
PRESS

BREATH OF ANGEL
PUBLISHED BY WATERBROOK PRESS
12265 Oracle Boulevard, Suite 200
Colorado Springs, Colorado 80921

The characters and events in this book are fictional, and any resemblance to actual persons or events is coincidental.

ISBN 978-0-307-73012-1
ISBN 978-0-307-73013-8 (electronic)

Copyright © 2011 by Karyn Henley

Cover design by Kristopher K. Orr; cover photography by Mike Heath, Magnus Creative.

All rights reserved. No part of this book may be reproduced or transmitted in any form or by any means, electronic or mechanical, including photocopying and recording, or by any information storage and retrieval system, without permission in writing from the publisher.

Published in the United States by WaterBrook Multnomah, an imprint of the Crown Publishing Group, a division of Random House Inc., New York.

WATERBROOK and its deer colophon are registered trademarks of Random House Inc.

Library of Congress Cataloging-in-Publication Data
Henley, Karyn.
   Breath of angel / Karyn Henley. — 1st ed.
      p. cm. — (The Angelaeon circle ; bk. 1)
   Summary: In a land of angels and humans, shape shifters and sylvans, warring brothers have destroyed the only portal to heaven, stranding tortured souls on earth, and only sixteen-year-old chantress Melaia—half angel and half human—can restore it.
      ISBN 978-0-307-73012-1 (alk. paper) — ISBN 978-0-307-73013-8 (electronic : alk. paper)
   [1. Angels—Fiction. 2. Fantasy.] I. Title.
PZ7.H3895Br 2011
[Fic] — dc22

                              2011000430

Printed in the United States of America
2011—First Edition

10 9 8 7 6 5 4 3 2 1

*With gratitude to my Vermont College
of Fine Arts friends and mentors,
angels all.*

Camrithia

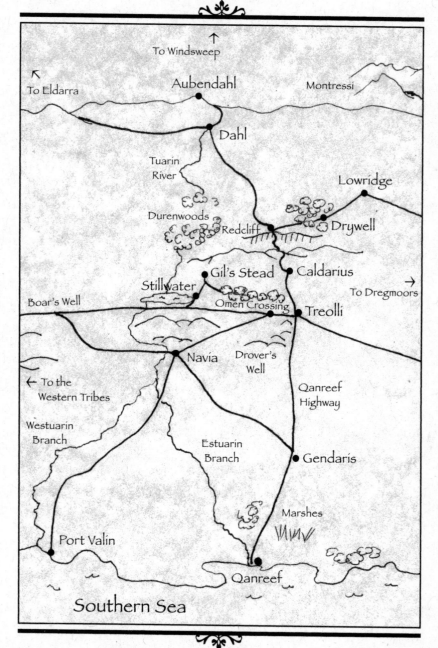

CAST OF CHARACTERS

Benasin: Advisor to the overlord of Navia.

Caepio: Leader of an acting troupe that travels Camrithia.

Cilla: Serving woman to the nobility at the palace in Qanreef.

Dandreij: The firstborn son of legend, who ate a seed from the fruit of the Wisdom Tree and became immortal.

Dreia: One of the Archae. Guardian of plant life, including the Wisdom Tree.

Dwin: Fifteen-year-old brother of Trevin and aide to Lord Rejius.

Earthbearer: One of the Archae. Guardian of ground and underground; also known as the Lord of the Under-Realm.

Esper: A sylvan earth-angel. Wife of Noll.

Flametender: One of the Archae. Guardian of fire.

Gerda: Dwarf. Angelaeon. Wife of Gil.

Gil: Dwarf. Angelaeon.

Hanamel (Hanni): High priestess of the city of Navia.

Iona: Fourteen-year-old novice priestess from Navia.

Jarrod: Nephili. Priest in the city of Redcliff. Admitted to the ranks of Angelaeon as Exousia, a warrior and keeper of history.

Laetham: King of Camrithia.

Livia: A servant-messenger of the lower order of angels.

Melaia: Sixteen-year-old priestess and chantress of the temple at Navia.

Noll: A sylvan earth-angel. Steward of the Durenwoods.

Nuri: Twelve-year-old novice priestess from Navia.

Paullus: Tavern-keeper at the Full Sail in Qanreef. An angel not committed to Angelaeon or malevolents.

Peron: Six-year-old novice priestess from Navia.

Pymbric (Pym): Armsman to Main Undrian.

Rejius: The king's physician.

Seaspinner: One of the Archae. Guardian of water.

Silas: Overlord of the city of Navia.

Stalia: Daughter of the Firstborn of legend. Became immortal after eating a seed from the fruit of the Wisdom Tree.

Trevin: Twenty-year-old kingsman who serves Lord Rejius.

Undrian: A comain of Camrithia. Commander of men-at-arms.

Windweaver: One of the Archae. Guardian of wind.

Yareth: Son of the overlord of Navia.

Zastra: Queen mother of Camrithia.

THE ANGELAEON

FIRST SPHERE: The three highest ranks are not strictly angels but winged heavenly beings who serve in the presence of the Most High.

CHERUBIM
Guard light and
sound (music)

SERAPHIM
Personal servants
of the Most High

OPHANIM
Guard celestial
travel

SECOND SPHERE:

KURIOTES
Regulate duties of
lower angels and
govern worlds

ARCHAE
Guardians of the
world's elements:
wind, fire, water,
plant life, and earth

THRONOS
Negotiators and
justice-bearers

THIRD SPHERE:

EXOUSIA
Warriors and
keepers of history

ARCHANGELS
Guardians of people
groups; influential in
politics and commerce

ANGELS
Messengers

WORLD SPHERE:

NEPHILI

The "clouded ones"; half-angel, half-human

SYLVANS

Elflike earth-angels; inhabit forests and woodlands

WINDWINGS

Winged horses

BREATH
OF
ANGEL

CHAPTER 1

The prick of the thorn drew blood, but Melaia smiled. The last ramble rose of the season was well worth a pierced thumb. She carefully drew the blossom from the vine that clung to the side of the temple. As she breathed its rich, sweet scent, she sensed someone watching and looked up, expecting to see one of the novice priestesses. She saw only dry leaves skittering across the flagstones of the walled courtyard, along with a black feather, no doubt from a bird scavenging seeds in the woodpile.

Then a haggard young man stepped through the gate, and Melaia drew back. The chill autumn breeze riffled the edge of his dirt-stained cloak, revealing the corner of a journey pack and the hilt of a dagger.

Melaia gave him a tentative nod.

"I've come—" His voice was dirt dry. He wiped his fist across his mouth.

"I'll fetch water." Melaia tucked the rose into her waist sash and headed for the stone urn by the arched doorway. "Travelers are always welcome at our temple. We've pallets if you wish to stay the night." She would have to check with the high priestess, but Hanni rarely turned away weary travelers.

"My thanks," the man croaked.

Melaia flipped back her loose honey brown braid and dipped a pottery cup into the cool water. "I'm chantress here, always eager to hear new tales from travelers."

The young man looked too weary to tell tales. Or too ill. His dark-ringed eyes darted from one afternoon shadow to another, and he cocked his head as if he heard something beyond the walls.

"We're healers here as well," she offered.

For a moment his wild eyes focused on her. Then he glanced above her head, and his hand went to his dagger.

But he never drew it.

A hawk, larger than any she'd ever seen, shot like an arrow past Melaia and sank its talons into the stranger's chest. The man's raw screams pierced the air as the hawk's beak knifed at his throat.

Melaia stood stunned and speechless. But as the hawk flapped its great wings and lifted the man a handbreadth off the flagstones, her senses surged back.

She snatched a branch from the woodpile and swung it at the hawk. The raptor screeched and dropped the stranger. "Fight!" she yelled at him. "Fight back!"

But it was the hawk that fought, its wings beating at her stick as its claws snagged the man again. At last Melaia struck a solid blow to the hawk's head, and it skidded sideways. She chased after it, but the raptor took to the air, quickly rose, and soared away over the domed roof of the temple.

Melaia flung aside the stick and fell to her knees by the bloodied man. Then she covered her mouth and swallowed a bitter taste. "Most High, have mercy," she croaked. Seeing wounds so deep and blood flowing freely, she wasn't surprised that the stranger's mistlike spirit had emerged from his body. As a death-prophet, she could see the shadowy echo writhing around his form as he struggled to live.

"Mellie? Is it safe?" Dark-eyed Iona stood in the temple doorway, holding back the other two novices. At fourteen, she was the motherly one, although Melaia was two years older. Curly-haired Peron, still baby plump at six, peered around Iona, clutching her skirts, while twelve-year-old Nuri broke away from them and ran across the yard, her usual dimpled smile gone.

"Is he dead?" Nuri asked.

"Not yet," Melaia told her. "Take Peron and fetch a basket of plumwort. And water."

Nuri stared at the man's wounds. "We saw the hawk."

"Go!" said Melaia. "I need plumwort to stanch the bleeding."

As Nuri dashed away, Melaia wondered why the high priestess hadn't appeared. "Where's Hanni?" she called to Iona.

"Summoned to a birthing. The weaver's wife." Iona nervously twisted the end of her black braid.

"Then come help me carry the man inside."

Melaia hesitated. She was often called to the bedside of the dying to confirm the moment of death, but never had she been required to reach through a spirit to touch someone. Of course, other people did it all the time, she told herself. They just couldn't see the struggling, mistlike layer. She took a deep breath, grasped the man's bloodied cloak, and pressed it to the gashes in his chest. His spirit pooled around her wrists, vibrating like a throat quivering with speech.

"Can you hear me?" Melaia asked, keeping pressure on his wound.

The stranger's spirit thrummed frantically, as if he were trying to say something.

"Where's the plumwort?" Melaia yelled.

Nuri ran across the yard, sloshing a jar of water. Peron trotted behind her with the basket of plumwort. Iona knelt at the man's feet, her mouth moving silently in prayer.

Melaia reached for the plumwort, but the man's spirit slid off his body, thinned into a stream, and seeped through a crack in the flagstones. A sudden, grim silence fell over the yard. Melaia shook her head at Nuri and Peron and closed the man's green-flecked eyes.

Peron stuck out her lower lip. "I was too slow."

"No, I was." Nuri's shoulders drooped.

"No one's at fault," said Melaia, but she couldn't help thinking that the man might still be alive if she had only laid into the hawk sooner. "Let's get him inside." She lifted his upper body. For his bulk he was surprisingly light.

Iona lifted his legs. "Starved twig-thin," she said. "Poor man."

They carried the stranger to the sanctuary altar, the bier for those who could afford no better. Melaia took a deep breath, wishing Hanni were there. "Iona, find me a winding-sheet," she said. "Peron, go with Nuri. Fetch more water and scrub the courtyard."

"But it's bloody," said Nuri. Peron wrinkled her nose.

"Would you rather clean the man's body?" asked Melaia. Nuri and Peron scrambled out the door. Iona followed.

Melaia gently eased the man's cloak from his chest and winced, wondering where Hanni would begin. She exhaled slowly. "Start with the easiest," she murmured.

She untangled his pack from one forearm. As she slipped it free, she noticed the end of a small scroll clenched in his fist. "First the pack," she told herself, glancing around. Her gaze fell on a shelf of incense bowls. She stashed the pack there, then turned back to the altar-bier and froze.

The stranger's cloak had fallen back and, with it, a long, white, blood-stained wing.

Melaia's knees almost buckled. "An angel?" she whispered. It couldn't be. Angels were found only in legends. Chanters' stories. Bedtime tales.

Iona's voice echoed down the corridor. "Do we need more water?"

Melaia jerked the cloak back around the man.

Iona strode in with a bundle of white linen. "Do we need more water?"

"We need Hanni," said Melaia.

"You look as if you've seen the man's ghost." Iona looked around. "Has he returned?"

"Just go get Hanni."

ↄ৵ঽ

Distant drums signaled the closing of Navia's city gates and the change of watch on the walls. On the altar-bier in the temple, the winged man lay serene and clean, covered in white linen up to his chin. Melaia didn't often sit with the dead, but as she lit the oil lamps behind the bier, she decided that tonight she would request a vigil. She hoped the high priestess would join her, for she had a night's worth of questions to ask.

But so far, the high priestess hadn't returned. She had sent Iona back to say that the birthing was a difficult one and she must stay with it, although she was upset at the news of a death in the side yard. Hanni intended to stop by the overlord's villa and bring his advisor, Benasin, back to the temple with her.

As Melaia held the flaming twist of rushweed to the last wick, she eyed the three girls munching their supper on a reed mat across the room. With Hanni gone they had asked to stay with Melaia instead of eating in the hearthroom down the hall. She was glad for their company. She felt as shaky as they did, although she hadn't told them about the stranger's wings. She wanted Hanni's opinion first.

Melaia tossed the spent rushweed into the brazier in the center of the room and stirred the coals into flame. For a moment she watched the smoke curl up and drift like a dying spirit out through the roof hole above. Except dying spirits always drifted down, not up.

"I'm saving my scraps for the chee-dees," Peron said, scooping her crumbs into a tiny hill.

"Fetch your crumb jar from the storeroom, then," said Melaia. "When you've finished cleaning up, I'll tell a story."

Peron stared warily at the dark corridor that lay beyond the bier.

"I'll go with you." Nuri slipped one of the lamps from its niche. With an uneasy smile she guided Peron to the corridor, giving wide berth to the bier.

Iona stoppered the olive oil. "Peron is telling tales again. This time it's about two falcons scaring away her songbird friends."

"She must have been inspired by the hawk in the yard today." Melaia stacked the empty wooden bowls and glanced at the stranger who should have eaten a meal with them tonight.

"Peron said the falcons were darker than closed eyes," said Iona.

"I can picture that." Melaia lifted her harp from its peg.

"And they had people hands." Iona rolled her eyes.

"That I can't picture," said Melaia. "Too ghoulish."

Iona laughed. "With such an imagination Peron will surely become a chantress."

A shriek came from the corridor. Peron darted into the room, hugging her crumb jar, with Nuri on her heels. Both girls were open-mouthed and wide-eyed.

Behind them limped a sharp-nosed, beardless man wearing a cloak fashioned completely of feathers—brown, black, and an iridescent blue that glinted in the lamplight. The skin around one of his round gold eyes was blackened, and a scratch jagged across his brow.

Melaia went cold, head to toe. How had the man entered? Had she left the side door unbolted?

Nuri and Peron ran to Iona, and all three huddled by the wall. Melaia stifled her impulse to join them. Hanni had left her in charge, so in charge she would be. She had fought off a murdering hawk. She had prepared a bloody winged man for burial. She would stand up to this intruder.

She strode to the brazier, her hands clammy as she clung to her harp. "This is the temple of the Most High," she said, hoping he wouldn't hear the quaver in her voice.

"So it is," he hissed, limping to the bier. "I believe I noticed that."

"What's your business here?"

He raised an eyebrow. "Surely you're not the high priestess."

"She's the chantress," blurted Peron.

"Ah. Singer of songs, soother of sorrows," he crooned.

"If you're here for our treasury box, take it and be on your way," said Melaia.

"I have unfinished business with the high priestess," he said.

"You can find her at the overlord's villa," said Melaia.

"No doubt." With a gloved hand he slid back the sheet that covered the corpse. He smiled at the gashes, then studied Melaia. "Chantress, play your harp for me."

Melaia gaped at him. "You have no right—"

"Or let me play it," he said. "The little girl can bring it. The one who feeds the birds."

Peron's eyes grew round as the supper bowls, and she shrank behind Iona's skirts.

Melaia hugged the harp tighter to her chest and glared at the man defiantly, even as she fought back a fear that curdled in the pit of her stomach. How long had this swaggerer been spying on them?

His unblinking gold eyes stared back at her. "I do not take disobedience lightly." His voice was ice. "Send the girl with the harp or play it yourself."

Melaia swallowed dryly. She felt her courage fall as limp as the poor stranger in the yard. Keeping her eyes on the intruder, she sank to a bench by the brazier and positioned the harp in her lap.

"Let us hear the tale of the Wisdom Tree," he said. "You know it, don't you, Chantress?"

Melaia scowled at him and motioned for the girls to join her. As she fingered the melody, they silently gathered around, and she breathed easier. Together they were safer, with the brazier as a barrier between them and the bully. She turned her attention back to the harp, and over the music she spoke the tale.

In a time long ago, there lived a tribal chieftain whose firstborn son was a wealthy trader, his second-born a lone hunter. Each year at harvest festival, his sons vied to present him with the best gift. The Firstborn always gave perfumes, musicians, slave dancers, the treasures of his trade. The Second-born presented partridges, deerskins, lion-claw necklaces, the spoils of the hunt. But the Second-born thought his gifts paltry compared to those of the Firstborn. So he set out to seek the greatest gift of all.

Far and wide he journeyed, to no avail. At last, weary and discouraged, he lay to rest in the shade of a tree as tall and wide as the tower of a citadel. The Wisdom Tree it was, bearing fruit that granted the eater knowledge and cleverness.

Peron popped her thumb out of her mouth and chanted, "Within this tree stood the stairway to heaven made wholly of light."

"Exactly," said Melaia, glad that for the moment the tale was distracting Peron from the intruder, whose gold eyes held a hungry glitter. Melaia continued:

An angel named Dreia, guardian of the Tree, saw the Second son lying there and asked the cause of his despair. When he told his tale, she pitied him and gave him the juice of one fruit. "This will grant you knowledge and cleverness to find the right gift for your father," she said. As he sipped the juice, the man's eyes brightened. "I know the perfect gift," he said. "A fruit from this Tree."

Dreia hadn't intended to give the man a whole fruit. Its seeds were precious, carried by angels into the heavens to plant wisdom trees in worlds among the stars. Yet the man was handsome, his entreaties eloquent.

At last Dreia said, "You may take one fruit if you vow to bring me the first creature that greets you when you arrive home. This I shall send over the stairway as payment. Moreover, you shall return the three seeds of this fruit, for they are strictly forbidden to mortals. Should you fail to repay your debt, the Tree itself shall exact payment in breath and blood."

The Second-born agreed to the bargain, for the one who always greeted his homecoming was his old hunting dog. Taking his dog and the seeds back to Dreia would be good reason to see the beautiful angel again. So he carried the fruit home.

While he was still afar off, he saw, bounding across the field to greet him, his young niece. "Uncle!" she cried. "Terrible news. Your old hunting dog has died."

The Second-born fell to his knees and wept, not for his dog, but for his niece, the only daughter of the Firstborn, now to be payment for his debt.

Melaia paused as the intruder slipped off his gloves. His fingernails were long, curved, and sharp. Talons. Her pulse pounded at her throat. His blackened eye, his scratched brow, his feathered cloak, his limp.

She had met him before. As a hawk.

"Is there no ending to the tale?" He smirked at her recognition of him and stroked the corpse. "I favor endings."

Melaia felt foggy, as if she were in a dream. She tried to gather her thoughts.

"The Second-born knew only one way to escape his debt," Iona prompted.

"Yes." Melaia cleared her throat and forced out the words.

The Second-born knew he had to destroy the Wisdom Tree.

Dreia saw an army approaching, the Second son in the lead, betrayal in his heart. She gathered what angels she could. Some plucked the remaining fruit and hastened over the stairway to celestial worlds. Others stayed behind to defend the Tree. But these were not warring angels. The best they could do was save some of the wood as the Tree fell and was plundered by men who wanted pieces for themselves.

"That was the end of the stairway," Nuri said.

"And the end of angels in our world," added Iona.

"But the brothers planted the seeds of the Wisdom Tree," offered Peron, "didn't they?"

"They did." Melaia set the harp aside. "The brothers learned that cultivating wisdom takes patience."

The girls chimed in, "Wisdom, over time, is earned."

The hawkman hissed. "A pitiful ending and woefully false." He pointed a taloned finger at Melaia. "Remember this, Chantress. The Second-born abducted his niece and headed for Dreia. But fortune was with the Firstborn, for I discovered the treachery in time to rescue my daughter. To ensure that the Tree never collected on the debt, I destroyed it. My daughter and I ate the seeds, round and shiny, red as blood. We became immortal!"

"You're trying to haunt us with our own tale." Melaia took up a poker and stabbed the coals in the brazier, determined not to show her fear. "There were three seeds."

"So there were," said the hawkman. "The third I crammed down my brother's throat. Now he owes his debt for all eternity. And it is my pleasure to make sure he never repays." He grinned at the dead man. "Son of Dreia, this night you are destroyed."

He snatched up the corpse, and its wings unfolded. The girls shrieked and ran to Melaia.

The hawkman dropped the body back to the bier as if it had burned him. Then he cursed and shoved it to the floor. He scanned the room. "The man had a pack. Where is it?"

"Maybe he lost it in the side yard." Melaia felt her face grow warm at the half lie.

But the man didn't press his search. Instead, he stiffened and stared at the front door, his head cocked, listening. Melaia heard only wind, but the hawkman slowly retreated, tense as a cat backing away from danger. He glanced from the door to the window to the roof hole, where smoke drifted into the night. Then he hurtled toward the brazier, and his body contorted.

All of Melaia's instincts screamed at her to run, but she stayed her feet, clenched her jaw, and gripped the poker with both hands. As the hawk leaped into the flames, she swung with all her might.

She struck only air as he rose in the smoke and vanished.

CHAPTER 2

Melaia was still gaping at the roof hole, watching smoke swirl away, when Benasin, the overlord's advisor, barged into the sanctuary like a dog on the hunt, his windblown dark hair giving him a wild look.

The high priestess swept in after him and slipped off her gold-trimmed blue cloak. She paused to catch her breath, her almond-eyed gaze trailing him around the room as he inspected every nook. "You run like a young man, Benasin," she said. "What did you sense?" When he gave no answer, she turned to Melaia. "What's happening?"

The other girls all spoke at once, pointing at the roof hole. "Strange man—" "Gold eyes—" "Up there—" The words bobbed like apples in water.

"And the other man, he has wings," said Peron, pointing at the stranger on the bier.

"The cloaked man called him Dreia's son," explained Melaia. "He started to take the body, then changed his mind."

"No wonder in that." Benasin squatted beside the corpse. "Your visitor saw the wings and knew his mistake. Dreia's son doesn't have wings."

"Who is the winged man?" asked Melaia.

"I intend to find out," said Benasin. "He's one of the angels, that's certain."

"Angels are real, then." Nuri frowned at Melaia. "You said your stories were just legend."

"I thought they were." Melaia knelt beside Benasin. "You spoke of Dreia as if she's real."

"She is," said Benasin. "Legend is often based on truth."

"But according to legend, Dreia is an angel," Melaia pointed out. "So her son would be too. Wouldn't he have wings?"

"Mellie, for once try to hold back your questions," said Hanni.

"It's all right, Hanamel," said Benasin. "The girls deserve answers for what they've seen."

"You have answers?" asked Hanni.

"Some." Benasin gently lifted the corpse and laid it back on the bier. "To start, few angels have wings. This one happens to be an Erielyon, one of the lower ranks of angels. A simple messenger. Erielyon are the only winged angels."

Iona stepped gingerly toward the bier. "I've never seen an angel before."

"How would you know, if they don't have wings?" asked Nuri.

"I wish I had wings." Peron snuggled up to Melaia and put her thumb in her mouth.

"That would make you the lowest rank," said Nuri. "I'd rather be higher."

"How many ranks are there?" Melaia stroked Peron's silky hair.

Benasin eyed Hanni. "You've not schooled your charges in the histories?"

"It's all I can do to train them in herbs and rites. We've little time for histories. As for angels, they should stay in tales." Hanni sank to the bench at the brazier and stared weary eyed at the stranger.

"But the tale of the Wisdom Tree," said Melaia. "Is it in the histories? Is it true?"

"The part about no more angels in the world is obviously wrong," said Iona.

The girls began guessing which parts of the tale were true, which false. Hanni flapped her hands at them as if shooing chicks. "Off with you now. To your prayers and pallets."

As Melaia herded the girls out, Hanni caught her arm. "You'll be wanted here," she said. "Iona will take charge."

Melaia followed Hanni to the bier, where Benasin was examining the angel's wounds. Melaia cringed at the sight of the gashes. Even though she had cleansed them, it took all her willpower to keep from turning away.

"Hanamel told me about the hawk." Benasin glanced at Melaia. "You saw the attack?"

"Hanni was at a birthing. The girls came running when they heard the screams. I don't know how much they saw, but…" She bit her lip. A hawkman sounded imaginary. Yet before tonight angels had existed only in legend. "The man who was here tonight is the hawk that killed the angel."

Benasin's face hardened. "You're sure?" He searched her eyes.

"His face was scratched, and he limped," said Melaia. "It was my doing. I chased away the hawk with a stick."

A smile flickered at the corners of Benasin's mouth. "Shameful, being beaten away by a priestess." He drew the sheet over the Erielyon's chest.

"But a hawk who becomes a man?" Hanni shook her head. "It can't be."

"You're right," said Benasin. "He's more likely a man who becomes a hawk."

"Wonderful." Hanni held up her hands in exasperation. "Why now, Benasin? Why here?"

"Should I know the why of it?" he asked.

Hanni shook a finger at him. "Don't trifle with me. You're one of them. You're—" She glanced at Melaia.

Benasin raised his eyebrows.

Hanni's gaze locked onto Benasin's. "You're an angel, and you know more than you're saying."

Melaia stared at Benasin. "Do you have wings?"

He glanced over his shoulder. "I had none the last time I looked."

"Benasin is not an Erielyon," said Hanni.

"Angels are of different races," said Benasin. "For the most part they move about undetected."

"And they live extremely long lives," said Hanni.

"But they can be killed." Melaia eyed the Erielyon.

"True," said Benasin. "Angels can be killed in physical form, which is how most appear in the world these days. But if they can avoid getting themselves killed, then, as far as I know, their time here is unlimited. I tend to think of myself as immortal." Benasin stroked his close-trimmed beard. "This winged one was no doubt a messenger. Did he say anything before he died?"

"He tried." Melaia shivered at the memory of his vibrating spirit. "He carried a pack." She retrieved it from the shelf and handed it to Benasin.

He drew out a thin, palm-sized wooden box.

"A money box," said Hanni.

"A codex, rather." Benasin lifted the lid and thumbed through leaves of papyrus. "A book." He closed the wooden cover and held it out for Hanni to see.

Melaia leaned in to look. A *V* with a line running straight up the center was carved into the ruddy cover.

"The sign of the Tree," said Hanni. "I guess I shouldn't be surprised."

"I know this book," said Benasin. "It's Dreia's. I expected her to send her son here, not the book. It seems, instead, that we have the book and not the son."

"You expected Dreia?" Hanni's mouth dropped open.

"You know Dreia?" Melaia asked.

Benasin made no answer as he leafed through the book.

"He knows her quite well," Hanni said as if it were an accusation.

"You assume I know more than I'm telling," said Benasin. "I assure you, I know very little."

"I'm aware that angels can't know things that depend on human choice." Hanni narrowed her eyes at him. "But don't you have insight into the spiritual realm?"

"Are you worried Dreia will come here for her book?" asked Benasin.

"An angel dies in our courtyard, an intruder frightens my girls, says he has unfinished business with me, and disturbs a corpse." Hanni paced to the brazier, then whirled around. "Who under the Most High has unfinished business with me?"

"Who indeed?" muttered Benasin.

Melaia glanced back and forth between Benasin and Hanni. She had never seen the high priestess so agitated. Both Hanni and Benasin seemed to have forgotten she was present.

"It's my duty to protect this temple and my priestesses," said Hanni. "I do not wish to be mixed up in the disputes of angels. You of all people—of all—"

"Beings?" Benasin seemed amused.

Hanni huffed. "You of all the creatures that roam this wild world should understand."

Melaia bit her lip. Hanni's sharp, direct observations intimidated most people, but Benasin was unruffled. He obviously knew he had to brave some thorns to reach Hanni's soft side.

"Dreia is an enigma to me," said Benasin. "She's always coming up with these sayings." He thumped the book.

"I'm not talking about sayings, and you know it," said Hanni. "I thought I was done with angels."

"Except for me?" he asked.

Hanni rubbed her forehead and sighed. "Except for you. Yes. But I do not want this, Benasin." She pointed to the Erielyon. "Do something. Take the corpse."

Melaia cleared her throat. "There's one thing more." They both looked at her as if she had just arrived. "When I cleansed the body, I saw a scroll in his fist. I left it there."

Benasin set the book aside and uncovered the corpse.

"It will be tight bound by now." Hanni joined Benasin, who worked with the angel's fist.

As Melaia looked on, Benasin inched a crumpled scroll from the angel's grip. He unrolled it and read, "Now is payment due in full."

"Well enough, then," said Hanni. "It's no secret that you wager, Benasin. I would say your debts have caught up with you."

"I've paid all. All but one." Benasin looked askance at Melaia. "You have no debts, have you?"

"Me?" Melaia blinked at him. "I've never wagered or borrowed—"

"I thought not. Yet the messenger was approaching you with the scroll."

"I was the only one in the yard." Melaia tried to rub the chill from her arms. "Besides, he didn't give it to me."

Benasin tucked the scroll into his waist pouch. "Did I not say Dreia was an enigma?" He took up the book again. "I'd like to sit here awhile to see if this book yields any answers. With your permission, Hanamel."

"Of course," said Hanni. "And you'll take the Erielyon's body? Tomorrow?"

Benasin eased himself onto the bench by the brazier. "I'll think on it."

Hanni bolted the front door. "You may retire now, Mellie."

"I thought I would keep vigil." Melaia retrieved her lap harp from the bench. "I'd not be able to sleep anyway. I've seen two angels today."

"Three." Hanni headed to the corridor. "Only an angel can kill an angel."

As Hanni's footfalls faded, Melaia frowned at Benasin. He looked up. "The man who killed the Erielyon…," she said. "He claimed to be the firstborn son of legend. So he wouldn't be an angel, would he?"

"You listened well."

"But Hanni said—"

"Hanamel hears what she wants to hear. She'd like to stuff the dangerous, unkempt world into a pouch and pull the drawstring closed. To keep life tidy. Safe. In her control. Today the drawstring was cut and the bag opened."

Melaia hugged her harp. She had never thought of Hanni in that way.

"Hanamel was wrong on at least two counts," said Benasin. "For one, as you surmised, an angel can also be killed by an immortal."

"The Firstborn is truly immortal, then?" asked Melaia.

"As well as his daughter and his brother, the Second-born."

"And Dreia was truly the guardian of the Tree?"

"She was." Benasin closed the book and patted the bench beside him.

Melaia sat with her harp in her lap, basking in Benasin's presence. She had often thought that if she could choose a father, she would choose him. He was

generous with his money and his encouragement, firm as well as kind, not easily ruffled, and so wise that even Hanni went to him for advice. Besides that,
he always smelled of cedar, warm and woodsy.

"You asked about angels' ranks," he said. "The highest rank are celestial
beings but not truly angels. Dreia is of the Archae, who are in the second rank.
The Archae guard the elements of the world: wind, fire, water, earth, plant life."

"But I thought Dreia guarded the Wisdom Tree."

"She did. She called it her temple. But her guardianship extended to all
plants of the world." He stared into the embers in the brazier. "Tragic was the
day the Second-born asked for the fruit of the Tree; tragic the day Dreia gave it
to him."

Melaia stirred the coals. "Now the brothers are immortal."

"As is their feud."

"Perhaps they will kill each other."

Benasin snorted. "Don't think they haven't tried. Dreia's only hope is to
restore the Tree and its stairway."

"And if she fails?"

"Then your world, and the angels trapped in it, will continue to descend
into the ever-deepening savagery of the immortals' feud."

Melaia squatted at his feet with a new notion. "Would you teach me about
the spirit world?"

He chuckled. "And what would Hanamel say to that?"

Melaia shrugged. "I'm to be high priestess after her. I should know about
the histories. Didn't you say so yourself? I want to know what Hanni can't tell
me."

"Or won't." Benasin patted her head. "First let me take care of the Erielyon's
body for Hanamel. Then we'll see."

"You said Hanni was wrong on two counts. What was the second?"

Benasin glanced at the corridor. "That, for the moment, is better left
unsaid."

CHAPTER 3

Melaia scanned the sky as she led Iona and Nuri into the stubbled field outside Navia to gather wild herbs. Iona was pensive, Nuri talkative—each in her own way reflecting the unease they had all felt since the visit of the cloaked man. Seven days had passed since he had vanished in smoke. Six days had gone by since Benasin had left to take the Erielyon's body, book, and scroll north, where he intended to find Dreia and some answers.

In that time, no one had seen the hawk or the gold-eyed stranger. Still, Melaia shrank from every shadowed corner in the temple, and outdoors she continually eyed the sky. Today two dark birds circled high above, but their flight appeared choppier, their wings more pointed than a hawk's. It was little comfort. She rubbed the goose bumps on her arms.

"I spy plumwort!" Nuri crowed, her dimpled face beaming. She headed toward a patch of purple green leaves. "I'll fill my basket first!"

Melaia glanced at Iona, wondering if she would take up the challenge, but Iona clearly thought Nuri's ways childish. She sidled up to Melaia. "Hanni told me I'll soon be a full-fledged priestess like you. Has she mentioned where she'll send me?"

"No, but with your strong gift of mercy and skill in herbs, you'll be honored wherever you go." Melaia fought a pang of envy. The temple at Navia trained priestesses for service in outlying towns, but as the next high priestess, she herself would stay in Navia, although she felt ill prepared since discovering Hanni had neglected the entire subject of angels and the unseen world. Melaia was eager for Benasin to return so she could press him to school her.

"Perhaps I'll be sent south." Iona knelt to pick orange-berried dreamweed. "I've heard stories of the great sea. I'd like to see ocean waves."

"So would I." Melaia gazed north at the hills on the horizon. Navia was said to be the navel of the kingdom of Camrithia, an equal distance from every border. But it could have been on the moon for all she knew. Only travelers' tales had told her about the rest of the world. The Southern Sea, the hills of Aubendahl, the Davernon River. Winding highways and jovial inns, rugged fortresses and royal palaces. As she watched a cart trace the north road and disappear over a hill tinted with autumn gold, she remembered how she, too, used to dream of where she might be sent as a priestess.

Melaia tugged up a clump of pungent golden-berried saffroot, chiding herself for indulging in childish musings. The fields always made her feel this way. Dreams of journeying stirred and stretched and resisted being sent back to bed. She wondered if Hanni ever felt the desire to leave Navia. How did a high priestess conquer such yearnings?

"Look what I found!" Nuri ran toward them, waving a long black feather that glinted an iridescent blue in the sunlight.

Iona turned to Melaia. "From your hawk?"

"My hawk?"

"You know," said Iona. "The hawk that attacked the angel."

Nuri handed over the feather and ran back to her basket. Melaia shivered as she ran her finger along the edge of the plume. It was as long as her forearm. She eyed the two dark birds circling overhead and slipped the feather under her waist sash like a sword.

⟡

Peron danced up to Melaia the moment she returned to the temple with the older girls and their full herb baskets. "Hanni wants you at once, Mellie," sang Peron, twirling her cloth doll.

"I found a treasure for you," said Nuri. "Melaia has it."

As Nuri followed Iona to the storeroom, Melaia slid the feather out from under her sash.

Peron shrank back, her eyes wide. "Did you see them too?"

"Who?" Melaia set the feather on a bench.

"The hand-birds. I saw them today, but Hanni said not to talk about it."

Melaia took Peron's hand and walked her down the corridor. "Tonight I'll help you with your bird story. We'll put it to song."

"But it's not made-up."

"The birds seemed real, didn't they?"

"They flew down when I was feeding the chee-dees." Peron wrinkled her nose. "They don't have bird feet. They have hands. People hands."

"Of course they do." Melaia thought of the two birds circling the field. No doubt Peron had seen them and invented a story to tame her fears. As Hanni had done with angels. Keep them imaginary and keep them safe. "The next time you see these birds, call me," said Melaia. "I want to see them too."

"Then you can chase them away." Peron skipped ahead to the door at the end of the hall.

"Maybe that's my new gifting," Melaia muttered.

Peron tiptoed into the stillroom, where spicy sweet herbs hung in bunches from the ceiling. Melaia entered clearing her throat, knowing Hanni didn't like to be taken by surprise.

Hanni glanced up, swirling a fragrant potion at a table cluttered with flasks, bowls, and pouches. She nodded at Peron, who began crushing dried herbs in her own small mortar.

"The overlord requests your presence," Hanni told Melaia. "Right away." She poured the golden potion into a small vial and handed it to Melaia.

"Is he ill?" Melaia swirled the vial.

"Probably his stomach again. Take him that saffroot potion. But it's your music he's requested. You know how it soothes him."

Melaia nodded. Music seemed to be an antidote to the cares that racked the overlord. He was one of her favorite patients. Not so his son, Yareth. The arrogant, moon-pale young man made her skin crawl. She hoped Yareth, feigning illness, hadn't asked his father to call for the chantress.

"Quick now." Hanni waved her out. "Go and wash. Wear your blue cloak."

Melaia lost no time cleaning up. With the vial of saffroot tucked into her waist pouch and her harp slung across her back under her priestly cloak, she crossed the flat rooftops that connected the city all the way to the town square. There she descended to the road and made her way to the overlord's villa.

A stern-faced servant led Melaia up two flights of stairs and along one of the upper porches. When he stopped at an arched doorway, she peered over his shoulder. Lord Silas, the overlord, a pale, shrunken man, sat staring at his folded hands, which thumped a shaky beat on his lap as if he were measuring his thoughts. Across from him sat a sun-browned, noble-looking young man, clean-shaven, with chestnut hair and the king's emblem of a white lion on his dove gray cloak.

Yareth, sly eyed and pale as ever, saluted Melaia with his goblet from where he lolled against the sill of a latticed window. She quickly returned her attention to the kingsman, deeming him to be about the same age as Yareth, who at twenty-one should have already stopped leeching off his father and begun pursuing his fortune in the world, as the kingsman obviously had.

"The chantress, my lord," the servant announced. Without looking up, Lord Silas motioned for her to enter.

As Melaia stepped into the room, the kingsman glanced at her. His dark, alert eyes held hers for only a moment, but she hardly breathed, as if in that one glimpse he had read her soul. When he turned back to the overlord, she let out her breath. Priestesses were free to accept a suitor's interest, but Hanni had never done so, and Melaia reminded herself that she intended to follow the high priestess's path.

"And if King Laetham does not revive, what then?" the kingsman asked the overlord. "If you agree to support Lord Rejius, he can offer your son a high position at Redcliff."

"A position at court, Father," said Yareth. "Of course we'll support Lord Rejius."

Lord Silas thumped his folded hands on his lap. "I shall give the offer serious consideration. I'll send Yareth to Lord Rejius if my answer is yes."

"Very well," said the kingsman. "But know that the time is short. Dregmoorian raiders have already made forays into Camrithia."

"I know, I know," Lord Silas droned. "We need a king who can defend us, yet with King Laetham ill and no heir to the throne, we must face the possibility that the king may no longer be able to lead. And so on and so on. Do I have it right?"

The kingsman sat back in his chair. "That you do, sir."

"In that case—" The overlord turned his rheumy gaze to Melaia. "Welcome, Chantress."

Melaia bowed. "Lord Silas."

"Our guest is an envoy from Redcliff," said the overlord. "I told him about the harp that hangs in Benasin's quarters. I want you to play it for us. You know the harp I mean?"

"I do, but..." She saw the harp every time she accompanied Hanni to visit Benasin. She had even asked to play it, but he had never allowed her to so much as touch it. "Without Benasin's permission—"

"Benasin is away at the moment," said Lord Silas.

"I brought my own harp." Melaia shed her cloak and slipped the harp from her back. "Might it do just as well?"

"May I see it?" asked the kingsman.

Melaia handed him the harp. He plucked two strings with his right hand, which, she noticed, was missing its small finger. Then he ran his hand over the frame. "It's certainly sturdy." He gave it back to her. "I'm sure it suits your purposes. But I had hoped to see something fit for a king. Lord Silas says this other harp is quite regal."

"I said it appears so," said Lord Silas. "Mind you, I myself have never heard it. But our chantress can remedy that." He waved Melaia out. "Fetch the other harp."

With no choice but to obey, Melaia trudged to Benasin's quarters one floor down, off a columned corridor. A warm cedarwood scent welcomed her into the dim room, its only light drifting in from the open door. As her eyes adjusted, she looked around with new curiosity, knowing an angel lived there.

She stepped to a small writing desk, cleared of all but a jar of ink, a wooden goblet, and a mottled feather. Brown, black, and iridescent blue, the feather's colors shifted as she held it to the soft light. Its quill had been sharpened and was stained with ink. "Benasin writes with a feather instead of a reed," she mused. No doubt he, like Nuri, had found the feather in the field.

Melaia replaced the feather, then ran her finger around the rim of the wooden goblet. A pulse of heat shot up her arm. As she jerked away, a spider crept around the foot of the goblet and paused. She blinked at it, then realized it wasn't a spider but the tendril of a vine.

She tingled with guilt. What had she done? She was intruding in a sacred chamber. Maybe Hanni was right. Angels were best left to themselves.

Trembling like a reluctant thief, Melaia crept to the far wall where the harp hung. It was slightly larger than her own, but she easily lifted it from its peg. She could feel the intricate runes carved in the soundboard. That, she expected. She didn't expect the heat of the wood, like that of the cup. She shoved the harp back onto its peg and rubbed her palms together.

The room darkened, and Melaia glanced at the doorway. Yareth stood there in silhouette. "My father sent me to make sure you didn't lose your way."

"I know the way." Melaia took down the harp and hugged it to her chest. It hummed with energy, its pulse matching her own heartbeat, which she feared was loud enough for Yareth to hear as she made her way to the door.

He didn't step aside but crooned into her ear. "You could heal me."

"For your ailment you don't need a priestess."

"Oh, but I do."

Melaia slipped the vial from her pouch and shoved it into his hands as she sidled past him. "Try saffroot."

Yareth snorted. She strode down the corridor, her skin prickling as he followed in his uneven gait.

When they returned to Lord Silas's chambers, he and the kingsman were intent on a small bag that rattled as the kingsman shook it. In one smooth motion the kingsman upended the bag and swept it across the tabletop. Two stones clattered out.

"Mine out first!" crowed Lord Silas.

The kingsman laughed. "You've bested me twice now. Shall we play again?"

"No, mark the score. Our harper is here."

Yareth strutted unevenly across the room and filled his goblet.

Melaia made her way to a stool, hoping the kingsman would not ask to hold this harp.

"Ah," he said. "You spoke true, Lord Silas. I've never seen such rich, ruddy wood. Highly polished too. A worthy harp indeed."

"I thought you'd find it interesting," said Lord Silas. "Such workmanship is not often seen these days. Let us hear its tone, Chantress."

Melaia cradled the harp in her lap, then noticed a leaf, green as spring, on a small stem at the base of the frame. Her stomach knotted. This harp was truly an angel's treasure. She hoped Lord Silas would be content to hear one song and let her return the harp to Benasin's room.

As she bent to the strings, the harp's calm energy flowed through her. Hands curved, she rolled one chord and let it ring. The tones shimmered within her like light. She let herself ease into the music, then began springing notes to life. Her fingers hugged the strings, climbed up, and leapfrogged down as her hands danced, at one with the harp, at one with the music, which swirled within her like shimmering colors of light. When she had flung out the final chord, she bowed her head and leaned into the vibration of the wood. She had never played such music before.

As the last breath of the song lingered in the air, the kingsman tossed a pouch of coins onto the table. "The king's gold. For a harp worthy of him."

Melaia stiffened in alarm, and she sent a pleading look to the overlord. "Benasin should be consulted."

"Why?" Yareth picked up the pouch and tested its weight in his palm. "With this much gold, Benasin could buy a dozen harps."

Lord Silas eyed the kingsman and thumped his hands on his lap. "I assume you mean to have the harp for the king's healing?"

"The royal physician believes music might aid the king's recovery." The kingsman sipped from his goblet.

"Then I shall send the chantress as well," said Lord Silas.

Melaia's mouth dropped open.

The kingsman coughed on his wine. "I would not deprive you of your chantress," he said.

"I insist," said Lord Silas. "The chantress has soothed me well. She will be Navia's envoy to Redcliff, my gift to the king."

"Might I suggest that the high priestess be part of this discussion?" said Melaia.

"What is there to discuss?" Yareth chuckled. "One harp, one chantress in exchange for a pouch of gold. Payment has been made. All that remains is for the goods to be delivered."

Lord Silas scowled at Yareth. "Excuse my son. He could use a lesson in tact. The truth is, I grant a great gift to the king by sending him my chantress."

"I'm sure the high priestess will be happy to take up the matter with you tomorrow," said Melaia. "In the meantime I should return the harp to Benasin's room."

"If you wish," said Lord Silas. "But you must come for it early on the morrow. I believe the envoy intends to leave for Redcliff by midday, is that not so?"

"No later," said the kingsman.

✦

"You're not even angry!" Melaia had never yelled at the high priestess, but she was close to it now. She stomped down the corridor to the sleeping quarters with Hanni right behind her. The other girls scattered to their chores.

"I don't deny that Lord Silas should have consulted me." Hanni's almond eyes were stern. "He also should have consulted Benasin. I'm appalled that he didn't, and I shall certainly take up the matter with him."

"In the meantime I'm donated like property?" Melaia dug through a chest and pulled out a journey bag, the one she had meant to help Iona pack.

"Try to see it as the other girls do." Hanni folded her arms. "In essence, you're simply taking a post at the temple in Redcliff."

"Without my consent or yours." Melaia stuffed her sleep shift into the pack. "And what about my duties here?"

"Iona can take over. I was already considering sending you out in her place."

"But I thought—"

"I know. I chose you to take over my position because you alone, of all the girls I've trained, came to me under uncommon circumstances."

"I was a foundling. Left on the temple doorstep. That's nothing uncommon."

"Mellie, sylvans brought you here."

"The woodspeople. You told me that." Melaia scooped up her comb and a pouch of anise seed.

Hanni sat on a stool and studied her hands. "I didn't tell you that sylvans are earth-angels."

"Earth-angels?" Melaia plopped down on her mat, gaping at Hanni.

"Minor guardians who never enter the heavens as other angels do."

"Why didn't you tell me before?"

"I meant to. I would have." Hanni paced to the window and stared out. "I lived for a time with the sylvans in the Durenwoods. They trained me in herbs and healing. But those woods shelter secrets, Mellie. It was there that I met a dark angel, a malevolent. He was a hunter, and I became his quarry. I vowed I would never again have anything to do with sylvans or the Durenwoods or the games of angels."

"But Benasin—"

"Is simply a friend. We've long had an unspoken agreement to keep the affairs of angels out of our friendship."

Melaia drummed her fingers on the mat. Questions crowded her mind, but little time remained to find answers. "What about the sylvans who brought me here?"

"I turned them away. Refused to listen to them. But I couldn't refuse the girl child they brought me. I couldn't turn you away. I wanted to save you from the woods, from the angels. It's no life for a human." Hanni eased down to the mat beside Melaia. "A child found by angels is said to be gifted with wisdom and insight. I chose you as my successor because I assumed you would have an innate spiritual sensitivity that other girls would not have."

Melaia's shoulders drooped. "I disappointed you."

"Never, Mellie." Hanni stroked her cheek. "The Erielyon's death made me rethink my decisions."

"That makes no sense."

"Mellie, going to Redcliff may be your escape."

Melaia frowned. "From what?"

"I don't know. I told you I refused to listen when the sylvans brought you to the temple. Now I can't shake the fear that the Erielyon's scroll was meant for me."

"'Now is payment due in full'? What does that have to do with you?"

"I was your age when I pledged to spend a number of years serving with the sylvans in the Durenwoods. After my experience with the dark angel, I broke that pledge and returned to Navia. Perhaps the sylvans want your service to pay for the years I owed them."

"Then I'll serve." Melaia sat tall, undaunted, even eager. What better way to learn about angels?

"I'll not allow it," said Hanni. "I can't condemn you to repeat my past. Angels can take care of themselves and their own affairs. The more you can distance yourself, the better."

Melaia didn't argue. She had no choice anyway. She was headed for Redcliff as the overlord's gift.

CHAPTER 4

Gray clouds scudded across the sky as a wagon rattled north out of Navia, followed by the kingsman on his dappled horse. Seated snugly in the bed of the wagon, Benasin's well-wrapped harp at her feet, Melaia fought the urge to look back. She feared the kingsman would think she was distressed over leaving Navia, which she was. Worse, he might think she was ogling him, as did every other girl they passed. Iona had practically swooned.

So Melaia gazed glumly ahead down the road. She should be rejoicing. Only the day before she had dreamed of traveling. But leaving town freely was one thing. Being sent unwillingly was another matter.

Her throat tightened at the memory of the girls gathered in the temple doorway, watching her leave: Iona standing tall as the eldest now, Nuri chattering advice to mask her own distress, Peron waving her doll furiously, and behind them Hanni, her hands clasped at her chin.

Melaia had finished packing with Hanni at her shoulder trying to press a year's worth of instruction into one evening.

"Bide at the temple if you have a choice in the matter," she had said. "I know the high priest there. Jarrod. He can counsel you." Hanni had held up three fingers. "This is the sign of the Tree. You saw it on Dreia's book. It's a greeting between angels and their supporters. Avoid those who use it."

Bumping along in the back of the wagon, Melaia could not recall all of Hanni's advice. Nor could she see this journey as a promotion to a new position at Redcliff. Under the circumstances she felt too keenly that she was being shipped off like property. She blinked away tears and stared at the back of the driver, Gil, a big-eared, bush-bearded dwarf with close-set eyes, who had been commandeered by the kingsman to transport them to Omen Crossing.

As the wagon headed uphill, Melaia gave up her resolve and glanced back for one last look at Navia. The stolid, whitewashed dome of the temple curved like a rising moon above the flat rooftops. Only the tower of the overlord's villa rose higher, its parapet set with strangely shaped stones that looked like hands beseeching the sky.

Two dark birds soared past the tower. As Melaia watched them circle the sky above the fields, the kingsman trotted up to the wagon. The red lining of his cloak rippled as he rode, leaving the hilt of his dagger in clear view at his side.

He nodded toward the birds. "Draks. Spy-birds."

Melaia hadn't intended to talk to him, but she found his half smile disarming. "They're not hawks?" she asked.

"Not hawks, Chantress. Would you like to see one?" Without waiting for an answer, he held his gloved hand high and whistled. One drak circled closer. After two more whistles, the drak descended, hesitant, to his glove. The falcon-like bird was a dull black with ghostly gray eyes.

Its feet were taloned human hands.

Melaia recoiled in shock and disgust, staring at the stubby, hair-tufted fingers gripping the kingsman's glove. "Most High, have mercy," she muttered. Peron had been right.

"Success!" The kingsman laughed as he grasped the leather cords that dangled from the bird's leg. Then he plucked a ruddy morsel from a pouch and fed it to the drak. "I work with the birds, but they don't always come when I call." He looked at Melaia, and his smile faded. "You've truly never seen draks."

"Their feet…"

"Draks were once human souls. Didn't you know?"

Melaia shook her head, wondering what else she didn't know. "And the hands?"

"Belong to the person whose soul is within the bird."

For a moment Melaia couldn't speak, and when she did, her voice grated. "You said they're spy-birds."

He shrugged. "Some people skilled in the dark arts mix oil and water in a scrying glass, a clear jar. The pattern in the oil reveals what the drak sees." The kingsman loosed the cords, and the bird flapped up to join its companion.

"Who watches through the eyes of that drak?"

The kingsman eyed her for so long that she wanted to look away, but she was determined not to back down. He didn't appear angry, just pensive. At last he said, "As priestess, you may have been taught to speak your mind boldly, but you've asked a dangerous question. I suggest you keep such queries to yourself at Redcliff."

"Mind my own affairs?"

"At court, my lady, that will be the only sure way to keep your beautiful head." He nudged his horse and trotted ahead.

Melaia, her face hot, looked back longingly toward Navia. But Navia was gone, and when she turned around, so was the kingsman.

The north road wound through rocky fields and stone outcroppings. "Goat country," Gil called it. Melaia spotted herders in the distance now and then, and once they had to stop while the bleating animals trotted across the road. The kingsman often galloped out to talk to the herders, "fishing for news and scouting for danger," as Gil put it.

Gil turned out to be quite talkative. Melaia learned he was a wheelwright from a stead near a town called Stillwater. His wife, Gerda, was also a dwarf. He missed her home cooking terribly. Patting his paunchy stomach, he said, "See how thin I'm growing? Gerda will worry over me for sure when I get home. I guess she'll have to fatten me up, eh?"

Melaia laughed at his rotund figure and wondered if he might answer her nagging questions. "Are draks really made of human souls?" she asked. "Are they spy-birds?"

"I know only what the kingsman told you," he said. "I'm doing nothing wrong, and I've no reason to think anyone's hunting me, so I pay them no mind. But your kingsman friend, being from Redcliff, may not be so fortunate."

Melaia eyed the kingsman on a hill to the west, silhouetted against the setting sun, releasing a drak from his hand. How could he work with such creatures?

As dusk fell, Gil turned the wagon toward a stand of trees an arrow's flight east of the road. "Drover's Well," he said. "Named for nomads who wandered these parts in times past."

Another small band of travelers had already settled near the well: two men with black braids and two women, one wrinkled and gray, the other dark with long, loose hair and darting eyes. The younger woman tended a pot that hung over the common firepit. All four of them stared warily at the newcomers. But when Gil hailed them, the old woman gave a toothless grin, and the taller man, who had a furrowed face, spoke an obvious greeting, although Melaia couldn't understand the language. The other man never looked up but rocked back and forth as he huddled near the fire, staring with glazed eyes.

"Dregmoorians," said Gil.

Melaia tried to look pleasant, but she wasn't sure she should encourage their acquaintance. "Are they raiders?" she asked.

Gil chuckled. "Raiders make themselves scarce until they're on the attack. These are most likely refugees from the Dregmoors. You've heard of the blight?"

"Failing crops, rivers drying up," she said.

"It's hit the Dregmoors hard," said Gil. "That's why they raid. They've lost their own crops and cattle."

As Gil helped Melaia out of the wagon, the kingsman trotted up. He dismounted, led his horse straight to the Dregmoorians, and began conversing with them as he rubbed down his mount.

"I'll be baked!" said Gil. "The kingsman speaks Dreg." He began rummaging through the packs in the bed of his wagon.

Melaia took her pack and drew out a cloth-wrapped loaf Hanni had given her.

"Save your bread," said Gil. "You've a longer journey than I. You may need it. Besides, my Gerda always packs more'n I can eat. You're in for a treat. Salt-meats, dried fruits, crisp bread. Most like, I'll have enough for the Dreggies as well." He handed Melaia a bundle. "Take this to the fire and lay it out. Food makes friends, my Gerda says."

Melaia felt the intense gaze of the family as she lugged the bundle, along with her harp and journey bag, to a spot near the firepit. As she unwrapped the food, she motioned to the family that they were welcome to some. By the time Gil and the kingsman finished tending to their horses and returned to the fire, everyone was dipping Gil's crisp bread into the common pot of thin lentil soup. Everyone except the glaze-eyed man. The old woman fed him.

Gil paced the perimeter of the camp, munching on his wife's provisions and eying the deepening twilight. The kingsman stretched out beside Melaia and took a handful of raisins.

"The overlord called you Chantress," he said. "Is that the name you go by?"

She laughed. "My name is Melaia."

"Ah, then, Melaia. I don't suppose you have a dagger? Nor that you'd know how to use one?" He popped the whole handful of raisins into his mouth.

She looked sideways at him. "Priestesses are peaceful."

"Brigands are not."

"You don't trust the Dregmoorian family?"

"They may not be the only ones around tonight. Gil's keeping watch right now. I'll take over in a while. As for our fellow campmates, it's best not to trust them."

"But you trust Gil."

"Do I?"

"Gil trusts you," Melaia pointed out.

"Does he?"

"But it's important to have people you can trust," said Melaia. "Don't you want me to trust you?"

"Ah, Chantress. Melaia. You strike directly at the heart of a matter, don't you?" The firelight danced in the kingsman's dark eyes as he searched hers.

Melaia had never known someone's gaze to be so disconcerting. She had to look away. For a moment they ate in silence except for the crackle of the flames and the chomping of the horses. She thought of Hanni and the three young priestesses in Navia, who would be preparing for sleep. On a hot night they sometimes slept under the stars on the flat roof by the dome of the temple, but none of them had ever slept in a camp in the wild. Such freedom made her tingle with excitement edged with fear. She was not at all certain she would be able to sleep here with Dregmoorians and Gil and…

She turned to the kingsman. "What name do *you* go by?"

"Scoundrel. Rogue. Ruffian. My brother calls me Slow-Wit."

"That, you're not." Melaia laughed softly. "What do you want me to call you?"

"At this very moment?" He eyed her and leaned close, murmuring, "It's a word more properly used by a mistress than a priestess." He snapped a round of crisp bread in two and handed her half.

Melaia narrowed her eyes at him as she took it.

"Forgive me." He leaned back with a roguish half smile. "The priestess in you brings out my honesty."

"Your name, sir kingsman." She pointed her crisp bread at him. "I'm requesting your name."

"Trevin." His smile seemed true and honest. Worthy of trust.

"Trevin, then. Where did you learn to speak Dreg?" She crunched the point off her bread.

"At Redcliff. It's required of an envoy."

Over the wood-lapping flames, the tall man called to Trevin and pointed at Melaia. Trevin rose to a squat, and she watched as the conversation went back and forth between the two.

Then Trevin turned to her. "When the old woman asked about you earlier,

I told her you're a priestess. She wants you to pray for the one who sits as still as a stump."

"What's wrong with him?"

"He's gash-drunk."

"Gash?"

"A thick, earthy drink with a putrid smell."

Melaia wrinkled her nose. "Why would anyone want to drink it?"

Gil paused nearby in his pacing. "There's a merchant, name of Baize, who's been traveling the roads trying to peddle gash. Nasty stuff. He claims it restores life, renews youth. He was drummed out of town by the folk at Stillwater."

"The merchant's selling a half truth," said Trevin. "Gash does restore youth. For a time, anyway. See how young the drunk looks? In truth, he's the other man's father. Husband to the old woman."

Melaia stared at the drunk. He appeared sculpted, young and perfect as a statue. His skin was so smooth, he looked as if he were modeled of dun-colored clay.

"That's the bane of the drink, eh?" said Gil. "You grow young looking even as you waste away."

"That's what the old woman said." Trevin nodded toward where she sat watching them intently, wringing her hands. "Her husband developed a fierce craving for gash, couldn't do without it. Now listen to him."

The man's labored breathing rasped loudly over the snap of the flames.

"In the end, I hear, gash hardens a person from the inside out." Gil took up his pacing again.

"I'd say he's dying," said Trevin.

"He's not. Not yet." Melaia saw no sign of the drunk's spirit leaving him. "I should play some music. It might revive him." She reached for the harp.

But Trevin placed his hand on hers. "No harp. The only valuables we display are our daggers."

"Which I don't have."

"Because you're armed with your prayers. Go pray for the man. I'll stand by with my dagger."

Melaia skirted the fire and knelt before the unseeing clay man. Angels, draks, gash—the world was not as she had imagined it. Not at all.

CHAPTER 5

Melaia roused herself from a doze in the back of Gil's wagon. The slant of the warm sun told her it was nearing midafternoon. She wondered if the Dregmoorian family had journeyed to Navia as she had suggested, hoping Hanni might have herbs that could help the gash-drunk father.

She peered around Gil's squat, cloaked form. The road ahead curved into woodlands. Throughout the day they had slowly passed from rocky hills to fields of yellowed grass and into a scattering of gold brown trees, while Trevin ranged to and fro around them. His dappled horse seemed as eager to run as Gil's was to plod. Apparently impatient with the slowness of their travel, Trevin had galloped down the road ahead of them.

"Gil?" Melaia scooted to the side of the wagon where she could better see his bush-bearded face. "Have you ever been to Redcliff?"

"That I have. Me and my family." His slow nod matched the gait of his horse. "Back when times were good, the king held a yearly harvest festival in Redcliff Valley. This very time of year, it was. Common people swarmed in like ants to a banquet. They'd buy and sell and barter. There was music, dancing, gaming, and good drink, strong or otherwise. My Gerda and I often took our boys. Gerda sold cakes and breads, I mended wagon wheels, and our boys spent every coin we made."

"But there's no harvest festival now?"

"Redcliff is much changed." Gil smiled at her, but his close-set eyes looked sad. "As you're headed there, you should know that the whole city is stewing in a pot of misfortune. Latest news is that Lord Beker, the king's trusted advisor, disappeared a fortnight ago. Presumed dead, so the rumor goes. Murdered by someone in the king's own court."

"So the king has no advisor?"

"The king's physician stepped into that position, I hear."

"What ails the king?"

"Melancholy. Queen Tahn died in a fire some months ago. She was with child, the king's only heir, and he grieves himself to death about it. And I wager the queen's death was no accident. What I'm saying is that the kingsman is right. At Redcliff, you'd best keep your wondering to yourself."

In spite of the warm sun, Melaia pulled her cloak tight. An advisor murdered. Maybe the queen and her unborn child too. How would the unexpected arrival of a chantress be received? At least she might have a friend in the priest Hanni knew. Jarrod. And Trevin. Could she count him as a friend?

"Omen Crossing's around the next bend," Gil announced. "That's where I'm to leave you. The town of Treolli's a short walk east."

"Where's Trevin?"

"He'll likely show up any minute now," said Gil. "But don't worry. I'll not leave you on your own. If worse turns to worst, you're welcome to come to my stead."

"If he's gone off and left me, I'll return home to Navia." She was surprised that the thought disappointed her, although taking the harp back to Benasin would be a relief. Redcliff quickened her pulse; Navia rested her soul. She would be hard-pressed to make a choice between them.

"Keep a sharp eye," said Gil. "We're coming to Omen Crossing. It's said that whatever you spy first at the crossing is the omen for your journey."

As the wagon rounded the curve, the crossing signpost came into view. Trevin leaned against it, watching his horse crop the grass nearby.

"Is that a good omen?" asked Melaia.

"Depends on who's interpreting it," said Gil. "Seeing as how there's none of those blasted spy-birds about, I'd say it tends toward the good."

"I'd be happy never to see another drak."

"Could be that's part of Trevin's training to be a comain. That's the highest rank of kingsman, you know. Each comain leads a group of men-at-arms. A worthy profession it would be, eh? Main Trevin. Has a nice tone to it. Sure as sure, the king could use some good men these days."

"So Trevin is a good man?" Melaia studied the kingsman, who had seen them coming and was coaxing his horse back to work.

"Hard to say." Gil scratched his bushy beard. "I've not known him any longer than you. If Gerda were here, she'd advise you to trust no one. That's a valuable piece of advice, given you free." He patted his chest with three fingers and winked.

She eyed him quizzically. "Are you an angel?"

"You know the sign?"

"I heard about it once."

"Angels make it. Or friends of angels. If you're a friend, you make the sign back to me." Gil reined his horse to a stop beside the post that pointed west to Stillwater, east to Treolli.

Melaia wondered if she should make the sign of the Tree. She could hear Hanni advising her to avoid those who use it. Yet Melaia had enjoyed Gil's company. She felt safe in his presence. He had truly been what he had said: a friend. But to make the sign of the Tree herself? Should she?

A breeze shivered through the golden trees, stirring their leaves into a restless *Shhhould shhhee? Shhhould shhhee?* Melaia stared at the woods, amazed to hear her own thoughts in the shush of the leaves. She shook her head, attributing the sound to her wild imagination.

Trevin strode to the wagon. Melaia gave him the harp, and Gil handed down her pack.

"Are we in the Durenwoods?" she asked, peering between the trunks into dimmer, deeper woods.

"That's northwest of us," said Trevin. "You'll see the edge of it from Redcliff."

As Melaia climbed down, Gil said, "Remember Gil and Gerda. Our stead's north of Stillwater a ways. Always open to friends." He tapped the seat with three fingers.

Melaia did the same. "Friends," she said.

For a time she watched Gil's wagon roll away west. Hanni would be grateful he was leaving, but she felt sad to see him go.

"Ready, Chantress?" Trevin finished securing the harp to the packs on his horse. "The caravansary isn't far. I'll walk my mount from here." He took the reins of his horse, and they headed down the dirt road. "I've already ridden ahead and procured us a room."

"Us? Just you and me?"

"I'm afraid they won't allow the horse upstairs even if we could get him there."

Melaia smiled.

"Your priestly cloak will be of some protection to you, as is the king's insignia on my own," he said. "But a lady traveling alone, rooming alone, is not safe. The comain in charge of protecting these roads disappeared months ago, likely murdered. Since then, all routes, especially the eastern ones, have become much more dangerous. We'll travel with a caravan the rest of the way." He pointed ahead.

Melaia could see where their road widened and ended at the caravan route. A string of laden donkeys plodded south, but at this distance they appeared to be a small carving come to life. A spark of anticipation danced within her. If she could forget she had been treated like chattel, she might dare to call it a feeling of freedom.

She studied Trevin out of the corner of her eye. As an envoy he no doubt felt such freedom every time he journeyed. Except perhaps now.

"You didn't intend to return to Redcliff with a chantress, did you?" she asked.

His mouth eased into an amused smile. "My orders did not include a chantress."

"So I'm now a burden to you."

He raised his eyebrows. "You were the gift of the overlord. I'm simply the envoy. It's not my place to refuse a gift. So *burden*, I think, is not the proper term." He grinned. "Perhaps *challenge*."

Melaia smiled at his direct, steady gaze. "It's a challenge for me as well."

Together they stepped into the flurry of travelers coursing the broad highway south to Qanreef and north to Redcliff.

Voices clamored, horses clopped, harnesses jangled, and donkeys brayed. Melaia and Trevin joined carts, goat herders, and fieldworkers headed toward Treolli, a walled city on a distant hill warmed by the late afternoon sun. At the foot of the hill stood a stone fortress with latticed windows high in the walls and a double-arched entrance, where a buxom woman with flowing sandy hair held a long spear as if it were a staff.

"That's our caravansary with the innkeep at the gate," Trevin called over the din. "Stay close."

Melaia wove through the crowd with Trevin and his horse. The innkeep studied the travelers entering her domain as if to make sure they were acceptable guests. She nodded at Trevin and smiled at Melaia, who hoped the woman was pleased to shelter a priestess.

They passed through the arches into a square yard open to the sky, surrounded on the upper floor by a walkway and the enclosed rooms of the inn. On the ground level, open stalls lined the walls. These were already overrun with horses, donkeys, and goats as well as travelers. A man was lighting torches on brackets. In the center of the yard, a fire blazed in a shallow pit. Travelers were warming themselves and cooking their evening meals, and the aroma of roasting meat mingled with sweat, smoke, barley beer, and animals.

Trevin handed a coin and the reins of his horse to a youth. Then Melaia followed him upstairs to a small, dark room furnished with two straw pallets and a chamber pot. On the east wall the window's latticed shutter stood open. While Trevin went to fetch an oil lamp, Melaia closed the lattice, trying to trick her mind into believing it would diminish the chill. Then she dug bread and cheese out of her pack. Trevin returned carrying not only a lamp but also a skin of wine and two cups. As Melaia handed him some bread and cheese, a cheer went up from the courtyard below.

"We're in for a noisy night," said Trevin. "A troupe of actors is staying here. They've already begun entertaining in the yard." He poured wine into the cups.

Another cheer sounded. Melaia took her supper out to the rail overlooking the yard, and Trevin joined her. As they ate, they watched the actors, who juggled and sang and then slipped on masks to pantomime a tale.

In the middle of the tale, there was a commotion at the archways. The innkeep led in four unkempt swordsmen who bore a wounded man on a litter. The audience turned its attention to the newcomers, and the performance trailed to a close as the swordsmen began their own tale. Melaia couldn't hear the talk, but she could feel the tension in the air. Travelers checked their swords and daggers. Some stationed themselves at the entrance while the litter was laid near the fire. Others stood around and gawked as first one person and then another bent over the wounded man.

Trevin set aside his cup and headed downstairs. Melaia fetched the harp and unwrapped it, thinking he would call for the chantress, but instead he strode to the archway and fell into a discussion with the watchmen.

She carried the harp to the courtyard anyway and elbowed through the onlookers until she reached the wounded man. She could see his spirit edging his body.

Just as she started to offer her aid as chantress, a hand grabbed her upper arm so hard she gasped in pain.

Trevin tugged her back and muttered into her ear, "What do you think you're doing?"

Melaia pulled her arm free. "The man needs healing music. He might revive."

Trevin grabbed her again and hurried her toward the stairs. She tried to slip from his grasp, but he held tight. "Don't call attention to yourself," he muttered between his teeth. Not until they were in their room with the door closed did he release her. "Do you value your life at all?" he said. "To thieves, a harp like that is worth slitting your throat in the middle of the night, priestess or no."

Melaia's face was hot with anger and shame, and she was glad of the dim light. She jerked the cover around the harp. "I happen to be a death-prophet," she said, "and I know that man is dying. I can see his spirit departing. I might be of some help."

"Not this night." Trevin paced in front of the door, eying her. "You can see spirits?"

"Of the dying."

"If they're dying, then playing your harp does no good."

"Sometimes the dying recover with the music, and their spirits settle back into their bodies. But even if they die, music can ease their passing."

"A noble thought," said Trevin, "but one best set aside for tonight."

"How was the man wounded?" asked Melaia.

"Raiders. Three of the men regularly patrol this stretch of road. The other two are scouts. One of the scouts ran into a Dregmoorian outrider and was nearly cut down before his comrade reached him and joined the fight. He felled the outrider but was too late to help his friend."

"*I* could have helped him." Melaia rubbed her arm, feeling completely useless. What good did it do to keep a lifesaving gift hidden? Or to have an angel's harp and keep it shrouded as if it were dead? It went against her upbringing, her training, her instincts.

"I'm sorry if I hurt you," said Trevin, "but that harp does not belong to you. For that matter, as a gift of Lord Silas, you may not even belong to yourself."

Melaia narrowed her eyes. "I'm not a slave."

"As chantress serving at Redcliff, you may find little difference." He poured himself a cup of wine. "But I have a thought. You might keep that harp if you know where I could find another like it."

Melaia sighed. "I don't." She wondered if Benasin did.

"It's made of kyparis wood," said Trevin. "Quite rare. You might expect to see something like it in a palace, but at Navia?" He laughed softly. "I'd wager this harp is the only piece of kyparis you've ever seen."

"You think Navia is a backward village, don't you?" said Melaia. "But it's not. I've seen a cup made of kyparis and a book covered in it as well."

"Then you're ahead of me. Not backward at all." He saluted her with his wine. "I'll be on the porch. I want to see what's happening in the yard. That should give you time to ready yourself for sleep. When I come back in, I'll lie here beside the door. With my dagger." He slipped out with the cup and wineskin.

Melaia sank to one of the straw pallets, which was thin and moldering. She blanketed herself in her cloak and used her pack as a pillow. The sounds and smells here were frightfully different from those in the peaceful temple at Navia, and she sorely missed the comforting presence of Hanni and the girls.

As she listened to the tide of voices rise and fall in the courtyard, she thought of her training. She knew what to do in cases of grief, illness, birthing, and temple rites, but she had no idea what to do in cases of attractive kingsmen. And she was sorely bothered by something Trevin had said. He had voiced a thought of her own, one she had never let out of its cage.

Slave and priestess, both were bound. Neither was free.

Melaia drew the harp close, slipped her hand beneath the overwrap, and touched the wood. Warm and thrumming, it soothed her soul. But she didn't allow herself sleep until Trevin returned and she was certain he meant to settle himself at the door.

⟦❧⟧

She awoke shivering with cold. The night was dim, only soft charcoal moonlight drifting through the latticework. She tucked her cloak tighter around her feet and drew the harp closer. Animal sounds and smells permeated the night air, and scratching sounded at the outside wall.

It stopped, started again, stopped again. Rats? She curled her toes. No, bigger. Foxes? Wolves? Draks?

She sat up and murmured, "Trevin?"

A thin line showed under the door where he should have been blocking the light. For a moment all was silent. Then the scratching began again.

"Trevin?"

She listened for his breathing. Nothing. She eased out of her almost-warm mat and crept around the cold, drafty room, squinting into the shadows, drawing away at the touch and smell of the chamber pot, feeling for him, afraid she would find him, afraid she wouldn't.

When she was certain Trevin wasn't in the room, she tiptoed to the door and eased it open. It squeaked. A sandy-haired young man about Nuri's age straightened and blinked sleepily at her from where he had been leaning against the doorframe.

"Who are you?" asked Melaia.

"I'm yer guard, miss," he croaked. "The kingsman paid for extra protection tonight, and my mam put me to the task."

"Who's your mam?"

"Why, the innkeep, miss. She says I'm to let no one in or out of this room until the kingsman says, and if there's trouble, I'm to call for her."

"So no one's been in or out?"

"No one, miss. I'm trusty."

"Yes, I can tell." Melaia closed the door and leaned back against it. If no one had been in or out, where was Trevin?

The scratch came at the window. Then a sharp click, and the lattice silently swung open to reveal a thick silhouette against the airy darkness of the night.

"Trevin?" she asked.

The silhouette jerked upright. "Rogue, scoundrel, and ruffian, remember?" He stretched and rubbed his arms.

"Which is it tonight?" She paced back to her pallet, folded her arms, and faced him. Whatever he was stuffing into his pack clinked. "Where did you go?"

"To the privy."

"Out the window?"

"Can you see in the dark?" he asked.

"Of course not."

All she could see was his angular face dusted by a trickle of pale moonlight. But she could tell that he jerked something off a finger and stuffed it into his pouch. Then he slipped off his cloak and shook it.

She huffed. "You climbed out the window to go to the privy? There's a chamber pot in the corner."

"Great ghouls, lady. Can't you be somewhat discreet?" He ran his hand through his hair and sighed. "I'm sorry. I'm accustomed to court life, where those who want to keep their positions choose to feign a blind eye, a deaf ear, and a *mute tongue*."

"You mean they pretend not to know anything."

"Exactly. So you'd best learn the lesson now, or you'll have more trouble than your priestly vow of integrity is worth."

She set her jaw and glared at him, wishing she could see in the dark. It was impossible to read his face. "Trust no one," Gil had said, but if she couldn't trust *anyone*, she might as well return to Navia on the morrow. She was certain the kingsman would have no complaints as long as she left the harp with him. But deserting her mission would mean snubbing the overlord, clearly disobeying Hanni, and most important, giving up on the possibility that she might truly help the king.

"All right," she said. "When I get to Redcliff, I'll do as you say. But for now—please understand—I need to know I can trust you."

"Can I trust you?"

She was taken aback. "Of course you can trust me. I'm a priestess."

"I'm not talking about creeds or vows. I'm talking about you. Can you be smart enough to know when keeping your mouth shut will save your own neck? And mine?"

"I…I don't know." She sank to her pallet.

"You're never less than honest, are you?" He leaned against the window frame. "Let's start with something small. A raiding party is camped two ridges away. Their plan was to attack us at dawn."

"That's something small?"

"Mouth shut."

She pressed her lips together and folded her hands in her lap.

"I found a lookout and impressed upon him the importance of taking a message to their leader, forbidding him to attack us." He tied two corners of his cloak to the bottom of the lattice. The moonlight split into shards as he closed the lattice, leaving the cloak hanging out the window.

Questions filled Melaia to bursting, but she swallowed them.

"I hope that works," he said. "We'll know when the cock crows."

"Does the innkeep know?" she blurted, then covered her mouth.

"A question worth asking. She doesn't know I left, but she knows raiders are near. Weapons are gathered, the city alerted. She's placed a couple of archers on the roof." He squatted in front of Melaia, took her hand, and slipped a hilt into it. "A knife," he said. "Sharp. Just in case."

A rush of warmth ran through her at his closeness. A new way to ward off the chill, she thought, immensely glad he couldn't see that she was flustered.

"You've never held a knife." His voice smiled.

"Only a kitchen knife."

"It's not so different. With a kitchen knife, you don't swing it about, right? If you must use this knife, be deliberate. You'll probably get only one chance to strike, so hit hard and up. Throat, eye, midchest under the ribs if there's no breastplate." He released her hand. "Lay it somewhere nearby while you sleep."

The chill of the room returned full force as Melaia realized what he was saying. Stab someone? She closed her eyes against the vision of what the hawk had done to the angel in Navia. To be the cause of such bloody wounds—she couldn't do it.

She shoved the knife under her pack and wiped her clammy hands on her skirt. "If the raiders don't come," she said, "I'll return your knife tomorrow."

"Keep it. It belonged to the man on the stretcher." Trevin dragged his pallet to the wall under the window and lay down.

"He died?" Melaia curled up on her own pallet, wrestling with both sadness and guilt. She might have helped him. Might have saved him. She'd never know.

"I should tell you I sometimes fight terror-dreams," said Trevin. "If I wake yelling, feel free to shake me. Slap me if you need to."

She rose on one elbow. "Truly?"

"Another question." He yawned. "Ah, well. You're wise not to trust me."

CHAPTER 6

The cockcrow woke Melaia. As the caravansary came to life, animals brayed and nickered, people coughed and spoke tersely. She sat up and rubbed her eyes. Trevin already knelt at the window, peering out the openings in the latticework. She took a pinch of anise seed and crunched on it, releasing the clean, sharp sweetness. Then she joined Trevin at the window and squinted through a half circle at the thread of light edging the horizon.

"Nothing yet." Trevin's breath smelled of anise. "They'll attack as the sun blinds us full on."

"If they attack." She fingered the gray and red sides of his cloak knotted around the base of the lattice. She craned her neck to see if she could tell which side was displayed on the outer wall.

Trevin tugged her back down. "Some things you're safer not knowing," he said.

She started to question him, then bit her lip as a new thought hit her. If she wanted to trust him—and she did—maybe it truly was better not to know. This morning she didn't want to go back to Navia. She liked this new freedom and the prospects of a new life. Surely for a priestess, affairs at Redcliff would not be as difficult as Trevin had portrayed them.

"There." He shot up like a bird released from a snare. "On the ridge. An outrider."

Melaia scanned the ridge under the pale-green-and-pink-streaked sky, marveling at how Trevin spotted anything so far away.

"He rode down into the cover of the trees," said Trevin.

"But the sun's not fully up yet."

"Soon now. The rest of the raiders are hidden, watching for the outrider's signal."

Melaia hardly breathed. The caravansary churned with bumps, bangs, shouts, and the complaints of restless animals. Footsteps sounded overhead. Then the sun blinded her. She shaded her eyes and thought of the knife under her pack, but she couldn't pull herself away from the window to get it. Trevin's hand went to his dagger, but he made no other move as the minutes crawled by tortoise slow.

The world outside kept its silence as the sun rose. Trevin stared out the window. "The outrider again. Back up the hill." He turned to Melaia, grinning. "They'll not attack."

"So you sent the raiders home empty-handed."

"Not likely." He began untying his cloak from the lattice. "They'll not go home without plunder of some kind."

"Will they attack our caravan as we travel north?" She noted that the gray side of his cape was toward the wall, the red side facing out. A signal for the outrider?

"Don't worry about the caravan." Trevin pulled in his cloak. "I strongly suggested the raiders go elsewhere."

"You have that kind of authority?"

"I'm an envoy of someone who does. I sent them south."

"South?" She gaped at him.

"That's better than north." Trevin slipped on his cloak, gray side out. "Pack up, and let's get downstairs. The caravan master will want to leave as soon as he judges it's safe."

"And you'll tell him it's safe to journey north, because you sent the raiders *south*. Toward Navia."

Trevin whirled, his finger to his lips. "I'll not tell him, and you'll not tell him." His voice was low and stern. "No one is to know what you've seen and heard. If you let it slip, I'll be forced to deny it and say that you and I…kept each other warm last night. *All* night." He grabbed his pack. "I'll meet you at the bottom of the stairs."

Melaia glared after him, then turned and took her time gathering her belongings. Let him wait.

⁓❧⁓

Amid clanking and jangling, neighing and lowing, the caravan assembled outside the caravansary walls.

Melaia perched on the front seat of the actors' wagon beside the troupe's stout leader, Caepio, whose eyes still held the dark puffiness of interrupted sleep. His actors, covered in cloaks, lay snoring in the back. Everyone in the caravan wore a similar groggy gaze, thanks to a short, worrisome night. Melaia suspected her eyes looked the same.

Trevin, leading his horse, walked up to her and held out a dried apricot. "This cost me dear," he said, "but I mean it to be a guilt offering from a ruffian."

Melaia took the golden leathered fruit. "For what?"

He lowered his voice. "For being rude to you last night—and this morning."

"Your apology is accepted," she said. "I absolve you of wrongdoing."

"That sounds official." He half smiled.

"It's one advantage of having a priestess nearby."

"I sent a messenger to Navia to warn them of raiders," he said. "It's the best I can do."

Melaia hoped it would be enough. As she took a rich, sweet bite of apricot, a shout went up from the caravan master. Trevin mounted, and when the procession began snaking north toward Redcliff, he trotted ahead. Two draks glided high above. Melaia took some comfort in the fact that the birds didn't look her way.

The innkeep, watching from the archway with her spear, held three fingers to her heart as the actors' wagon passed. Caepio nodded to her and held up three fingers himself.

Melaia studied his drowsy face with its spot of dark beard in the center of his chin. "Are you an angel?" she asked. "Is the innkeep?"

He blinked at her sleepily. "Are you?"

Melaia laughed. "No, but I've met two. Maybe three."

"Ah. Well, I was raised by an angel, though I can't claim such a role myself. As for the innkeep, she's a true angel and worthy. Which is why her inn is tolerably safe. The malevolents sense her light—an emanation of color, I'm told. At any rate the malevolents usually keep their distance."

Melaia recalled Hanni mentioning a malevolent. "Who are malevolents?"

Caepio squinted at her. "Do my ears trick me, priestess? You know two angels but have no knowledge of malevolents?"

Melaia stared at her hands clasped in her lap atop the wrapped harp. "A fortnight ago I thought that after the fall of the Wisdom Tree, angels no longer lived in this world."

"You've not heard a true and honest actor tell the tale then." Caepio straightened and held up his forefinger. "Ah!" he began. Then he slumped. "Methinks it too early in the day to tell tales. Even true ones."

"I'm a chantress myself. I've told the tale a score of times. But I think I learned the ending wrong. Does it have to do with malevolents?"

"Aye, it does, Chantress. You see, when the Wisdom Tree came to its despicable end, and the stairway to heaven with it, many angels were stranded in this world. Trapped, as it were. Some swore allegiance to the Second son. Or was it the Firstborn?" Caepio tapped the spot of beard on his chin. "Possibly both. There's some disagreement about it. At any rate, those angels who reject the Tree are called malevolents."

"What do malevolents look like?" she asked.

"No different from any other angel. I could be one, masquerading as an actor." He raised one eyebrow and regarded her with an evil eye. "But I'm not." His sleepy-eyed grin returned.

Melaia laughed. "So why do malevolents reject the Tree?"

"As it happens, Chantress, I've never felt like venturing close enough to a malevolent to ask. There's great enmity between them and the Angelaeon—

those are angels loyal to the Tree. Other than that, all you need to know is to stay clear of the affairs of angels."

"Are the raiders malevolents?"

"My guess is there's a malevolent staging the raids. Maybe more than one. The raiders themselves are controlled by their dependence on gash, I hear. You know about gash?"

She nodded. "Do malevolents drink it?"

"They don't need to. Physically, angels grow to their prime and age no further."

Melaia thought about the Erielyon, Benasin, the innkeep. All in their prime. "Do you know anything about a debt between angels?" she asked.

"All I know about debt is seeing my fleshly father hauled to debtor's prison, thus my adoptive angel parent. But I suppose angels have debts as much as humans do. Though if it's an angel collecting, I'd not wish to be the debtor."

Melaia curved her hand around the harp in its wraps, wondering if it could be the payment for a debt. If so, it should be in Benasin's hands, not hers. Perhaps he was back in Navia or tracking her to Treolli. She drummed her fingers, thinking of the raiders headed south. Would Trevin's message arrive in time? What would Hanni and the girls do?

"Do you journey to Redcliff—or beyond?" asked Caepio.

"Redcliff. I'm sent by the overlord of Navia to play the harp for the king."

"The harp I saw yesternight? You intended to play for the wounded man, didn't you?"

"I thought my music might soothe him, help him heal."

"With that harp methinks you might resurrect him from the maws of death." Caepio's puffy eyes widened. "I saw the runes carved into it. They indicate its power. Do you know what they spell?"

Melaia shook her head.

"*Dedroumakei.* 'Awaken!' If the runes speak true, I'd have liked to see the harp awaken the warrior yesternight." Caepio glanced sideways at her. "You'd not consider joining our troupe, would you? We'll be at Redcliff for a time.

After that, we journey to Navia. Then it's south to Qanreef. With that harp—and a pretty chantress as well—we could keep any audience awake."

"I'm pledged to Redcliff at the moment," said Melaia.

Caepio placed his hand on his heart as if he had been wounded. "Pledged to another." He sighed, then grinned. "Truly, if you ever wish to be free of the priesthood, you'd be welcome in our troupe."

"Are you always traveling?"

"We circle 'round the kingdom. But when the wind blows cold, like birds we hie ourselves south, where the king keeps his winter palace. So I suppose we'll renew acquaintance with you there."

Melaia nodded, but she wondered if a priestess would overwinter with the court or be expected to bide the cold season at the temple in Redcliff. Where would a kingsman who worked with draks spend the winter?

❧

That night they camped at Caldarius, where steam curled up into the cold air, rising from two pools formed by hot springs bubbling out of the ground. One pool lay on a ledge and cascaded into a second pool below. Melaia stood transfixed, watching the steaming waterfall.

Trevin stepped up beside her, rubbing his right hand where he was missing his small finger.

"Does your hand hurt?" asked Melaia.

"Just an old habit," he said, clasping his hands behind his back. "This place smells like gash."

Melaia wrinkled her nose. She had to admit that the pools held a sharp, rather putrid smell. But she had heard traveler's tales of Caldarius and had always wished she could see this place. Torches were lit around the pools so everyone could bathe. The prospect of being clean excited her. And in hot water, no less.

She was not disappointed. Women went first in the upper pool, and she returned relaxed and wet haired to the spot Trevin had chosen by one of the campfires. He was waiting for her, keeping watch over their valuables.

He eyed her, his mouth in its winsome half smile. "How was it?"

"Like liquid sunshine." She loosened her cloak now that she was near the fire. "I wish I could have stayed in longer, but I started to doze. One of the other women told me to get out before I drowned."

"Wise." Trevin rose. "I'll have to remember to do the same." He took his cloak and his dagger with him but left the rest of the packs for Melaia to watch.

She ran her fingers through her drying hair and gazed into the fire, wondering what Hanni and the girls would say when she told them she had not only seen this magical place but had also bathed in its hot waters. Her throat tightened. When would she see them again?

A gust of wind sent the flames undulating upward, and for a moment Melaia glimpsed the form of a woman in joyful dance, her arms over her head. She twirled, rising in the fire, and disappeared in sparks. Like the hawkman who had left the temple through flame and smoke.

She blinked at the deep orange blaze. The figure was either a product of her weary imagination or of her gift as a death-prophet. But dying spirits never danced with joy, nor did they rise. They sank into the earth in grim despair.

"I'm tired," she murmured. "Tired and imagining." The hot water had soaked her with drowsiness, body and mind.

But Trevin was counting on her to watch their packs until he returned. Perhaps chewing on dried figs would help her stay awake. She tugged her journey pack out of the pile. It snagged Trevin's pack and tipped it sideways, spilling out a small scroll, two metal pegs, a finger-sized spiked tool, and a ring. As she quickly slid everything back into the pack, the ring caught the glint of the campfire.

It was a signet ring. Bearing the image of a hawk.

CHAPTER 7

Melaia rode beside Caepio again the next day and was regaled with tales and songs. His actors joined in. She even told a few stories herself, glad to occupy her mind with something besides raiders storming Navia and Trevin riding out to scout for danger. But between tales, she found herself worrying anyway, watching for Trevin to appear over a hill or in the road ahead.

At last Melaia decided it was just as well he kept his distance. She was full of questions for him, questions that would reveal she knew what he carried in his pack. She didn't want him to think she was a snoop. But, then, what *did* she want him to think? And what should she think of him? The trees shifted in the wind. *Shhhould shhhee? Shhhould shhhee?*

In the late afternoon the actors' wagon slowed as the caravan headed up a hill. "We're close enough to camp to smell it, gentlemen," Caepio said to his troupe. "I smell supper. Maybe a bit of performing." He turned to Melaia. "Keep your eyes sharp, priestess. At the top of the next rise, you'll spy Redcliff."

High above, two dark birds zagged across the road—west, east, west. Then they headed north and disappeared over the hill. Trevin was nowhere to be seen.

The matter of his signet ring had nibbled at her all day. Why the image of a hawk? Did it have anything to do with a hawkman? She had tried to see nothing, hear nothing, say nothing, but the question kept returning like an itch. She decided it wouldn't hurt to ask Caepio if he knew what the image of a hawk signified.

"I've a question," she said.

"Ask away." Caepio sat tall and raised his chin in a scholarly fashion.

"As you know, I'm ignorant in a great many matters," she said.

"Not ignorant, my priestess. What say you, gents?"

"Ill-informed, perhaps," called one of the actors.

"Unenlightened," suggested another.

"Empty-headed?" ventured a third.

"You're the empty head," Caepio shot back. "No, my priestess, the word for you is *innocent*."

"And you've been enlightening her, I suppose?" asked Trevin.

Melaia jerked around to see him riding up beside them. Her cheeks burned at the thought of the question she had almost asked.

Trevin laughed. "At the rate we've all been educating you, you'll be a wise old woman by the time we enter Redcliff." He nudged his horse and cantered up the hill, where he stopped and dismounted.

"Now what was your question?" asked Caepio.

"Never mind," said Melaia. "I'd best stay innocent."

As they crested the hill, a cheer shot up from the actors. Redcliff Valley lay ahead, rippling with golden grasses. The highway before them stretched across the center of the valley, which was scattered with camps. At the far side the highway became a bridge that soared into a line of red clay cliffs. Atop the cliffs stood the mass of ruddy square towers that formed the city of Redcliff.

Melaia caught her breath at the sight of the magnificent red city. The lowering sun painted its western edge with a fiery glow. She tingled all the way to her toes, awed, excited, petrified.

Trevin signaled for the wagon to halt, calling, "The chantress will ride the rest of the way with me."

Melaia kept her mouth shut but raised her eyebrows in question.

"There's still some distance to cover," he explained. "I want to reach the city gate before it closes for the night."

He took Melaia's journey bag and the harp and tied them onto his own packs while she said good-bye to the actors.

As Caepio headed over the hill, Melaia turned to Trevin's horse and then shrank back. How did one mount such a large creature?

Trevin tugged the last knot, turned to her, and burst into warm laughter. "You should see yourself. You look appalled. Shall I guess you've never ridden?"

"Never," she squeaked. "I suppose it's too far to walk?"

"Unless you want to walk by the light of the moon and arrive in Redcliff for breakfast. I myself crave supper and my own bed."

Melaia took a deep breath. With Trevin's instructions and help, she mounted the horse after just two tries. She shifted her skirts and cloak to the least awkward feel as Trevin settled in behind her. At his direction she wove her fingers through the horse's mane.

Then he nudged his mount into a walk. Melaia clenched the stiff horsehair and felt Trevin's arm draw snug around her waist, his breath at her ear. She knew she would take pleasure in it if she were not terrified of tumbling off.

"Breathe," said Trevin. "Relax. Ride with the movement, not against it."

Melaia exhaled slowly. "You'd have more luck telling a stone to turn to water."

Trevin laughed again and clucked to the horse. Their easy gait down the hill slowly gathered speed. The actors cheered when they passed, but Melaia didn't respond, for she clung to the horse's mane as if it were all that stood between her and death. Despite her fear she thrilled to the feel of the wind in her face and the scent of grasses as they swept across the valley.

Soon they slowed to join the last of the throng crossing the bridge and funneling through the city gate. Melaia at last felt steady enough to look back at the valley. To the east, lights winked like flickerflies.

"Is that where the caravan camps?" she asked.

"That's an unwalled city of sorts," said Trevin. "Made by people fleeing Dregmoorian raiders or the blight. Or both."

Melaia wondered if Hanni and the girls were fleeing raiders. "Gil said raiders attack because the blight destroyed their crops and cattle."

"That's the common notion. Dregmoorians have plenty of gold and gems, but they can't eat gold."

"In that case why don't they buy food from Camrithia? Why do they raid?"

"They did buy food for a while. But the blight creeps across our land too. We've little to spare, and we're storing our excess for the time when our fields look like theirs."

"But surely the king—"

"Chantress, remember what we talked about? This isn't a time for questions, and these are not your concerns."

Watch-drums sounded the closing of the gates, which creaked and scraped as portal-keepers began easing the huge ironclad doors closed. Trevin nudged his horse around a slow cart and pressed ahead of stragglers surging through the grand archway. Once they were within the city walls, he pointed out an inn with a savory smell of stew drifting out, the street of metalsmiths where the odor of smoke and hot metal lingered, the alley of carpenters scented with pungent wood shavings, and the lane of perfumers where sweet and spicy fragrances mingled. Melaia marveled at the maze of streets and wondered how long it would take to learn her way around.

At a second wall, a rough-hewn guard grinned at Trevin. "You've not got enough ladies? You're bringing 'em back with you now?"

Melaia narrowed her eyes at the man.

"She's a priestess," said Trevin as the guard opened the gate for him.

"So you're holy now, are you?" the guard laughed.

"Don't mind him," said Trevin. "He's not mean, just slack mouthed." He loosed the reins, and his eager horse carried them into the inner ward. Ahead stood the towering red-clay palace. Royal stables lined the east wall. The round-domed, earth red temple backed up to the wall on the west.

"I'm to stay at the temple," said Melaia, easing her grip on the horse's mane.

"Are you expected?" asked Trevin.

"No, but temples are open to wayfarers, and Hanni, high priestess of Navia, knows the priest here."

Trevin dismounted and helped Melaia off the horse. She opened and closed her stiff fingers.

"You'll be sore tomorrow, no doubt," he said as he untied her pack.

"I'm sore tonight." Melaia patted her rump, then took her pack from Trevin and shouldered it. "And the harp?" she asked.

"Perhaps I should keep it." Trevin rubbed his left hand over his right. "As proof I didn't return empty-handed."

"But I was sent with the harp." Melaia shifted, uneasy. As far as she was concerned, the harp still belonged to Benasin, and she was its protector. "I really should play it a bit before I face the king. I'd like to feel somewhat at home on its strings." She frowned. "You know the harp is safe with me."

Trevin hesitated. Then he untied the harp. "Are you sure you want to stay here?" he asked. "I can find you a room elsewhere."

"The temple is fine. I'm a priestess, remember?"

Trevin handed her the harp, then dug into his waist pouch and pulled out his wagering stone. He pressed it into her free hand and closed her fingers around it. "I'll be back on the morrow with instructions about the harp. But if you need me, bring this to the palace and ask for me." He pointed out a tower on the east front of the building, which now looked blood red against the darkening sky. "I spend much of my time in that tower, in the aerie."

Melaia nodded. "Tomorrow then."

She fingered the *T* carved into the wagering stone as Trevin crossed the courtyard and handed off his horse to the stableboy. Then she tucked the stone into her waist sash and turned to the temple, which towered over her. It was at least twice the size of the Navian temple. She felt the impulse to call Trevin back, to accept his offer of finding her a room elsewhere. Then she thought of Hanni's friend within and climbed the stone steps to the columned porch.

Taking a deep breath, Melaia ducked through the temple's arched entrance. A low-ceilinged corridor curved both right and left. Straight ahead through a wide doorway lay a lamp-lit altar room much like the sanctuary in Navia, except that it was larger and the lamps were made of brass cut in patterns like latticework. The light that escaped them mottled the haze of nose-tingling incense.

Melaia tapped a small gong with the mallet that hung from a cord beside it. From behind one of the columns encircling the sanctuary, a sallow-faced priest emerged. His long hair was tied back at the neck, as was the custom of male priests, and his hands were hidden deep in the folds of his blue and gold robe. His close-set eyes flitted across Melaia as if to evaluate her worthiness. In an oily voice, he asked, "What is your business here?"

"I'm a chantress sent from the overlord in Navia. You must be Jarrod."

His eyebrows arched. "I'm Ordius."

"Is Jarrod here? Do you know Hanamel, high priestess of Navia?"

"Jarrod is no longer here," said Ordius. "And I know no one from Navia."

Melaia's shoulders sagged. "Could you provide me a room?"

"How long do you expect to stay?"

"I don't know. I was sent to play for the king. I may be asked to stay elsewhere after tonight."

Ordius gave one nod. With a hand decked with jeweled rings, he slipped a torch from its bracket and beckoned her to follow. They passed down the curved corridor and climbed a flight of stairs. Halfway down the hall, he ushered Melaia into a small stone-walled chamber, bare except for a stool and a table that held an unlit clay lamp. A latticed window was opposite the door, but only the dark of night showed through.

"Is there no mat?" she asked. "Where do I find water? And the privy?" From the way the priest scowled at her, she decided to leave asking for food until the morrow.

"Water and privy are in the courtyard out back. I'll bring a mat." The priest thrust the torch into a bracket in the corridor and was gone.

Melaia carried the palm-sized clay lamp to the torch flame and lit it. In the small circle of lamplight, she padded back into the room, feeling completely alone. It was too quiet here. A scratching noise on the outside wall would be welcome tonight. How comforting it would be to see the shutter opening and Trevin climbing in.

She set the lamp on the table and peered through the lattice. To the right a portion of the palace was visible, some of its windows flickering with light. To the left loomed a black shadow, which she assumed to be the city wall, for above it stretched the star-strewn heavens and a half moon.

Lifting her face toward the sky, she closed her eyes and breathed deeply of the savory smells that hung in the air. She wished she had let Trevin select a room for her, somewhere with a brazier and a hot supper, which he was probably enjoying right now, no doubt with a bevy of young ladies vying to keep him warm tonight.

When she opened her eyes, she found herself staring at the moon. Across it glided the silhouette of a hawk.

CHAPTER 8

After a cold, fitful night on a thin mat, Melaia was relieved to see the slant of morning sun streaming through the lattice, creating shadows in lacy patterns on the opposite wall. She opened the shutter and gazed at the palace but could summon no more than a sense of foreboding.

She chided herself. Any priestess would count it an honor to be assigned a post at Redcliff. Besides, she had longed to see the world outside Navia. But that was when she sat safely at home, dreaming of travel and adventure. Now that she was actually in Redcliff, staring at the unknown, she felt like a child again nervously preparing to sing for the overlord for the first time.

She leaned out the window and studied the square towers. Above the tallest hung the king's flag—a white lion on a dove gray field—snapping in the wind. A drak flapped out of the highest window of the east front tower, followed closely by a second.

"The aerie," murmured Melaia.

She stared at it for a moment, hoping Trevin would lean out and look her way. When no one showed, she withdrew and went to the courtyard to find the privy and make her ablutions. Then she went to the sanctuary for prayers and knelt before the altar, trying to ignore the stifling incense.

"Chantress!" the priest snapped.

Melaia rose and faced his scowl. She had heard there was sometimes rivalry between male priests and their counterparts. She wondered if her presence somehow threatened him.

"Word has come from the palace." He folded his arms, drummed his jeweled fingers, and stared down his nose at her. "An escort will come for you late this afternoon. You're to play for the king before he retires tonight."

"I'll be ready." Melaia tried to appear serene and composed as her stomach roiled. This was not Navia, and the audience would not be an aging overlord.

She returned to her room, mentally scrolling through the songs that seemed to soothe Lord Silas, hoping they would do the same for the king. It seemed too much to hope that the harp's music would heal him completely. Then again, there was no predicting what effect such a harp might have.

When she stepped into the room, she was surprised to find a breakfast of bread and fruited wine on her table. And a dried apricot.

She looked at the lattice. It was open, but she had left it that way. He may have simply delivered her breakfast to the priest while she was in the back courtyard. She smiled as she bit into the tart, leathery fruit. Another guilt offering? For what? Maybe he would tolerate that one question.

After eating, Melaia unwrapped the harp. The pulsing energy of the wood brought back memories of Benasin's dim room, the clink of Trevin's coin purse on the overlord's table, Yareth's sneer, her jolt when the overlord announced he would send her to Redcliff with the harp. Now here she sat, preparing to play for the king. The king! She ran her hand over the runes carved in the thrumming soundboard. *Dedroumakei.* "Awaken!" Perhaps Caepio was right. An angel's harp might be exactly what the king needed to shake off his melancholy forever.

She squinted at the harp's base. Where one living leaf had been, now three had sprouted. Never had she seen leaves on the harp when it hung on Benasin's wall. She wondered if he trimmed them when they appeared. She dared not try to snap them off herself. It was enough to hold stolen property. She didn't want to add to her guilt by damaging the harp.

She sighed, rolled a chord, and began to play a simple tune. Halfway through, a thump sounded at the window. She looked up, her heart pumping eagerly.

Then she recoiled. A drak sat on the sill, its hands spread in a human grip, its ghostly gray eyes ogling her. It occurred to her that Trevin might be watching through the spy-bird's eyes, but the creature was hideous.

She plucked a dissonant chord and said, "Begone!"

The drak sidestepped across the window ledge, bobbing its head. A gust of wind ruffled its dark feathers.

Melaia set the harp aside and shooed the bird. "Out! Begone!"

The drak leaped into the air with a screech, and she closed and latched the shutter.

꽃

Midafternoon, Melaia went to the back courtyard to wash. She returned to her room, braiding her hair, but stopped short just inside the doorway. Benasin's harp was in the hands of a cloaked, broad-shouldered woman whose dusky hair was twisted and pinned loosely at the back of her neck.

The woman looked up, then held three fingers over her heart. "Greetings," she said. "Are you Melaia, chantress from Navia?"

"I am." Melaia released her half-plaited braid and cautiously stepped into the room. "Are you an angel?"

The woman placed a finger to her lips and said softly, "Not everyone should know."

"The priest let you in?"

"I told him I'm a friend of yours. I hope that's not too far off the mark." She tilted her head and studied Melaia. "I'm here as a friend."

Melaia studied her as well. The woman had a noble nose, a high brow, and long fingers.

"I'm Livia," she said. "I knew the Erielyon who died at the temple in Navia."

"Did you send him?"

"I didn't even know he had gone to Navia. Nor did I know he had died." She looked down and cleared her throat. "Not until Benasin returned the body."

Melaia went back to braiding her hair. If this angel was a friend of Benasin, she was probably trustworthy.

"My friend Pymbric traveled with Benasin back to Navia. I followed soon after. Of course, in Navia, Benasin discovered that Lord Silas had sent you to Redcliff with a possession Benasin highly values." Livia patted the harp. "This is it, is it not?"

"I tried to dissuade Lord Silas—"

"But gold had the louder voice. So I heard."

"You were in Navia?" asked Melaia. "All was well? No raiders?"

"I saw no sign of raiders."

Melaia breathed easier. "And Benasin. Is he here?"

"He and Pymbric are on their way. I'm here to get you and the harp safely out of the city."

"And return to Navia?"

"To the Durenwoods."

Melaia dropped her braid, and the end unraveled. "It's the harp, isn't it?"

Livia frowned.

"'Now is payment due in full.' The harp is the payment for a debt, isn't it?"

"If only it were that simple." Livia smiled sadly.

Melaia stepped to the window and fingered the latticework. Of course it wouldn't be that simple. It was angel business. Which she was supposed to avoid. She sighed. She had no claim to the harp. Yet there was no reason to remain in Redcliff without it. She placed her hand on the form of Trevin's wagering stone tucked in the fold of her sash. She would have to give it back, say good-bye. Her throat felt pinched just thinking about it.

She turned to Livia. "I can't leave Redcliff just yet. I'm to play for the king this evening. An escort is already scheduled to come for me late this afternoon."

"A good reason to leave now." Livia wrapped the harp.

"Before the escort comes?"

"You'd be foolish to stay behind and try to explain why the harp is gone."

"But the king is ill with melancholy, mourning for Queen Tahn. My music always soothed Lord Silas when he was in a low mood. With Benasin's harp I might revive the king. Wouldn't that be worth the wait?"

Livia patted the stool. "Let me finish your braid."

Melaia hesitated, then sat.

Livia combed through her hair with her long fingers, the way Iona had always done. "The king's melancholy is no mood," she said. "It's guilt, pure and simple."

"For what?" Melaia picked at the crumbs left from breakfast.

"For banishing his previous queen under false accusations."

"What was she accused of?"

"Infidelity." Livia began rebraiding. "It happened many years ago. The queen hated court life and took extended trips to the countryside. When the king got her with child, he thought the father to be some lowborn countryman. I'm told that he only recently discovered the truth, and it cut him to the core. It was far too late to make amends. By that time he had been married to Tahn for several years."

"And then she died in a fire." Melaia gasped. "Do you think the king arranged it?"

"Not in my estimation. Queen Tahn was with child. His only heir. He would hardly destroy his heir."

"Unless he meant to bring back his previous queen," suggested Melaia.

"She's dead now," said Livia. "Perhaps her son as well. So you see, King Laetham's melancholy is of his own making."

"So you're saying I should leave him to his illness because he deserves it? What about Camrithia? We need our king whole, don't we?"

"Hold still." Livia smoothed a strand of hair. "I'm simply saying kingdom affairs can—and will—roll on without you or the harp. The king has a physician."

"But music often cheers the ill," said Melaia. "And this harp seems to have strong power. The runes say 'Awaken.' It truly might help the king. Surely when Benasin arrives, he'll agree."

"I don't intend for Benasin to know I'm here. I must keep a certain distance, or he will sense me."

"Why don't you want him to sense you?"

"Because I don't trust him. He's neither malevolent nor Angelaeon. We traced him to the Dregmoors. An informant there claims he's the Second son of legend." Livia tied off the braid.

"Second-born!" Melaia thought of Benasin prowling the temple on the trail of the Firstborn. Recognizing Dreia's book. Claiming Hanni had been wrong on two counts, first about who could kill an angel. And second? Of course: thinking Benasin was an angel.

"If he's the Second-born," said Livia, "he was involved in destroying the Wisdom Tree and our stairway to heaven. Surely you can understand my caution."

Melaia looked askance at Livia. "The Second-born didn't destroy the Tree. The Firstborn did."

Livia shrugged. "There are many versions of the tale."

"You can believe this one," said Melaia, although she doubted the wisdom of revealing she had heard it from the Firstborn's own mouth.

"Whatever the tale, the harp is not Benasin's," said Livia. "It belonged to Dreia."

Melaia gaped at her. "Why did Benasin have it?"

Footsteps echoed down the hall. Melaia and Livia fell silent.

Ordius appeared at the door. "An escort awaits the chantress downstairs."

"She wasn't expecting anyone until later," said Livia.

"Shall I send him away?" asked Ordius.

Melaia pictured Trevin leaning against the archway, his dark, alert eyes watching for her to appear. "Ask him to wait," she said.

As the priest's footsteps faded, Livia said, "I suggest you tell the escort you're ill."

"Would he believe that? Do I look ill?" Melaia snatched up the wrapped harp. "I feel like a game piece on a playing board. Have I no choice in this matter?"

"Unfortunately, you have every choice. As a rule we angels avoid interfering with human will, so I'll not tell you what to do. But I warn you, malevolents have no such compulsion. And there *are* malevolents here, Chantress."

Melaia hesitated. Last night the path ahead had seemed simple. Now it held all sorts of uncertain twists and turns. The only simple, certain thing she knew was the task she was sent to accomplish. And Trevin was waiting. "I'll decide what to do when I return," she said. "Until then, I'll mind my own affairs and play for the king. Then at least my duty here will be done."

Before Livia could protest, Melaia strode out. As she descended the stairs, she wondered why Trevin had come so early. She couldn't help smiling at the thought that he might want to spend time with her.

But when she reached the columned porch, her shoulders drooped. A beardless youth about Iona's age, black curls falling rakishly across his forehead, waited for her. She chided herself for thinking Trevin would have the time or inclination for such a menial chore as escorting her.

"You're the chantress?" the youth asked.

"I am." Melaia drew her blue cloak around her.

"I'm here for the harp," he said.

Melaia frowned. "I thought I was to bring the harp myself."

"I'm to take it to the chamber where you'll be playing."

She stood tall. "As chantress, sent by the overlord of Navia, I'm responsible for this harp. If you'll lead the way—"

"Dwin!" Trevin loped across the courtyard. "Scoundrel!" He grabbed the youth by one arm. "What are you doing?"

"The very thing *you* should—"

"Begone." Trevin shoved him toward the stables. "Go curry a horse."

The youth shot a teasing look at Trevin. "I just wanted to see her while I had the chance. If you need any help—"

"I don't," said Trevin.

The youth sauntered away.

"My brother, Dwin." Trevin watched him until he disappeared into the palace rather than the stables. Then he turned to Melaia. "I suppose you were surprised to see him."

"I was surprised to see anyone this early." She noted the way Trevin's right eyebrow lifted slightly when he smiled.

"A misunderstanding. But since it's early yet, let me show you the palace." Trevin reached for the harp. "May I?"

Melaia handed it to him, and they strolled across the flagstones. She wondered if Livia was watching.

"Do you have brothers and sisters?" asked Trevin.

"I have novice priestesses. They serve quite well as sisters."

"You're lucky to have no brother. Dwin can be a thorn in the foot."

"Tree-vun!" A leather-faced, bulky man rode up on a sleek black horse. "Ye'll see the birds in this even?"

"I'll be there," said Trevin.

"Ye make sure he is, missy." The leather-faced man leered at Melaia before he reined his horse away and galloped out of the courtyard.

Melaia shuddered. "Who was that?"

"Vort. One of our two talonmasters," said Trevin. "They're like falconers. You've met one of their birds."

"Draks." Melaia wrinkled her nose.

As they walked, Trevin seemed lost in thought.

"I had a wonderful dried apricot for breakfast this morning," she said. "Another guilt offering?"

"I thought perhaps I should pay in advance." Trevin's face was inscrutably pleasant as he gazed at the palace entrance. "A friendly reminder," he said. "No more questions."

"I'm sorry. It's my nature." She eyed the great bronze doors. "Maybe I should apologize in advance in case I forget."

"Don't forget."

She clamped her mouth shut, fighting a pang of homesickness as they climbed the steps to the palace. Thus far, Redcliff was a disappointment. Even Trevin was obviously distracted, his mind on his duties. Or on someone watching them. Or on the young ladies falling all over themselves for his affection.

She made up her mind. After Benasin arrived, she would let him sort out the business with the harp, and she would return to Navia.

A porter ushered them into a columned entryway. Directly ahead stood a pair of tall, gilded doors. Trevin edged one open, and Melaia peeked into the cavernous great hall adorned with ornately painted walls and a colorful mosaic floor.

"This is where the king would normally take his supper if he were not ill," said Trevin.

"So I'll not be playing here." Melaia raised her eyebrows to make it a question.

Trevin's mouth turned up slightly. "You'll not play here tonight, no."

He closed the doors and led her down the west corridor, where polished red marble columns lined both sides like sentries. Up a staircase, down another corridor they strolled, passing servants intent on their tasks. Melaia tried to think of how to ask where they were going without making it a question.

A woman's angry yell echoed down the hall. Servants scattered, and Trevin tugged Melaia into an alcove.

"Zastra," he whispered. Melaia started to ask who Zastra was, but he placed a finger over her mouth. "Queen mother," he whispered.

"How dare you touch my scrying jar!" screamed Zastra.

"Just to clean, Great One," squeaked another voice.

"You spoiled the image!" Zastra yelled. "I'm watching for Dreia. I leave for one moment, and I come back to nothing! Out!" A slap echoed down the corridor along with a whimper and running feet. A red-cloaked woman swept past them, muttering, one hand choking the neck of a large, clear jar containing a colored liquid.

When her footsteps had trailed off into silence, Melaia whispered, "Dreia! Here!"

"What do you know of Dreia?" asked Trevin. Then he held up his hand. "Don't answer. You've obviously told the tales. Dreia is not here."

"But Zastra said—"

"Zastra is crazed. Believe me, Dreia is not here." Trevin led her out of the alcove and down the corridor in the opposite direction from the way Zastra had gone. He was tense, his eyes not meeting hers.

Melaia sighed. "Maybe you could show me to a room where I can practice and rest."

"We're almost to the king's tower," he said. "You'll like the view."

Melaia trailed Trevin up one flight of stairs after another, then onto a roof like a small courtyard, its walls waist high. The king's white-lion flag flapped in the wind from a pole in the center. Trevin nodded to a guard, who then retreated into the stairwell.

Melaia gaped at the landscape that spread out around her. "You're right," she said. "The view is no less than astonishing." She turned in a slow circle. Forest to the west. Mountains to the north. Plains to the east. The highway they had traveled just the day before was now a ribbon crossing the valley and hill to the south. "You must love it up here. It's a bird's perch."

"The highest of Redcliff's towers." Trevin strode to the east wall and looked toward the aerie.

Melaia stepped to the south side of the parapet. Looking down on the grasshopper-sized people in the courtyard below proved dizzying. She held to the edge of the half wall and lifted her gaze to the horizon. Navia was out there, somewhere past the ruddy rows of houses, the city wall, the golden valley, and the dusky hills beyond.

Trevin's hands slipped around her waist. Her heart lurched, and she twisted around to face him.

"I'm not ready," she gasped.

He backed away, his hands raised. "I...I'm sorry."

"You startled me, that's all." The reason for the apricot, she thought. In case she rebuffed him.

Trevin strode back to the east wall of the parapet and stood there, rubbing his right hand. A drak sailed past, then glided up to join another.

Melaia watched Trevin's jaw clench and unclench. "I didn't mean to offend you," she said. "I just wasn't ready."

"Nor was I." He didn't look her in the eye, just took her arm and walked her back to the stairway. The guard climbed back to his post.

They descended the stairs in silence, Melaia apprehensive at the swelling wave of unease she sensed in Trevin. She missed his quick, disarming smile. Now it felt as if he wore a mask.

As they wove their way back through the corridors, she said, "Before I play for the king, I need to know if my presence is unwelcome. I intend to bring greetings from Lord Silas, but I don't want to offend anyone."

"Don't worry about the king." Trevin kept his eyes on the corridor ahead. "Ask no questions. Do as you're told."

"See nothing, hear nothing, say nothing."

"Pawns," he muttered. "We're all pawns." He pointed ahead. "I'll show you the aerie." He sounded less than eager.

Melaia wondered if he was concerned about what she would think of the aerie since she had shrunk from the drak on their first day out of Navia. She wasn't eager to see the birds again, but she determined to abide the sight for his sake.

They climbed a steep stairway. Then Trevin placed his hand on her back and ushered her into the aerie, which was sharp scented even with the south window standing open. At the far side of the room, Dwin rose from a bench in front of three large cages, two of which were empty. In the third sat two draks, their human hands clamped over a branch, their gray eyes staring at Melaia.

"Welcome, Chantress."

The smooth, deep voice sent chills slithering down Melaia's spine. She turned to see a gaunt man emerge from a shadowed alcove. Sharp nosed. Beardless. A cloak of feathers, brown, black, and iridescent blue.

"Meet the king's physician," said Dwin. "Lord Rejius."

CHAPTER 9

Holding his hands as if in prayer, Lord Rejius tapped his taloned forefingers together and studied Melaia with his round gold eyes. "A little chantress far from home?"

She felt the blood drain from her face. Firstborn. Angel murderer. She glanced at Trevin, recalled him urging the Navian overlord to support Lord Rejius. She clenched her jaw, fighting an angry shame. Oh, yes, she *had* been empty-headed. Yet she still had a task to do, and here stood the king's physician.

She swallowed the lump in her throat and said, "I've been sent—"

"I know why you were sent," said Lord Rejius. "But all I requested was a harp. Unwrap it, Trevin. Make certain she hasn't deceived us."

"It's not I who deceived," she hissed, glaring at Trevin.

Stone faced, he strode to the bench, unwrapped the harp, and shoved it into Dwin's hands. Then he plopped onto the bench, his back to Melaia, while Dwin carried the harp to Lord Rejius.

Melaia plucked Trevin's wagering stone out of her sash and fingered the *T* on it. His warnings about her questions now made a great deal of sense. As did the hawk on his signet ring. No doubt the insignia on the red side of his cloak was also a hawk. She threw the stone at Trevin as hard as she could. It missed, clanked off a cage latch, and spun at his feet. The hawkman chuckled. Trevin didn't move.

Lord Rejius examined the harp and crowed. "This is the one! Well done, Trevin. Except for the fact that I have no need of a chantress, and you didn't have the mettle to push her off and watch her fly."

Sweat broke out on Melaia's forehead. The dizzying view from the highest tower. Trevin's hands on her waist. It all washed back, leaving her with a sick feeling in the pit of her stomach. He had paid for absolution in advance, fully aware that he meant to murder her.

"How do you propose to get rid of her now, *son*?" Lord Rejius drew Dwin close.

"Son?" Melaia muttered.

Trevin glowered at the hawkman. "I'll return her to Navia."

"You have no more imagination than that?" Lord Rejius grinned coldly.

"She can tell the overlord she played for the king and was dismissed," said Trevin.

"But that ending is too dull, is it not, Chantress?" The hawkman cocked his head. "Surely she deserves more, Trevin, as do you. A happy ending, perhaps one in which she spends the rest of her life with you. Wouldn't you like a drak of your own? One with the hands of a harper?"

Trevin rose so fast his bench toppled, but Lord Rejius curved his taloned hand around Dwin's neck. Dwin held still, his eyes fixed on Trevin, who froze, glaring at Lord Rejius, his fists clenched.

The hawkman released Dwin and stepped toward Melaia, his gold eyes gleaming. "Which cage do you want, Chantress?"

She edged back, aware of the stairwell behind her. Her mind screamed for her to run, but the hawkman's eyes held her. She couldn't even look toward the swift footsteps echoing up the stairwell. It was only when she heard a familiar voice call her name that she turned.

Benasin swept through the door, and she darted into his arms, feeling like the small girl in Navia who had greeted him at the temple, bumped into him at the market, taken messages to him from Hanni. He appeared weary, sweaty and huffing, but he had the same wild, hunting eyes she had seen the night he paced the Navian temple searching for the intruder. This time he pegged his prey.

"Dandreij." Benasin leaned on his walking stick. "I'd heard the king's physician was Lord Rejius, but I didn't suspect it was you."

"I would have provided a more fitting welcome, brother, but I didn't sense your coming." A menacing smile spread across Lord Rejius's face.

Melaia glanced back and forth between the two, as did Trevin and Dwin. Firstborn, Second son—the legend alive before her eyes. The aerie filled with animosity as thick as the air of a gathering storm.

"I suggest we meet in private," said Benasin.

"No witnesses?" Lord Rejius laughed. "We've nothing to hide, have we? Hear this, one and all. I hold two harps and a certain angel you love, Benasin. I'm sure you heard of her recent tragic death."

"I did." Benasin raised his chin defiantly, and Melaia felt him tense.

"One by one I've taken everything you've ever desired." Lord Rejius casually examined his talon nails. "I believe Hanamel is next on my list."

"Hanni?" Melaia whispered.

The hawkman's eyes flicked to her. "Though I must say, this chantress becomes more interesting by the moment. I like the way she clings to you, Benasin." He motioned to Trevin. "Open one of the empty cages."

As Trevin took a ring of keys from a peg, Melaia felt Benasin firmly grip her arm. She let him draw her behind him. "Hanamel is only a friend, Dandreij," he said.

Trevin shifted uneasily, keys in hand, intent on the conversation.

"Only a friend?" said Lord Rejius. "You underplay your attachments. But I believe I befriended her first."

Benasin snorted. "I think not."

Melaia wrung her hands. She couldn't tell what was truth. She knew Hanni relied on Benasin, yet how close they were, she didn't know. She certainly couldn't remember Hanni mentioning Lord Rejius. Or Dandreij, for that matter.

"I assume you have some purpose in posing as King Laetham's physician." Benasin's voice was low and calm. "Could it be that his melancholy is your doing?"

Lord Rejius raised his eyebrows. "I'm crushed you would even think such a thing. The king fell into melancholy on his own. I only had to answer the call for the most skillful physician that could be found. Though Queen Tahn never did quite trust me."

"And now she's dead." Benasin's words echoed Melaia's thoughts. She saw Dwin snatch the keys from Trevin and unlock the cage himself. Trevin stood like a tensed wildcat.

"As you would assume," said the Firstborn, "melancholy again struck the king after Tahn's death. Woeful, isn't it? But convenient. I simply bring him the peace he so richly deserves. It's cruel to allow someone to linger too long, don't you think? The greater mercy is to bring such affliction to an end. After all, he is mortal. His future is finite here. He'll die sooner or later."

"Sooner happens to be to your advantage," said Benasin.

"Dear brother, I must look to the future. For Stalia's sake."

Out of the corner of her eye, Melaia could see Trevin and Dwin exchanging sharp words. She wished she had not left the knife in her pack at the temple. Everyone else had a dagger.

"You deceive yourself, Dandreij," said Benasin. "You're not providing for your daughter; you're exacting revenge."

Melaia bit her lip. Stalia. Daughter of the Firstborn. Of course. She was entangled in this too.

"You call it revenge," said Lord Rejius. "I call it justice. You thought you could take refuge in Camrithia, but Camrithia will soon be mine, and then where will you run? You know that wherever you go, I'll find you. Whatever you value will become mine." He pointed a single taloned finger. A thin bolt of thunderlight hissed out.

Melaia ducked as the bolt struck Benasin's right arm. With a sharp cry he stumbled back into her. She steadied him.

Trevin started toward them, then halted. Dwin grabbed the harp and carried it into the shadowed alcove.

Benasin cradled his wounded arm. "Revenge will eat you alive, Dandreij. Steal your human soul. Turn you into an animal. It's a trap. But you still have time to free yourself."

"Time?" Lord Rejius laughed. "What is time to an immortal? I have all eternity."

"Don't count on it," said Benasin. "When the Tree is restored—"

"A dream, brother. A delusion. Once I have the third harp, my eternity is secured, and I shall be free."

"You'll be bound," said Benasin. "Bound forever. Vengeance is a demanding slave driver, and you, Dandreij, are the slave. By your own choice, no less."

"And whose choice was it to abduct my daughter, to send her to an early death?"

"I've tried to explain—"

"So have I. Everything I do is for Stalia."

"Everything you do is for you."

"Your self-righteousness sickens me." Lord Rejius raised both arms. They shriveled and twisted sideways as black feathers emerged from his skin.

Benasin nudged Melaia toward the door. "Get out!" His own arms began to transform.

Lord Rejius's face contorted, more bird now than man.

"Out!" Benasin shoved Melaia, not with an arm, but with a wing. She ran.

The cry of the hawkman followed her down the stairs as he screeched, "Dwin! Take the girl!"

"I'm already after her," called Trevin.

Melaia stumbled down the stairs, retraced the torchlit corridor at a run, dodged servants, and headed for the entryway. But Caepio and his actors were milling around the door to the great hall, preparing to enter. Melaia groaned, knowing they would hail her if they saw her. Yet she couldn't turn back, for Trevin's footsteps echoed behind her.

Slipping into the shadows behind the marble columns, Melaia wove her way to the front doors, then dashed to the portal guard. "Lord Rejius needs help in the aerie!" she told him. "Quick!"

As the guard trotted toward the east corridor, she shoved a door open and made the same claim to the two outer guards, who were already gaping at the aerie window. A succession of screeches and squawks ripped the air. The guards rushed inside, and Melaia ran down the steps into the courtyard.

The few people in the yard, including the stableboy, stood like statues, gazing toward the aerie. Melaia grabbed the stableboy's arm. "I need help!"

He stared at her, wide-eyed. "If it's about the aerie, lady, I'll not get mixed up in it."

"Ho there!" a gate guard called out.

Melaia shrank behind the stableboy as the guard ran toward the palace, sword in hand. Trevin stood at the top of the steps, scanning the yard. Dwin shot out from the doors behind him.

"Am I needed?" asked the guard.

"We're looking for a lady," said Dwin. "A priestess."

The stableboy shifted.

"Don't," whispered Melaia, edging back behind him.

But Trevin had already spotted her. His gaze held hers for a moment. Then he turned to the guard and called, "Check the temple."

Melaia ducked into the stable. "What is he doing?" she murmured. Did he intend to take her himself? She glanced out the door, fully expecting to see Trevin loping toward the stables.

Instead, she saw Dwin hit him on the arm. "I can't believe a girl outran you," he griped.

"Maybe she didn't," Trevin shouted, shoving Dwin. "Maybe she's still inside." They both barged back through the bronze doors.

Melaia leaned against the wall and tried to catch her breath. The courtyard fell eerily quiet. No squawks. No yelling. Nothing. She wondered if it was too late to help Benasin. Livia was the only person she could think of who might be able to help, but getting to Livia seemed out of the question with the courtyard being watched and the temple being searched.

A squat, bandy-legged man with a weathered face stepped from a stall as horses bobbed their heads over the rails and eyed Melaia. "Agues and ailments, lady, you spooked too?" The man ran his fingers through his dirt brown hair, which stuck out like an unweeded garden. "All that racket. I was just calming the horses."

She stared at him, panting, wondering if she should run.

He grabbed a rag and wiped his callous hands. "I'm Armsman Pymbric. Or just Pym, if it suits you. And you're?"

She took a cautious step toward him. "Melaia. Livia told me about you."

"You know Livia?"

Melaia nodded. "She's at the temple, but the guards are there looking for me."

He narrowed his eyes. "Are you involved in the ruckus?"

"It's Lord Rejius. He attacked my friend Benasin in the aerie, and I ran."

"Benasin? I traveled in with him today. Just saw to his mount. He's in the aerie, you say?" Pym peered out into the courtyard.

"He's wounded. I have to go back and see if I can help him. And the harp is up there."

Pym shook his head. "I generally stay as far as I can from the quarrels of other men—and twice as far from the quarrels of angels."

"Not angels. Immortals."

"Danger, they are, either one." Pym fingered the hilt of a dagger that hung at his side. "But if it's Benasin in trouble…"

Melaia peeked out the stable door. Lord Rejius strutted along the top of the palace steps, directing the search. A guard headed to the stables, and she shrank into the shadows. "Is there another way out?"

Pym motioned for her to follow. They slipped past the stalls to the north side of the stables, where a door opened into a smaller courtyard. Keeping to the shadows, they crossed the yard and ducked into the palace through the servants' entrance.

"We'd best act like we know where we're going," whispered Pym. "Do you know the way?"

"East tower." Melaia strode ahead. "Front of the palace." She hoped she was going the right direction. All the hallways looked the same. Then she heard voices and flattened her back to the wall.

Trevin and Dwin emerged from a stairwell ahead and trudged the opposite direction. "We can't just leave him up there," said Trevin. "He may still be alive."

"He'll be dead by the time the guards come to take his body," said Dwin. "I can't believe the lady outran you. You should have let me take the chase. You're as slow as a hobbled mule." Their bickering faded with their footsteps.

Melaia dashed to the stairs and headed up with Pym right behind her. She edged into the aerie, which was deathly silent. One lamp burned low. All the draks were gone. The harp was gone. But Benasin lay in one corner, burned and bleeding. Melaia could see his spirit bordering his body.

"He *is* alive!" She ran to him and knelt. "We can carry him to the stables. Then when it's clear, the temple."

"How, lady?" asked Pym. "We can hardly move unnoticed as it is, much less bearing a wounded man."

She slipped her arms under Benasin and strained to lift him to his feet. Pym added his support, but they only succeeded in dragging him a short distance.

"Pym. Mellie. Leave me," Benasin groaned. "Let me lie." They laid him down.

Melaia watched his spirit in its death struggle. "I thought you were immortal," she said.

Benasin's eyes were closed, but the corner of his mouth twitched up. "Immortal. Yes."

"What do you need?" asked Melaia. "How can I help?"

He made no answer as he struggled to breathe.

She couldn't see him clearly through her tears. As she pulled his cloak around him the way she had done for the Erielyon, his spirit pooled around her wrists, not with the aloof vibration of a stranger's spirit, but with the intimate embrace of a friend. She began to hum a song of comfort, her throat so swollen she could hardly keep the tune.

Hoofbeats sounded in the courtyard, and Pym peered out the window. "Talonmasters. They're malevolents. If I may say so, lady, we'd best not be caught up here."

Benasin's hand abruptly grabbed Melaia's wrist. She gasped and jerked back, but his hand was a metal-cold shackle as his spirit rose and swirled around her like a mist, breathing. *The book. Get it.*

"Dreia's book?" She blinked back tears. With her free hand she searched Benasin for a journey bag, a pouch, but Lord Rejius had taken everything. Even his staff. "It's gone," she whispered. She stroked his hair away from his bloody, sweat-beaded forehead. His spirit would return, wouldn't it? He wasn't supposed to die.

Get the book, his spirit breathed. *Open—*

"Live, Benasin," she pleaded. "Live. Then you can get the book." His grip was uncomfortably tight, but when she tried prying his hand from her wrist, it only tightened.

You. Get it.

Her hand throbbed. In an effort to reassure him, she nodded. "All right. I'll get it. Just live."

Pym touched her shoulder. "The draks will be coming back to roost."

Promise... Open... Benasin's breath shuddered out.

"I promise," said Melaia.

Benasin's grip eased as his spirit broke away from his body.

"Benasin?" Melaia stared at the ribbon of spirit that streamed across the floor and disappeared. "No." Her whisper became a moan. "How can he die?"

"I don't know, lady, but I know how we can die. And it'll be none too pleasant." Pym paced to the door.

Melaia hesitated, Benasin's hand loose around hers.

"Lady?" Pym was halfway out the door.

Melaia pulled away and dashed after Pym, fighting sobs.

CHAPTER 10

Melaia and Pym had taken only two steps into the temple when she was grabbed from the shadows and jerked into the incense-laden sanctuary. Before she could cry out, a hand clamped over her mouth. She fought back, wondering why Pym was helping drag her to the other side of the room.

"Hush! It's me." Livia shook her.

Melaia stilled just as Ordius stepped from a side room, peered down the torchlit corridor, then slipped back into his quarters.

"Bats and beetles!" Pym whispered. "He's a pasty-pale grubworm."

"I've been frantic for you," whispered Livia, releasing Melaia. "Where's the harp?"

"The king's physician has it," said Melaia.

Livia pinched the bridge of her nose.

"And Benasin's been murdered," said Pym.

Livia looked up in alarm. "Murdered?" Her eyes welled with tears. "Who's next?"

"Can you help us get Benasin's body back?" asked Melaia. "And the harp?"

Livia wiped her eyes. "You're being hunted. We'd best try to save you." She shoved Melaia's journey pack at her, snatched up her own bag, and grabbed an oil lamp.

Shaken, Melaia followed Livia and Pym through a corridor and down stone stairs to a chilly chamber of catacombs. There they slipped past a row of vaults and wove around ancient burial masks and stone altars. Grotesque shadows leaped up at the reach of their lamp, danced across the walls, then sank back into thick, dank darkness. A stone coffin came into view. The carved figure of a woman lay on top, heaped with dry brown flowers.

"Queen Tahn," said Livia before Melaia could ask. Darkness swallowed the coffin as the lamplight moved on and found a waist-high door.

"The Door of the Dead," said Pym. "Clever, Livia, to go the way of coffins."

"Pray it's unguarded." Livia unbolted the door and edged it open. A rush of wind whistled in.

"Where are we going?" asked Melaia.

"The Durenwoods," said Livia.

Melaia pulled back. "Can't I return to Navia?"

"Navia isn't safe," said Livia. "You remember asking about raiders? After you left for the palace, I stepped out and wandered the marketplace, listening for news. You were right. Navia has been attacked."

Melaia's jaw dropped. "What about the temple? Our coffers hold very little, but raiders wouldn't know that. I have to go back."

"With raiders on the roads?" Pym drew his dagger and slipped out the door.

"Even if you made it to Navia, you've no guarantee that the city would be safe," said Livia. "Redcliff certainly isn't. Guards combed every corner of the temple in search of you. It took all my wits to throw them off track."

Pym glanced back. "The way is clear, and there's cloud cover."

"You're free to choose," said Livia. "Come or not." She held the lamp to the open door, and the wind snuffed the flame. Deep black enveloped them. The darkness outside was now lighter than the darkness within. Livia stepped out.

Melaia huffed. She couldn't scrabble around in the catacombs without light. She tugged her cloak tight at her chin and followed Livia into the night, concluding that, while angels might not force their will upon humans, they certainly could make it hard to go against their wishes.

Following Pym's bandy-legged gait, Melaia and Livia wove their way through the commoners' burial grounds, then headed across the field toward the dark line of the Durenwoods. Wind whipped their cloaks and misted them with fine rain.

Melaia's steps were steady, but her thoughts stumbled along, ranging from Hanni and the girls in Navia to Hanni's warnings about the Durenwoods. Were the sylvans, the earth-angels, truly waiting for a priestess to serve out Hanni's time? Would that be so bad? It would be a good way to learn about angels, Melaia thought. But would they keep her there against her will? And what about her foolish promise to Benasin? Was that another debt to be paid now? Nothing was simple anymore. Nothing.

After crossing the deserted caravan road, they approached the dark mass of swaying trees. At the edge of the woods, Livia whistled a birdlike warble. An echoing trill sounded ahead, and Livia took the lead, guiding them into the forest, which was as deep and dark as Hanni had said. But at least the tree trunks served as a windbreak, a shelter of sorts.

Shhhelter, shhhelter, swished the upper reaches of the trees. Waves of wind gusted through the boughs, and dry leaves pelted down. Melaia kept her eyes on Livia and the trail before her, but her ears pricked to the sighs and shivers and soughs of the trees. Surely this was a forest with dark secrets. The thought drew her and repelled her at the same time.

As they plodded on, Livia now and then whistled a short trill. An answer always rang from somewhere above. At last Livia slowed, apparently searching for something along a laurel hedge. After a few moments she pointed to an arbor that arched over a door hidden among the leaves. Placing the flat of her hand against the door, she bowed her head. The door unlatched with a click, and Melaia jumped. Her heart beat as if it were in her throat. Should she enter?

Shhhould shhhee? Shhhould shhhee? Melaia frowned at the echoing branches.

"What's your worry?" Pym asked her.

"Are you hearing your own thoughts?" asked Melaia.

"I'm hearing my own stomach," said Pym. "I hope there's food inside."

As Livia eased the door open, a warm, woodsy fragrance wafted out. Melaia wondered if choosing to enter this place would be her last act of freedom. She took a deep breath and let Livia usher her inside with Pym. The door clicked shut behind them.

"Welcome to Wodehall," said Livia.

Melaia strained to see in the darkness.

"Who's there?" A nasal voice drifted toward them, and a lamp flame flared in the hands of a sylvan, who padded down a curved staircase carved into the back wall. Thin green legs poked out from under his long bedshirt. A gray green beard vined from his chin to his waist.

Melaia couldn't help staring at this strange angel. Then he held the lamp higher, spilling light into the room, and her gaze turned to her surroundings. The room was circular and as wide as two of the king's great halls put together. The ceiling soared high overhead.

"Livia!" The sylvan's face wrinkled in a grin.

Livia smoothed back her dusky hair. "I'm sorry we've come unannounced, Noll."

"Twiddlesticks! You were announced by the lookout. He just had no knowledge of who you were. You'd never have gotten past him, you know, if you'd not given the whistle." He nodded at Pym and Melaia. "Who might these honorable guests be?"

"Armsman Pymbric." Pym saluted.

"Ah!" Noll nodded approval. "In service of which comain, may I ask?"

"Main Undrian. Until he disappeared, that is." Pym ran a hand across his hair, which promptly sprang back to its weedy state. "I'm in search of him. If you have any news, I'd be grateful to hear it."

"No tidings here," said Noll. "But if I learn anything in that vein, you'll be the first to know." He turned his pale green eyes to Melaia and squinted a smile.

"This is Melaia," said Livia. "Hanamel's ward."

Noll eyed Melaia. "Can it be?"

Melaia tried to picture a sylvan bringing her as a baby to the temple in

Navia. She knew she should greet Noll, but she couldn't find her voice, for the thought of Navia had reminded her of raiders at its gates.

"By the Ancient!" said Noll. He grabbed Melaia's hand. "Great glades! Esper!" he called. "Esper! Hurry down!"

"Did you get my message?" Livia asked.

"I did," said Noll, his twiggy fingers still around Melaia's hand. "I called for a meeting of the Angelaeon. The first of them has already arrived."

"Who is it, Noll?" Another sylvan bobbed down the stairs, green as the first, but this one an apple-plump woman with long white hair.

Noll leaned close to Melaia. "My wife, Esper." He called to the plump woman, "Livia and her friend Pym are here with Hanamel's ward, Melaia."

Esper rushed over. "Melaia? Bless us!" Her hands went to her flushed cheeks. "I last saw you when you were newborn!"

Melaia's heartbeat quickened. "You know who my parents are, then."

"We're a safe haven here. Your mother came to us knowing she was with child." Esper fanned her face with both hands. "Mercy me! Here we are, gabbing in the mid of the night. There'll be plenty of time for talk on the morrow. Come now. To bed with all of you. Ladies in bower rooms." She turned to Pym. "Do you think you could content yourself with a nook near the larder?"

"*Content* would indeed be the word for it." Pym patted his belly.

"I myself have always wished to sleep near the larder." Noll winked.

"Milkweed!" said Esper. "You'd not do much sleeping, and there'd be nothing left for meals on the morrow." She shuffled Melaia and Livia to the spiral staircase and led them up. In a chamber off the second-floor landing, Esper laid out a sleep shift for Melaia. Then she accompanied Livia upstairs.

Melaia changed into the shift, tired but frustrated that Esper had not revealed her parents' identities. Tomorrow, she thought. Tomorrow would bring answers.

As she sank into the mat and closed her eyes, she saw again the view from the top of the king's tower in Redcliff, felt Trevin's hands at her waist.

"I trusted him," she murmured. And he had taken her straight to Lord Rejius. I'm a fool, she thought. A shameful, empty-headed fool.

Outdoors the wind roared through the trees. *Shhhameful. Shhhameful.* She drew the covers over her head.

❧

Melaia awoke to muted voices drifting up from downstairs. After dressing, she padded onto the landing and gazed up the spiral staircase in awe. Boxy lanterns filled with glowing lichen lit the stairwell, which circled walls of red brown wood as high as she could see. What's more, she sensed the chatter of tree-thought, warm and vibrant, flowing just beyond her range of hearing. Stroking the polished ruddy wall, she realized Wodehall was a giant tree, and she was within its amazing, expansive, wondrous trunk.

Shhh, shhh, came the tree-thought, calming her spirit. Melaia inhaled the spicewood fragrance, which reminded her of incense. Surely this was a holy place, the temple of the woods.

"Why didn't Hanni like it here?" she wondered aloud.

"She did, pipit. For a time." Esper bobbed up the stairs behind Melaia, carrying a cloth-draped tray that smelled of fresh-baked bread. A grin brightened her pale green face. "You like our inn? Few kyparis trees have survived to this day. I'm proud to say that since the Wisdom Tree fell, Wodehall is the tallest."

"The Wisdom Tree looked like this?"

"Same type of wood. But Wodehall doesn't bear fruit. And the stairway of the Wisdom Tree was pure light leading to the heavens. Ours leads only to the lookout. Noll is up there now, keeping an eye on draks circling the woods this morn."

"Draks, here?"

"Spy-birds do appear from time to time. With the Angelaeon gathering, draks are to be expected."

"How many angels will be here?" asked Melaia, uneasy.

"Depends on how many answer the call," said Esper. "A dozen? A score? I hope they fill the whole of the common room."

Melaia thought of Hanni's warning, and her resolve cracked like an eggshell. "I have to go back to Navia," she said. "Today."

"But we've so much to talk about." Esper handed the fragrant tray to Melaia. "Be a dear and take Noll's lunch to him in the tower for me."

"Lunch? Have I slept that late?"

"Aye, pipit. Most likely you needed the rest. There's enough on the tray for you too, if you've a mind to eat. Just take it to the tiptop of the stairs."

Melaia headed up with the tray, wondering if this was Esper's way of keeping her here. What else would she find for Hanamel's ward to do? A day could easily turn into a week, weeks into months, months into years. Hanni had liked it. *For a time.*

At the top of the stairway, Melaia stepped out onto a landing that widened into a room half the size of the common room. Its walls extended upward the height of two more floors. But there was no roof. Instead, from the center of the room a second tree grew, thin trunked, straight and tall like a column. High overhead it sprouted into a broad-leafed canopy. Its leaves tossed wildly in a howling wind.

Noll clung to the top of the swaying trunk. As Melaia stared up, he glanced down. "Melaia! Find the bench and sit tight."

He scrambled through the leaves and disappeared. Other sylvans scampered around in the crown of the tree. Arrows zinged.

A drak broke through the canopy and hurtled down. Melaia scooted to the bench, trying not to spill Noll's lunch. The drak's spirit spiraled free as it fell, and its body thudded to the landing, an arrow in its heart, its eyes wide and staring.

Then it began to transform. A stem. Branches. Leaves. Within moments the drak had become a dark-stemmed bush with dull black green leaves and two gray eye-blossoms.

"Aha!" cheered Noll. "Another soul freed."

"To go where?" asked Melaia.

"That's the thorn of it. In the olden days it would have crossed the stairway to the heavens." Noll scampered down and studied the drak-bush. "That's a pretty one, if I do say so myself."

Melaia stared at the eye-blossoms and shuddered. "Do all draks become bushes when they die?"

"Any creature shot with sylvan arrows takes root and branches out." Noll eyed the tray and sniffed. "Might this be lunch?" He lifted the cloth. A loaf of bread lay on a bed of broad leaves. Beside it sat a pot of honey. He broke off a hunk of the bread, drizzled honey on it, placed it on a large leaf, and handed it to Melaia. Then he nodded at the drak-bush. "No need to worry. I'm steward of the Durenwoods, and I see to it that draks find a prickly welcome when they venture into the sylvan realm." He licked a drip of honey from one of his fingers.

"How far can you see from the lookout?" asked Melaia. "Can you see Navia? Do you have news from there?"

"Can't see that far," said Noll. "I heard raiders attacked, but I know nothing of how the city fared."

"I have news of Navia." Livia strode into the room, regal in her cloak. Over her shoulder she carried a large deerskin bag. She eyed the fallen drak as she circled it.

"And?" Melaia set aside her bread.

"Raiders broke down the gates," said Livia. "Some buildings were ransacked; others went untouched. I hear the temple looks as though someone turned it inside out. The high priestess has a great deal of work to do if she's to clean it up."

"She's not harmed, then?"

"She and the girls hid in the underground storehouse."

"I'll return to Navia right away," said Melaia. "They'll need my help."

"First, I have something to show you." Livia drew a thin, square board from the bag and set it on the bench beside Melaia. The design etched on top matched the carving on the cover of Dreia's book. The sign of the Tree. But a central path crossed from the crown of the Tree to the opposite edge of the board.

Noll leaned in to look. "I've not seen that in many a year."

"What is it?" Melaia stroked the etching.

"A game." Livia pulled a pouch from the bag and gently poured out a die and a set of miniature wooden figures, intricately carved. As she set them in marked squares at the foot of the tree, she called out their races. "Sylvan, Erielyon, dwarf, Windwing, human, Archae."

Melaia eyed them. Each figure was different from the others, but their races were obvious. Thin-limbed, long-nosed sylvans. Humans of various sizes. Winged, human-looking Erielyon. Potbellied, round-faced dwarfs and slick-haired, thin dwarfs. Winged horses, the Windwings. And five tall, fragile-looking Archae—two men, three women, each rising from a different base: water, earth, fire, an airy cloud, and a bush.

"They're exquisite," said Melaia. "Surely you don't let people actually play with this."

"Only special guests." Livia pointed to the figures nearest Melaia. "These will be your figures; the others mine." She handed Melaia a die. "We take turns rolling the die. You may move one of your figures the number of spaces equal to the number of dots on the die. Or you may split the move between any of your figures. The goal is to be the first to get all your figures up the tree, across the stairway to heaven, and into Avellan."

Melaia scowled. "Navia is in shambles after a raid, draks circle the woods, and you want to play a game?"

Livia shrugged her broad shoulders. "We'll make it a short game."

Melaia shook her head and rolled the die. It landed with two spots up.

"Move two spaces up the trunk," said Noll.

Melaia selected an Erielyon, a woman with wings. As she picked it up, a tiny green leaf sprouted from its base. She almost dropped the piece in her hurry to set it down. "Great shades!" she said. "This is like Benasin's harp. Enchanted somehow."

Livia threw the die and moved a sylvan five spaces ahead. The sylvan didn't sprout. She pointed to a dwarf. "Try this one."

Melaia rolled the die. As she moved the dwarf three spaces, a leaf appeared on it. "Which ones sprout?" she asked.

"The ones you touch," said Livia.

Melaia gaped at her.

"Try it."

With one finger Melaia touched a sylvan figure. It sprouted. She stroked a horse with wings. It sprouted. An Archon. It leafed at her touch. Melaia bit her lip. Had the harp sprouted at her touch as well? And the cup in Benasin's quarters in Navia?

Livia looked at Noll. "It's true, then."

"What's true?" Melaia's fingers tingled.

"And to think Esper hid it, even from me," said Noll.

"A secret well kept." Livia scooped up the game pieces and returned them to the pouch.

Melaia glanced back and forth from Livia to Noll. *Dark secrets in these woods.* She shifted uneasily, thinking she might as well settle one important matter. "I won't be allowed to leave the Durenwoods, will I?"

"You're free to leave any time," said Livia. "I told you, angels don't usually interfere with human will. But the freedom to go should be balanced with the freedom to stay, don't you think? I want to show you something that may help you make that choice." She headed out, motioning for Melaia to follow.

"Where are we going?" asked Melaia.

"Into the woods."

CHAPTER 11

When Melaia and Livia descended the last curve of the staircase into the common room, Melaia gasped. It looked as if the game figures had come to life. She saw no Windwing horses or Archae, but long-limbed sylvans milled around, helping Esper ferry drinks and food to round tables made from stumps. At many of those tables, plump, bushy-haired dwarfs huddled in conversation, now and then leaning back in boisterous laughter. Melaia saw Gil among them, although he didn't notice her. Then there were the more somber Erielyon, some with white wings, some with gray, seated on benches around the brazier. She couldn't help staring at their elegant wings and thinking of the Erielyon who died in Navia.

The conversations lulled as one by one the guests caught sight of Livia. Melaia could feel their gaze on her as she followed Livia across the room and out the door.

"Are they all angels?" asked Melaia.

"The Angelaeon, yes," said Livia. "Angels can embody any living form. When the Tree was destroyed, we were trapped in the forms we wore at the time. It just so happened that most of us were dwarfs, Erielyon, or human."

"What about sylvans?"

"Sylvans are sylvans, already earthbound and suited for the forest." She headed deeper into the woods.

"Which way is south?" Melaia looked around, wary.

"Navia is that way." Livia pointed. "But I wouldn't recommend leaving the woods just yet." She ducked under a branch. "Pym told me all he knows about the events of yesterday, which is very little. I want to know about Lord Rejius. What happened in the aerie?"

Dry leaves crunched underfoot as they threaded their way between the trees. Melaia told Livia about the Firstborn. "He's the king's physician, and he's poisoning the king."

"Shame." Livia cut her eyes at Melaia. "You heard him say so?"

Melaia nodded.

"You're lucky we got you out of Redcliff, then. He probably wanted you silenced."

"No doubt." A chill shivered through Melaia.

"What about Benasin?"

Melaia told her about the quarrel and the Firstborn's attack. "But I thought Benasin was immortal. I thought he couldn't die."

"Perhaps he didn't," said Livia.

A glimmer of hope warmed Melaia. "You mean his spirit might return to his body later?"

"Perhaps."

Melaia remembered the quarrel in the aerie, and her hope gave way to fear. "Lord Rejius said he would take everything Benasin cares about. He said Hanni was next. What does that mean?"

"Nothing good."

Melaia kicked a pile of leaves, fighting back panic. "I have to return to Navia. I have to warn Hanni."

Livia said nothing. She led Melaia across a plank bridge that spanned a bubbling stream and stopped in a grove of lindens. There she pointed out a tree with a carving in the trunk: a *V* with a third line running straight up the center.

"The sign of the Tree." Melaia gave Livia a puzzled look.

Livia ran her fingers over the mark, then stepped back, knelt, and placed her palms on the ground. "Dreia's body is buried here."

"Dreia? She's dead, then. Did Benasin know?"

"He found out before he returned to Navia, yes," said Livia.

"Guardian of the Wisdom Tree," Melaia marveled. "I've told the tale many times. You knew her well?"

"Well enough."

Melaia knelt. "The grave isn't old."

"Dreia was murdered only a few weeks ago. I believe she was on her way to Navia to meet you."

"Me? Why?"

"Melaia, we've all been searching for Dreia's son, but we should have been looking for her daughter."

Melaia blinked at Livia. When she finally found her voice, it came out in a whisper. "What are you saying?"

"You're Dreia's daughter." Livia placed a hand on her arm.

Melaia jerked back and rose, shaking her head. She felt as if she had been doused with a bucket of winter rainwater. "No. I was a foundling, left at the temple in Navia."

"By sylvans."

"Yes, but…" Melaia edged back from the grave. "You need someone to be Dreia's heir, is that it? You're so desperate you clutch at me. But I'll not be your stand-in. I'll not be drawn into the affairs of angels."

"I'm afraid it's too late for that."

Melaia darted into the woods and wove through the trees. "Livia's wrong," she cried. "She is."

Shhhee isss, shhhee isss, shhhee is. The whisper was shared from tree to tree.

Melaia swiped at the undergrowth only to see branches and vines part for her of their own accord. Her vision blurred with hot tears as her mind tumbled through signs she couldn't deny. The Erielyon approaching her in the temple yard. The Firstborn arriving to destroy Dreia's child. Benasin's harp alive in her hands. The sprouting game pieces. The trees echoing her thoughts.

And now she found herself dashing through the dark woods Hanni had warned against, going deeper and darker into the very place where Hanni was pursued.

Melaia's toe snagged a gnarled tree root, and she fell headlong into the loam. "It's not true," she moaned. "It can't be."

The woods around her seemed to moan as well, branches creaking in the wind.

An arm wrapped around her shoulders. "I myself found it hard to believe," said Livia. "Esper was the only one who knew the truth. She told me last night. Even Noll was surprised. But I wasn't ready to dismiss my own long-held belief in a son until the game figures sprouted. They always did the same for Dreia and no one else."

Melaia eased herself up and wiped her eyes. "But I'm not an angel."

"You're Nephili, a clouded one. The beings so hard for us to sense. Half-angel, half-human. Breath of angel, blood of man. Your spirit is angelic, the breath inherited from Dreia."

Melaia stared at her hands, at the veins that carried human blood. "Who was the man?"

Whoooo? echoed the trees. *Whoooo?*

Livia smoothed back stray wisps of Melaia's hair. "You were born at Wode-hall with Esper as midwife. She can answer your questions better than I."

Melaia stared into the sun-dappled shadows. "Hanni was right when she said these woods held dark secrets."

"Hanni can see it that way if she chooses. So can you. But I wouldn't say this secret is so dark. It kept you safe."

Melaia picked up a dry leaf and traced its edge. "Did Benasin know about me?"

"He was looking for a son when he came north. I assume he realized you were Dreia's child when he found the harp gone. It's made of kyparis wood from the Wisdom Tree, and he had bound it to his wall by enchantment. That's why he could leave it behind when he journeyed. Dreia instructed him to hold the harp until she sent her child for it."

"How do you know all this?"

"Pym has good eyes and ears for a human."

"Then the harp belongs to me?"

"In a way," said Livia. "The harps were Dreia's responsibility. Now they're yours."

Melaia recalled Lord Rejius in the aerie, the Firstborn taunting the Second. "Lord Rejius boasted that he holds two harps."

"Malevolents stole the other harp from Dreia."

"That's how she died, isn't it?"

Shhhee, said the trees.

Livia helped Melaia stand. "I'll tell you what I know as we head back to Wodehall."

As they walked, the undergrowth shifted to make a path.

"See?" said Livia. "Your mother's realm senses you."

"Her realm."

"She was Archon over the plant world," said Livia. "I met her up north and journeyed south with her a couple of times. She introduced me to my husband, Gailon. I thought of Dreia as a good friend, but some secrets she held close and never confided in me. When she visited, she never stayed long. I think she felt at home only in the wide expanse of nature. Surely she missed the Wisdom Tree. After it was destroyed, she never seemed to find rest."

They paused among the lindens where the grave lay. "Maybe she's at rest now," said Melaia.

"Her hope was in you."

"Why?" Melaia stared at the grave.

"Dreia felt keenly that she was to blame for the destruction of the Tree. She looked for the day when she could make amends. She knew only you could restore the Tree, but she was eager to manage the entire proceedings and see it done properly."

"Only *I* can restore the Tree? Don't angels have that kind of power? Can't the Most High intervene?"

"The Tree was destroyed by human will. What human will destroyed, human will must restore. Besides, the prophecy says the Tree will be restored 'by breath of angel, blood of man.' That means Nephili, Melaia, like you. Half-angel, half-human."

"But there must be other Nephili." Melaia circled the grave.

"There are many Nephili," said Livia. "But their inherited gifts vary. For years Dreia sought out strongly gifted Nephili using the game figures you saw this morning. When she found no one who could make the wood leaf out, she concluded she must be the one to bear the child. So, you see, you were conceived of a human father and born of an angel for the purpose of restoring the Wisdom Tree. When the Tree is restored, the stairway to heaven will rise once more, and we angels will be able to go home. For a while anyway."

"For a while?"

"We'll eventually get new assignments, go into other worlds."

Melaia could hardly comprehend it. She knelt and placed her hands on the firm earth over Dreia's grave. "Were you with Dreia when she died?"

"I last saw Dreia a fortnight before she died, when she left our home to travel to Navia. My son, Sergai, and one of his friends accompanied her. We knew she intended to pick up a harp on the way, one that matched Benasin's." Livia leaned against a linden tree. A gust of wind sent leaves sailing down. "All Angelaeon were aware there was some risk in the journey. The Firstborn has long coveted the harps. But he and his malevolents had been quiet for so long, no one imagined they would be watching. No one expected them to lie in wait for Dreia."

"Your son… Did he survive?"

"Sergai and his friend were the only two who survived the attack for the simple reason that they could fly. Dreia sent them for help." Livia stared at the grave, but she seemed to be looking far away. "One other angel, a warrior, accompanied Dreia. They had all been traveling together in a merchant's caravan when they sensed the presence of malevolents. They broke off from the caravan and headed toward the Durenwoods to minimize the danger to the merchant as well as to reach a place of safety. When Dreia saw they would be hard-pressed to reach the Durenwoods, she sent my son's friend to Aubendahl nearby, and she sent Sergai south. When the malevolents attacked, they spared no one. Not even the caravan. And somehow they tracked Sergai. Draks, probably. He died in Navia. In the temple yard."

A chill fell over Melaia. "That was your son? I fought off the hawk that killed him. Lord Rejius. The hawkman. He mistook your son for Dreia's."

"So the Firstborn is still looking for a son." Livia sniffed and wiped her eyes. "That, at least, is to our advantage."

Melaia could still see Sergai, the weary stranger—his cloak flapping, his hand flying to his dagger. Her eyes blurred with tears. "I'm sorry. I tried to save your son."

"Sergai knew the risks. Benasin brought back his body."

"That's when you met Benasin?"

"And why I followed him to Navia."

"Your son had a small scroll in his hand with the message 'Now is payment due in full.' What does that mean?"

"The Second-born owed a debt to Dreia, which he didn't pay. Maybe it was time for her to ask for payment."

"According to the legend, it's the Tree that will exact payment." Melaia paused. She had told the tale so many times the next words were as familiar as morning prayer. "In breath and blood." A chill came over her. "Is that me? Am I the payment?"

"Does it say breath of angel?" asked Livia. "Blood of man?"

Melaia shook her head. "Just breath and blood."

"Then I truly don't know. 'Breath and blood' could refer to any living creature. Benasin himself. The Firstborn's daughter. The whole human race, for that matter."

"Or me," said Melaia.

"Or you." Livia extended a hand. "It's time to make our way back to Wodehall."

Melaia took Livia's firm grip and rose, feeling very small and very vulnerable in a very dark wood.

CHAPTER 12

As Melaia and Livia neared Wodehall, Livia's pace picked up. Melaia's slowed. The thought of so many angels gathered in the common room rattled her. Was she supposed to consider them her people now? She gripped a sapling as if it could save her.

Ssssave, it echoed.

"Melaia?" called Livia, a stone's throw ahead.

"Are you going to tell the Angelaeon that I'm Dreia's daughter?" asked Melaia.

"Yes." Livia strode back to her. "You need our help, and we need yours."

"But there's still so much I don't understand," said Melaia. "Like why Lord Rejius wants the harps."

"Because when the harps are reunited, the Wisdom Tree will be restored and the stairway with it."

"And he doesn't want that to happen?"

"We believe the Firstborn wants to hold the harps as security. They're our only hope of gaining a path home to Avellan. If he controls our path home, he controls us."

Melaia picked at the bark of the sapling. "I should have listened to you at Redcliff. I took the Firstborn exactly what he wanted. Now he has both harps."

"There are three harps," said Livia. "Dreia's book tells where the third harp is hidden. Guard that book with your life. We have to find the third harp before the Firstborn does."

"But I don't have the book. Benasin took it north in search of Dreia."

Livia's face was ashen. "Did he have the book on him when he died?"

"Whatever he carried into the aerie, Lord Rejius took. I checked. But the book is all Benasin talked about before he died. He told me to get it and open it. He made me promise." Melaia rubbed her wrist.

"He definitely knew who you were, then."

Melaia squeezed her eyes closed. When Benasin entered the aerie, he knew. When he drew her behind him, he knew. When he told her to run, he knew. "He died to spare me," she murmured.

"That raises my opinion of him considerably," said Livia.

Melaia leaned her forehead against the sapling as her spirit groaned. It was her fault. If she had insisted on staying in Navia, Benasin wouldn't have died.

Livia linked her arm in Melaia's and drew her toward the arbor in the laurel hedge. "Surely Benasin wouldn't be fool enough to take the book to the palace," said Livia. "He probably stashed it somewhere."

"Then why didn't he tell me where?" asked Melaia.

"Maybe he did," said Livia. "Tell me again what he said."

Melaia remembered the swirling mist of Benasin's spirit. "The book. Get it. Promise. Open."

"Open," mused Livia, pausing at the door of Wodehall. "Why would he waste his breath telling you to open the book? Surely he'd trust you would do that naturally. Or perhaps—" Her face lit up. "Perhaps he said not 'Open' but 'Auben,' meaning Aubendahl. Benasin spent a night at the scriptory in Aubendahl on his way back to Navia. We'll ask Jarrod about it."

"Jarrod? The priest at Redcliff?"

"Until recently. He took refuge at Aubendahl, but he's sure to be here by now." She ushered Melaia into the cavernous common room.

As they crossed through the crowd, Melaia stayed close to Livia. She estimated there were at least forty angels present, maybe more. The air swirled with lively conversations, some low voiced and head-to-head, some light with the laughter of old friends renewing acquaintance. Esper and her sylvans ducked in and out of the larder with food and drink. Noll and Pym sat serenely beside the brazier: Noll smoking a long-stemmed pipe, Pym studying the group over the top of a mug clamped between his palms.

Partway up the curving stairs, Livia turned toward the crowd and held up three fingers. Talk dwindled as all across the room the Angelaeon raised their hands in the sign of the Tree.

Melaia, one step down from Livia, edged to the side of the stairs by the wall and tried to look inconspicuous, her hands clasped in front of her. *Shhhh,* came the tree-thought. *Shhhh.* Gil caught her eye and raised his bushy eyebrows. She nodded at him, knowing he was surprised to see her there and would be even more surprised when Livia introduced her.

"We're fewer in number than when we last met," said Livia.

A mop-haired man called out, "Some in my region claimed they were too busy with farm or trade to make the trip."

"In my part of the country, we're working to scrabble together some kind of harvest," said a big-eared dwarf. "Many have no wish to leave their families with the chore."

"The guardians," said a silver-haired woman, "will they come?"

"Windweaver was here last night," said Livia. "The guardians will attend us as they're able."

Melaia shifted, uncomfortable with the questioning glances the angels cast her way. She felt like an intruder.

"Dreia herself had hoped to address this gathering," said Livia. "By now you all know about her death. Fortunately, she sent for her child before she died." She drew Melaia up the step to stand beside her.

Murmurs rippled through the group. Gil grinned, and his shoulders bounced in a quiet laugh.

"Do you mean to say that's Dreia's child?" called a sylvan. "I thought Dreia had a son."

"Aye," said another. "Didn't she claim she had a son?"

"She did claim it," said Livia.

"Because she *desired* a son."

All heads turned toward a lanky, clean-shaven man who leaned casually against the back wall. His hair, the color of hay, hung like a horse tail over his shoulder as befitted a priest; the ebony hilt of a long knife protruded from his belt.

"The child I'm speaking of, Jarrod, is the one born to Dreia's task," said Livia. "That child was a daughter. Dreia claimed she had a son because she wanted to protect her daughter. It was an effective strategy."

"You're certain she's Dreia's child?" called a ruddy woman.

Jarrod folded his arms across his chest and narrowed his eyes at Melaia. "How much do you know?"

"I know that the high priestess at Navia told me to find a priest named Jarrod at Redcliff," said Melaia. "But the priest there didn't go by that name."

Jarrod raised one eyebrow.

"She's pegged you, Jarrod," said the big-eared dwarf. Chuckles sounded around the room.

"My identity is not so hard to discern," said Jarrod. "Tell me more."

"I was raised to be a priestess," said Melaia. "A chantress."

Jarrod gave one nod.

"I know you are all trapped here until the three harps are brought together again," said Melaia. "Then the Wisdom Tree will be restored, and you can climb the stairway back to Avellan. Or other worlds." She glanced at Livia for guidance, but Livia said nothing. Melaia turned back to the angels. "I saw the immortal Firstborn battle the Second-born at the palace at Redcliff."

Jarrod clenched his jaw. His hand drifted to the hilt of his long knife. "Lord Rejius. Lord Death," he said. "With immortals, waiting is nothing but part of the game. He waits; we move; he raises his ugly head. All he needs to do is sit back and wait for us to find the harps for him. Just as he did with Dreia."

"Are there not two more harps?" asked Gil. "Malevolents stole only one."

"Two," said Livia.

"Excellent!" Jarrod glared. "We bring the Firstborn one more harp, and we're at his mercy."

"Some of us haven't staked our lives on the restoration of the Tree," said the silver-haired woman. "We've coupled. We have families. We don't wish to cross to Avellan if it means leaving our husbands, our wives, our children behind."

"You're lulled into a slumber that aids the Firstborn," said Jarrod.

"Not so," said the woman. "We'll support the restoring of the Tree and the stairway. Just don't expect us to cross until our earthly families do."

Jarrod scowled. Murmured conversations boiled through the room.

Livia sighed and called out, "All I ask is your support. After all, none of us but Melaia can restore the Tree. But she'll need our help. Noll has agreed to supervise the sending and receiving of messages to the entire Angelaeon."

Noll rose at the brazier. "I ask three things of you." Raising his twiglike fingers one by one, he said, "First, choose whether or not to support us, and when you go back to your lands, give others a chance to join our cause. Second, be alert and subvert the malevolents wherever and whenever possible. Third, for those of you who can take a more active role, we'll need to branch out as spies and protectors where we can."

"We can't get too close, or they'll sense our presence," said a bald man.

"Come close as you can," said Noll. "Be ready to join the fray if it comes to that."

"How far will the Firstborn go to get and keep the harps?" asked the mop-haired man.

"He murdered Dreia," said Jarrod. "Need we know more?"

"He'll probably not wage a full-scale war," said Noll. "It's easier to take over by lopping us off one by one, as he did with Dreia and Sergai."

"Which reminds me," said Livia. "You Erielyon are never to show your wings." She narrowed her eyes at the Erielyon in the room, who quickly pulled their cloaks over their shoulders.

The room churned with comments and questions directed toward Noll. Livia didn't try to call them to order.

After everyone else retired, Melaia stayed downstairs, too stirred to sleep.

She helped Esper pack food for the morrow's journey to Aubendahl. Livia had questioned Pym and Jarrod about Dreia's book, but neither knew anything for certain. Pym said he had seen Benasin thumbing through the book before their visit to the scriptory at Aubendahl and not after, so it was agreed that the search would start there.

Melaia had suggested that Pym go to Aubendahl while she went to Navia, but Livia insisted that the book was now Melaia's, as was the responsibility of claiming it. Pym would check on Hanni, let her know about Benasin, and warn her about the Firstborn while Livia and Melaia traveled to the scriptory.

"Esper?" Melaia tucked a pouch of wilderberries into a pack.

Esper sighed. "I know." She stood back and eyed the pile of foodstuffs she had set out. "The packs are already bulging. I fear it's back to the larder for the rest of it. And I did so want to send some smoked fish with you."

"A small packet may fit. But I really want to know about my mother."

"She was a beauty, that one. But restless and full of worry for her babe." Esper dug through the pile of food. "Your mother took me aside and made me vow to hide your identity. I had no idea why, just that she seemed to think you were in some danger. If you were a boy, I was to say you were a girl. If you were a girl, I was to claim you were a boy. And she wanted your whereabouts kept secret. Hanamel had studied the herbs with us here, and I knew she lived at the temple in Navia. Just the place, I thought."

"So you took me there?"

"That I did, pipit." She handed a fishy-smelling pouch to Melaia.

"What about my father? Who was he?"

"That I wouldn't know. Dreia kept silent about it. I assumed she had her reasons, and who was I to pry? She was one of the Archae, you know."

"I know." Melaia wrestled the fishy packet into the journey bag and helped carry the extra food back to the larder. "One more question. Hanni didn't want anything to do with sylvans. Or angels of any kind. She didn't want me to come here. Something about a dark angel and the woods being full of secrets."

"She was scared out of her wits, poor dear." Esper covered a bowl of groundnuts. "She was out gathering some herbs when she met a man. The dark angel, she called him. No one but Hanamel ever saw him, but that was in the days when we had lookouts only at Wodehall. The woods were wilder then, so she usually insisted someone accompany her on her herb hunts. But one afternoon she ventured out alone. And there he was. She led him on a good chase, she said, but she couldn't shake him until another man came and fought him off. We never found either man."

"You think she imagined them?"

"We did at first. But when Hanamel discovered she was with child by the 'dark angel,' there was no denying it. The babe came too soon, though. Stillborn. Hanamel needed to leave the memories behind, so we took her back to the temple in Navia, where the high priestess could help her heal. Then when we needed a place for you, she came to mind. I thought you, too, might help her heal."

"Maybe I did. But she feared for me." Melaia wished she had insisted on going to Navia instead of sending Pym.

"No need to fear, pipit." Esper walked her out of the larder. "After those days we cleared out the woods east to west, north to south, and set up lookouts and signals."

"The whistle?"

"The All's-Well, we call it. So you can rest easy in your bed tonight, for sylvans are keeping watch."

Melaia headed upstairs, not at all sure she could rest easy. Within the space of a day, her whole life had turned upside down.

As Melaia reached the landing, she heard a soft patter of rain over the shushing tree-thought. But when she entered her bedchamber, her unshuttered window stood open to a still, clear night. Bewildered, she walked back to the landing and heard the patter again. She followed the sound to the chamber across from hers and gently nudged open the door.

At the far side of the room, Livia stood with her back to Melaia, bathing in water that rained from a myriad of holes overhead and drained out through holes in the floor.

Melaia knew she should tiptoe out and close the door, but she was rooted there, awed. It was not the waterfall. It was not even that Livia was naked. It was that Livia's nakedness was hidden by wings. Curved, white-feathered wings tapered down her back almost to the floor. Melaia had never really thought of Livia as Erielyon, but Sergai was her son, so of course she had wings. To see them close up was like standing before a life-sized figure from the board game.

Livia stepped out of the water, grabbed a towel, and turned around, drying herself. Melaia backed up.

"Oh!" Livia's eyes widened.

Melaia felt her face go hot. "I beg your pardon. I thought it was raining."

"No harm done." Livia rubbed down her arms.

"Your wings—they're beautiful."

"And quite helpful when I wish to fly. But Erielyon must be extremely cautious about showing our wings, which make it quite obvious we're angels. That's why most of us live far north of the kingdoms, well away from the more populous areas. While I'm anywhere but Wodehall, I keep my wings hidden, which means I must ask you to keep them a secret as well."

Melaia nodded and watched Livia slip on her gown. A slit down the back allowed her wings to be free. They folded in to fit close to her body. After she fastened a light cloak around her shoulders, she looked quite human, though her shoulders were broader than most.

Livia toweled off her dusky hair as she strode toward Melaia. "There is something you should know. The stairway in the Wisdom Tree existed not only for the Angelaeon but also for all beings in this world. At death, spirits are meant to cross the stairway into Avellan."

"Where do spirits go, then?" Melaia thought of all the dying spirits she had seen thinning and sinking into the ground, and even as she asked, she knew the answer. She whispered it at the same time Livia responded. "The Under-Realm."

"The blight, too, began when the Wisdom Tree was destroyed and we lost our connection to Avellan," said Livia. "It will only grow worse. Your mother guarded the way for angels to bring bounty to the land as well as inspiration for the landscape of the heart—music and art of all kinds. We hope you will open the way once again."

"But I was raised to be a simple priestess. I can't free the entire world. How is that even possible?" Melaia headed for the door.

"Do you want to know what I would tell my daughter?"

Melaia turned in surprise. "You have a daughter?"

"Serai. Twin to Sergai. She's your age."

Melaia felt a pang of grief for Serai, who must have felt her twin's death keenly. "What would you tell her?"

"Not to dwell on what she *can't* do but on what she *can*." Livia hung her towel on a peg. "Melaia, the longer you wait to give yourself to the task you were born to, the harder it will be to risk yourself."

Melaia looked down at her dirty, bare feet. "And if I choose to return to Navia and the temple?"

"The Angelaeon won't interfere with your free will. But can you truly return after all you know now? You were born for a greater temple: the earth, the trees, the sky."

Melaia half smiled. "That's a bit larger than what I'm accustomed to."

"That means you're moving toward your destiny. When you're going the right direction, life always looks larger than what you're accustomed to." Livia nodded toward the splashing water. "Towels are in the nook at the side of the room if you decide to try the indoor rain." She breezed out the door.

Melaia turned to the waterfall and watched the droplets form, gather weight, and splash down. Only in releasing itself to fall did the water offer its cleansing gift.

Melaia stepped to the nook and grabbed a towel.

he sun had set on the third day of their journey by the time Melaia and Livia climbed the trail to the entrance of the scribes' cave high in the Aubendahl Hills. Jarrod had insisted on accompanying them, but he spent most of his time out of sight. More than once Melaia had startled to see him standing rock-still in the path before them or stepping out suddenly from a grove at their side. Now he was up the hill somewhere, distracting a pair of draks, and she felt edgy, expecting him to emerge abruptly in front of them in the glow of the waning moon. But they reached the wooden door in the hill without him.

As Livia knocked, Melaia gazed out into the chilled night. Stars seeded the sky above the dark valley, broken only by a twinkling of light from Dahl, a town at the eastern end of the foothills. She wondered if Pym was in Navia yet. What would Hanni say at his news of Navia's chantress traveling not only to the Durenwoods but beyond, to the Aubendahl scriptory? Melaia inhaled the fresh night air. Never would she have imagined being here. She felt freer than she had ever felt in her life.

Until the distant scream of a hawk echoed through the hills and she remembered another height and the hands on her waist. She suddenly felt lightheaded. She sidled closer to Livia at the door, which was marked with the sign of the Tree.

Livia knocked again.

A peephole cracked open, and a brown eye glared out. "Who's there?"

Livia held up three fingers. "I'm of the Angelaeon and roomed here not long ago. Might I presume upon your hospitality again tonight?"

The door scraped open, and an ebony man, dressed in the belted linen robe of a scribe, saluted with the sign of the Tree.

"May we see the Dom?" asked Livia.

The doorkeeper nodded, and they stepped into a broad cave bathed by the glow of lamps on stands. With only two stone benches as furniture, the room seemed to be a receiving area. Three tunnel-like hallways led deeper into the hill. The doorkeeper retreated down one of them with a lantern.

Melaia watched the light bob away, feeling as if the expanse of her world had shrunk around her. The sense of freedom she had reveled in outdoors was rapidly turning into a feeling of being trapped.

"You feel closed in here too?" asked Livia. "We'll spend only one night if we find what we're looking for."

The doorkeeper returned with the Dom, a stooped, aged man.

"We were not expecting guests." The Dom's voice creaked like tree branches rubbing together. "But you are welcome." He squinted at Livia. "I remember you. Certainly, certainly. You were here not long ago."

"I've returned to fetch a book we think Benasin left here," said Livia.

"Certainly, certainly. Benasin sent you?"

"Actually, Benasin has died," said Livia.

"Dear me." The Dom's double chin wobbled as he shook his head. "There comes a time when the last word is scribed. I wish for our sakes that Benasin's last had not been writ so soon. A fine man he was. Certainly, certainly. Always a welcome guest here, you know." A smile crept across his face.

Melaia found herself bobbing her head along with him. "We're gathering some of Benasin's possessions," she said. "The book we're looking for is palm sized and has a wooden cover. Red brown wood, inscribed with the sign of the Tree."

"I know of such a book," said the Dom. "The first to be made here. At the request of a woman who wanted leaves of papyrus between wood. She insisted on scribing it herself and took it with her when she left. We've since made many books but none like that first one." He frowned. "Benasin said nothing about bringing such a book back home."

"Do you suppose Benasin hid it here for safekeeping?" asked Livia.

A smooth voice broke in. "Perhaps he placed it in your archives." Jarrod stood at the door, rebinding his long hair at the nape of his neck.

Melaia's back prickled. She wondered how long he had been standing behind them unnoticed.

"Jarrod!" said the Dom. "Back so soon?"

"I'm traveling with these two," said Jarrod.

"How fortunate for them." The Dom bobbed his head again. "You may be right about the archives, you know. In any case guests cannot stay at Aubendahl without seeing our archives."

The Dom led them to a spacious chamber where, at one end, scrolls peeked out of holes hewn into the cave wall and, at the other end, books lined shelves carved into rock. Three scholars glanced up from where they sat at desks, copying by the light of oil lamps. Then they bent back over their work.

With arms outspread the Dom waddled to the center of the room. "My domain."

Jarrod held a lantern to each row as Livia and Melaia inspected books and shifted scrolls. Most of the books were larger than palm size, but they inspected them anyway. The Dom muttered, "Gently, gently," whenever a book thudded back into place.

When the last shelf had been searched, Melaia slumped to a stone bench.

The Dom turned to Jarrod. "This book you seek. Might it be in your own collection?"

"Not likely," said Jarrod.

"It would be worth a look," said Livia, searching again through a stack of scrolls.

Jarrod rolled his eyes. "I know exactly what's in my collection." He handed the lantern to Livia. "I'm going to sleep outdoors where I can actually breathe."

Melaia watched him go, feeling jealous. She would have loved to sleep outdoors, although not in Jarrod's vicinity.

Livia slipped a scroll out of the stack and turned to the Dom. "May I take a few moments with this scroll?"

"Certainly, certainly." The Dom bobbed his head. "I'll ask the cook to prepare a small repast for you before you retire."

Livia set the lantern on a table and rolled out the scroll next to it. "A timely discovery. I intended to ask Jarrod to show you a version of this from his collection. He keeps chronicles of the Angelaeon, the history of our time in your world, but he's not ready to return to his scrolls."

"Why not?" asked Melaia. "Why do you allow him to speak to you so rudely? It maddens me."

Livia didn't look up from the scroll. "Jarrod is grieving." She motioned for Melaia to lean in.

Melaia scanned the faded script that spread like three fingers reaching down the page.

	Cherubim	Seraphim	Ophanim	
Kuriotes		Archae		Thronos
Exousia		Archangels		Angels

"This shows the order of Angelaeon," said Livia. "Three levels."

"Ranks of angels," said Melaia. "Benasin spoke of ranks."

"Did he? Did he explain the responsibilities entrusted to them?"

"Only the Archae, who oversee the elements, and the Erielyon. But I don't see Erielyon here."

Livia tapped the lower-right corner of the chart. "We're messengers, a common rank simply called angel. The truth is, the highest orders—Cherubim, Seraphim, Ophanim—are not strictly angels, for they carry no messages. In fact, they rarely leave inner Avellan and the presence of the Most High. If you were to see them, you'd wonder if they were living beings at all, for they appear quite different from anything to which you're accustomed.

"On the second level are rulers in the heavens and governors over worlds to which they're assigned. Kuriotes are lords of lower angels. Thronos are extremely humble; they're living signs of the justice of the Most High. Archae are lesser rulers who bring gifts and inspiration into the world and guard the world's elements."

"Dreia was of the Archae," said Melaia.

"Assigned to guard the Wisdom Tree."

Melaia nodded, thinking maybe that was why many of the Angelaeon were suspicious of her. Her mother had failed to guard the Tree and the stairway leading home. The Angelaeon had cause to be wary.

Livia ran her finger down to the lowest row. "Exousia." She tapped on the word. "Warrior angels and keepers of history. Like Jarrod. Then Archangels, who supervise kings and kingdoms and influence trade among nations."

"What powers do angels have?" asked Melaia.

"We're servants," said Livia. "Messengers and protectors. Our powers lie within the sphere of the tasks we're given when we're assigned to the world. It has been almost two hundred years since our stairway to heaven was destroyed. Except for the Archae's work, our tasks were completed long ago."

"But you fly. That's a power."

"I suppose flight could be considered a kind of power. And compared to most earthly beings, we do possess heightened senses of perception. Some of us are strongly gifted in sight, others in hearing or touch. We certainly sense each other's presence. But our greatest powers are wisdom, insight, strategy, even mercy. Most people don't label such gifts as power."

"Powers of the mind," said Melaia.

"And heart. Such powers serve our purpose, which is to guide and protect the worlds."

"But don't you have to use physical powers to protect?"

"Wisdom goes a long way toward protection. But, yes, we can fight physically, and most of us are well suited for it. We can destroy ourselves if we're not careful."

Melaia read over the ranks again. "So my mother was of the Archae. I wish I knew who my father was."

"Did you ask Esper?" Livia rolled up the scroll.

"She didn't know." Melaia sensed a presence and scowled. Jarrod. She turned to see him at the door. "Were you not able to breathe, even outdoors?"

Jarrod looked past her. "Livia, a runner has come with a message."

Livia stepped to the door, where she and Jarrod talked in low voices. Then Livia turned to Melaia. "I must leave at once. Jarrod will see you safely returned to Wodehall."

"You travel by night?" asked Melaia. "Who will see *you* safe?"

"I can fly by moonlight. I'm more safely hidden in the night sky."

❧

After a meal of barley stew, Melaia followed the Dom down a hallway with open cavelike doorways along one side. He ushered her through one, into a small chamber where a mat lay in a recessed ledge in the cave wall. "This is where Benasin slept when he was last here," said the Dom. He set a lamp in a small storage niche carved into the wall. "These are our best accommodations, Priestess. I hope you find them suitable. Jarrod will sleep in the next chamber." A bell tolled. "Our curfew. I bid you a good night." The Dom bobbed his head and ducked out of the room.

As his footsteps faded down the hall, Melaia tossed her pack at the foot of the ledge. "Confound it!" she growled, aggravated that Jarrod would be her company all the way back to Wodehall. On top of that, she felt stuffy and trapped here. She missed the outdoor undercurrent of tree-thought. Rocks were obviously not her heritage. But what grated on her most was the prospect of returning to Wodehall empty-handed.

"The book has to be here somewhere," she mumbled. She rummaged through the storage niche where the Dom had set the lamp. A chipped pottery cup. A scroll containing a prayer. No book.

Jarrod leaned into the room, his horse tail of hair draped over his shoulder. "Come and see the stargazers."

Melaia pressed her lips together, wondering if she should trust Jarrod. So far, her record of trust was less than stellar. She had trusted Trevin, and he had betrayed her. She hadn't trusted Livia or the sylvans, and they had shown her only kindness. Jarrod confused her. She didn't know what to think of him.

"Livia asked me to show you." Jarrod huffed. "I'm safe. I snarl, but I keep myself on a leash. At least around those I'm supposed to protect."

"All right then." Melaia trudged to the door. "Who are the stargazers?"

"Follow me."

Holding a lantern high, Jarrod led the way along the narrow corridor, deeper into the hill. Melaia wiped the sweat from her forehead and tried to imagine trees and fields. At the end of the corridor, they climbed stairs cut into the rock and emerged facing a starry sky over a bowl-shaped valley in the hilltop.

The night breeze cooled Melaia's sweaty brow. At last under the wide, wide sky, she took a deep breath, her gaze held by the heavens. She had once seen a jeweled veil displayed among a merchant's silks. The sky looked like a canopy of jeweled veils.

"Sit if you like. Or recline." Jarrod already lay on his back.

As Melaia eased herself down to the stone, she noticed the stargazers scattered around the bowl. They appeared to be dwarfs, but unlike Gil's bushy-haired race, their hair was dark and sleek, tied in tails or knots. Melaia recognized them as one of the angel races represented on the board game. Some of them lay on their backs like Jarrod, gazing up at the sky, their necks pillowed on stone supports. Others sat cross-legged at lap desks and held angular sticks to the sky as they eyed the heavens. Then they bent to mark on scrolls.

"Angels?" whispered Melaia.

"Angels," said Jarrod.

Melaia lay on her back too and hardly breathed. She raised her hand as if to stroke the heavens. "The stars seem close enough to touch," she said. "Stargazers must love it here."

"Probably," said Jarrod. "This is their work. They watch for the alignment of stars. At present, their foremost concern is the stars of this world's beltway, which align only once every two hundred years."

"That's important?" asked Melaia.

"Very," said Jarrod. "All worlds have beltway stars, receiving points for their stairways into the heavens. Once a stairway is received and established, the stars go their way, circling back from time to time to secure the stairway."

"But our world's stairway was destroyed with the Wisdom Tree," said Melaia.

"Almost two hundred years ago," said Jarrod. "Even if the Tree were already restored, the stairway won't rise until the stars of the beltway are aligned. Which will occur soon."

"How soon?" asked Melaia.

"The stargazers say we have maybe a year, no more than two, before our beltway aligns and the path is open to receive our stairway to heaven. How long the stars will stay aligned and the path open, no one knows. But if the Tree isn't restored before the stars journey on, then the stairway is lost for two hundred more years."

⌖

Melaia returned from stargazing frustrated. First, she had asked Jarrod if she could sleep under the stars, but he had said no, she needed to be in the cell the Dom had assigned her, which made it feel like a prison. Then she had very nicely asked if they might search his archives for Dreia's book, and he had brushed her off, saying he knew the contents of his archives. And that was that.

What did he drink, sour wine?

She blew out the lamp and lay back on the thin mat. It smelled loamy and warm, and as she pulled her cloak snug, she thought of Benasin sleeping there only a few weeks before. If only she had not gone to Redcliff, he would still be alive.

"The book," he had said. "Get it."

I would, she thought, *if I knew where it was.* Her throat grew tight, and she squeezed her eyes closed.

How late it was when Melaia awoke, she didn't know. She had shifted in her sleep and couldn't get comfortable again. Through the thin mat, she felt every bump in the rock beneath her, especially under her right knee. She kept rolling over that spot every time she fell into a doze. Finally she reached into the niche above the bed and felt for the lamp, then shuffled into the hallway and lit it by the flame of a lantern.

When she returned to her mat, she flipped it back. The corner of a stone jutted out just where her legs lay. With the flat of her hand, she tried to press it back into place. Instead, the stone dislodged. As she slid it out, she caught her breath.

Dreia's book lay beneath it in a small hollow.

She pulled it from its nook, held it in her palm, stroked the Tree carved into the cover, and felt the same life-pulse she had felt in the harp.

She set the lamp in the niche, settled back on the mat, and opened the book to the first page. Three words vined across it: *For My Child.*

Melaia stared at it, traced it with her finger, pictured Dreia writing it. "Mother," she murmured, listening to the sound, tasting it on her tongue.

As she turned the page, a leaf of papyrus fell into her lap, its top and bottom edge curling in memory of its former scroll shape. "Now is payment due in full." She shuddered and tucked the scroll into the back of the book.

Then she froze, her skin prickling. She was not alone. Jarrod?

She took a deep breath and looked up. On the other side of the chamber stood three mistlike spirits.

CHAPTER 14

Melaia hugged Dreia's book to her chest and stared at the three spirits. They didn't struggle or contort like spirits of the dying. Instead, they wavered like wispy water plants in a peaceful pool.

"I'm Windweaver," said a man with long white hair whose cloak billowed as though it were being blown by a breeze. He motioned to the spirit beside him. "This is Flametender."

The dark-skinned woman with wild copper hair nodded.

"And Seaspinner," he said.

The third spirit bowed, a woman with pale blue skin and short white hair like froth on a breaking wave. She said, "We've long awaited this moment."

Melaia knew she had seen Flametender before, in the campfire at the hot springs, but she said nothing. Her voice seemed to have gone into hiding. She couldn't even frame a question.

"We're the Archae, guardians of the elements within your world," said Windweaver. "Dreia was one of us, guardian of tree and flower, leaf and bough."

"Guardian, too, of the Wisdom Tree," said Seaspinner. "Livia requested that we come to you. To tell you about your mother."

"We looked forward to the time when Dreia herself would introduce us to you," said Windweaver.

"Which, of course, became impossible," said Flametender. "So we took it upon ourselves."

"We watched you grow up," said Seaspinner.

"In Navia?" Melaia found a tentative voice. "I never saw you there."

Seaspinner's laugh was like a splashing wave. "We can make ourselves present but unnoticed by the untrained eye. In water—"

"And fire," said Flametender.

"And wind," said Windweaver. "Dreia swore us to secrecy, but we carried news of you back to her."

"I never knew about her," said Melaia.

"That was her plan," said Seaspinner.

"To minimize the risk," hissed Flametender.

"As for who Dreia was," said Seaspinner, "she loved the changes of the seasons. She maintained the balance in nature."

"What most don't realize," said Windweaver, "is that because Dreia was guardian of the stairway, she drew creative energies from the heavens into the world, which I was able to carry on the winds. Inspiration, you call it."

"When the Firstborn killed her, he struck his first blow into the upper spheres of the Angelaeon," said Flametender. "Now her spirit is trapped with the spirits of all the dead in the Under-Realm."

"The realm of Earthbearer," said Windweaver. "He is also one of us, an Archon, but reclusive."

"Since the stairway collapsed, he has not deigned to meet with us," said Seaspinner.

"He finds himself busy with the plots of the Firstborn, who has taken a liking to Earthbearer's lair," said Flametender.

"Can't you free Dreia?" asked Melaia. "Surely Earthbearer can't hold an Archon."

"It's not Earthbearer who holds the spirits," said Windweaver. "It's the First-born. Because he chose to eat of the Tree, his immortality gives him certain—"

"Responsibilities," said Flametender.

"Which he perceives as rights," said Seaspinner.

"The Firstborn is held responsible for the spirits of the dead until the Tree is restored," said Flametender. "Then all are set free."

"By breath of angel," said Windweaver.

"Blood of man," said Flametender.

Seaspinner laughed. "You're everything Dreia hoped for."

"Except for courage and wisdom," said Melaia.

"We're here to encourage you," said Windweaver.

"And many will gladly share their wisdom," said Seaspinner.

"If you will listen," crackled Flametender.

"We'll be near," said Seaspinner.

"When we can," said Flametender.

"We're often present but unseen," said Windweaver.

The spirits began to fade.

"Wait!" said Melaia. "What now? The payment of debt? The third harp? Where—"

But the Archae were already gone.

As Melaia stared into the shadows, footsteps sounded in the corridor. She quickly blew out the lamp and lay down, holding the book close. Jarrod stopped in front of the open doorway for a moment, then continued down the hall.

༄

A firm hand shook Melaia from the depths of sleep.

"Up," said Jarrod. "Malevolents." He strode to the doorway and peered down the hall, his hand on the ebony hilt at his belt.

"In the scriptory?" Melaia scrambled out of bed and stuffed the book into her pack.

"Not yet. But approaching."

Melaia joined Jarrod in the hall, where he grabbed a lantern and led her away from the front of the cave. Agitated voices echoed up and down the corridor behind them. A banging sounded on the front door, and a barking voice demanded entrance. Melaia glanced back. The Dom shuffled toward the mouth of the cave, bobbing his head frantically. Scribes darted in and out of rooms like bees in a hive.

Jarrod took Melaia's arm and guided her through the kitchen into the larder. There he pulled aside a hide that hung on the wall. Behind it lay a gaping hole blacker than a moonless night. A dank smell wafted out.

"Our escape," he said.

Melaia peered into the darkness. "Is it safe?"

"Nothing is safe." Jarrod ducked into the hole and disappeared. Light from his lantern danced off the tunnel walls. Then he leaned back out, his horse tail of hair dangling over his shoulder. "Are you afraid to follow?"

"What about the scribes?" she asked.

"They'll let the malevolents in, allow them to search the caves, and answer their questions. They've got nothing to hide once we're gone."

Melaia didn't move. She felt rooted to the spot, paralyzed at the thought of entering such a narrow tunnel.

"You *are* afraid," he said. "So was Dreia."

"Is this your test of me, then?"

"I told you: it's our escape." He sighed. "When Dreia was here, she found it helped to think of the underground as the roots of your woods and forests."

"You knew her well?"

"No one knew her well." Jarrod slipped into the tunnel, obviously expecting her to follow.

"Roots of the forests," Melaia mumbled. She pushed her pack onto her back, then crawled into the tunnel, bracing her hands against the rough stone walls. Jarrod half crawled, half waddled ahead. She copied his movements awkwardly.

They did not go far before his light flooded a sparkling cavern. Elongated fingers of rock, pink and green, hung from the ceiling and jutted up from the floor.

"You'll find it a bit roomier for a while," he said.

Melaia slowed, grateful for the space and amazed to see that a desk and stool had been carved out of the fingerlike rock formation on one side of the room. Scroll niches and shelves of books lined the wall.

"Is this where you keep your archives?" she asked.

"The Angelaeon's archives, but I'm the keeper. And in case you're wondering, I checked it last night for Benasin's book." He slipped into another tunnel.

"I wasn't wondering," said Melaia, following.

This tunnel was large enough to stand in, but it was steep and slippery, and they had to watch their footing. Melaia couldn't tell east from west as they wound back and forth, 'round and 'round, always downward. It was cool, but sweat trickled down her front and back.

At last they emerged into another cavern, smaller than the first but with a pool of clear water at one side.

"I wonder what the malevolents want," mused Jarrod.

"Probably me. I know Lord Rejius is poisoning the king."

"Good."

"Good?"

"That means they don't know about Dreia's book." He lifted the lantern and gazed at Melaia. "Do they?"

Melaia bit her lip. At Treolli she had said, "I've seen a cup made of kyparis and a book covered in it as well."

"I told Trevin," she croaked.

"Who the drak droppings is he?"

"Son of Lord Rejius."

"Lord Rejius has a son now, has he? The way our fortune has been running, malevolents will find the book where we failed."

"No, they won't. I found it last night."

"And you have it with you?"

Melaia patted her pack. She kept the Archae's visit to herself.

Jarrod continued through the tunnel, this time so fast Melaia was hard-pressed to keep up.

Just when she began to think she was doomed to the bowels of the earth forever, fresh air began to mingle with the dank of the cave. Moments later they stood squinting in the bright outdoors. Melaia drank the air.

Jarrod shaded his eyes and scanned the sky. "No draks."

Melaia shuddered. "Lord Rejius threatened to turn me into one of those vile creatures."

"He would have had to transport you to the Dregmoors for that," said Jarrod, "but he could have done it. Or sent his son to do the job."

"No doubt his son would have complied." Trevin might have protested, but she had no doubt that, in the end, he would have done exactly as Lord Rejius wished.

Jarrod eyed the western horizon. "The river ahead should afford us some protection if we can make it there undetected." He headed to a rocky outcropping and after that a copse.

By the time they gained the cover of shoulder-high rivergrass, dusk had fallen. Only then did Jarrod pause. He broke off dried grass fronds, popped a few seeds into his mouth, and handed some to Melaia. She followed his example, chewing the sweet seeds and sucking nectar from the stems.

Then Jarrod stopped chewing. He crouched among the grasses and motioned for Melaia to do the same. Quietly he parted the stems and pointed at two riders headed toward Aubendahl at a full gallop, followed by two dark birds on the wing.

"Talonmasters," he said. "Malevolents from the Dregmoors." He closed the gap in the grass and crept south along the riverbank.

Melaia followed at his heels, anxious to reach the Durenwoods. It was terrifying to think they might be tracing her. Worse, she was afraid Lord Rejius had discovered Dreia's heir was not a son but a daughter.

⟍⟋

Jarrod's whistle split the quiet of the darkness in the Durenwoods. An answering trill rang from the treetops. "All's well," he said.

The night was so black that Melaia felt blind. All was not well. Not at Navia. Not at Redcliff. Not at Aubendahl. And not in her heart. She was small and weak and not at all brave. Why had she ever wanted to be free from the Navian temple? Life had been so much simpler as a priestess with just one city to care for.

Priestess. Priestess, echoed the trees.

Melaia clung to Jarrod's cloak with one hand and felt her way with the other. At last he came to a stop. A cushion of moss lay beneath her, and she gratefully sank to the ground. She could hear Jarrod scrabbling about; then a flicker of flame illuminated the hollow around them, formed by the ragged roots of a towering tree. The undergrowth was so thick it enveloped them in a dense arbor. Melaia could feel the pulse of the tree, strong and secure, but she warned herself that it might be a false sense of safety. Even the Wisdom Tree had been vulnerable.

Jarrod eyed her for a moment, then ducked out of the hollow. Melaia folded her arms around her pack, lay back in the moss, and found herself thinking about Trevin. She wished he were here instead of Jarrod. The old Trevin, her traveling companion. Not the Trevin of Redcliff, lackey to Lord Rejius.

She groaned. Her feet were numb, her bones were weary, and she wanted sleep. But when she closed her eyes, she saw again the talonmasters galloping toward Aubendahl.

Leaves rustled. Melaia jerked up in alarm. Jarrod sat a few feet away, splitting open a pealmelon with his dagger.

"Were you asleep?" he asked. "I thought you might be hungry."

Melaia rubbed her temples. "I must have dozed. Bad dreams."

Jarrod pulled the fruit in two and began scooping out seeds. Yellow juice oozed into the hollows of the melon.

"Where did Livia go?" asked Melaia.

"To Pym."

"Where was Pym?" She frowned as Jarrod shelled groundnuts over the melons. "Don't let the shells fall in."

"Don't worry." He tossed a handful of shells on the ground. "Pym went to Navia, remember?"

"So his message came from Navia? Is Hanni all right?"

"The message didn't say." Jarrod handed her half the melon and a fistful of groundnuts.

Melaia munched on the groundnuts, thinking of Hanni and the girls and the temple. She thought of the night the hawkman came and ordered her to tell the tale of the Wisdom Tree. He had asked for the end of the story, but as yet, it hadn't ended. She wondered if she would be part of the ending.

And what about Benasin? She eyed Jarrod, who was drinking juice from his pealmelon. "Would you know about the Firstborn?" she asked.

"Lord Rejius?"

"And Benasin, the Second son?"

"Perhaps."

"I thought Benasin was immortal, but I saw his spirit leave his body. He died." Melaia sipped the melon's flowery sweet juice.

"You're a death-prophet, then."

She nodded and took another drink.

"Did you see Benasin's body decompose?"

Melaia shuddered. "I've never seen anyone's body decompose."

"But you know they do. Yet Benasin doesn't. He has been killed before. His spirit wanders for a while, then reenters his body, and it lives again."

"Do angels do the same? Will Dreia return?"

"Angels are forms of light, invisible to human eyes unless the angel takes on a fleshly body—or near flesh, as with the Archae. If an angel's physical form is killed, the spirit remains but doesn't enter the body again except by divine directive."

Melaia licked a drip of juice from her finger. "But Benasin is different."

"His mortal body gained immortality," said Jarrod.

"So he's not dead." A great sense of relief washed over her. She had gotten Benasin killed, but she hadn't. She leaned back, suspecting she wasn't thinking too sharply. "Perhaps he'll go back to Navia." She eyed the juice. It coated her throat like honey.

"You can be sure Lord Rejius will transport Benasin's body to a place where the Firstborn holds advantage before Benasin's spirit reenters it."

Melaia licked her lips. Her tongue felt thick. "It's like a game."

"And the world is the prize."

"The prize…" Melaia blinked heavily. "You put dreamweed in my melon juice, didn't you?"

"Just to help you sleep. You seem agitated. We've a long journey ahead of us, and you'll make it easier if you're rested."

"And you?"

"I need to be alert and keep watch. I thought maybe you'd allow me to take a look at Dreia's book as I sit here."

"I've not even looked at it myself," Melaia said. Or perhaps merely thought. Or dreamed.

CHAPTER 15

Morning came with sunlight streaming through the branches of the forest canopy. Birds trilled their sunrise songs, and bushy-tailed squirrels foraged under leaf piles to gather winter stores. As Melaia tramped through the woods behind Jarrod, All's-Well whistles echoed from sylvan to sylvan, oak to elm.

Assssk. Assssk, the trees whispered as she wondered if Jarrod would let her ask a few questions. She decided the real question was if he would answer.

"Jarrod," she said, "what powers do you have?"

"What kind of question is that?" he asked.

"Livia said you're a warrior angel."

"I can protect you, if that's what you mean. I can wield a sword." He narrowed his eyes at her. "I'm death with a dagger."

"But those are human skills."

"Where do you think the sword came from?"

"Humans?"

"Their proud, lethal legacy."

"But the Firstborn can change shapes," she pointed out. "The Second-born too."

"Earth-magery. Sorcery. Alchemy. The immortals have had almost two hundred years to craft their chaos."

"You know a lot about it, don't you?"

"I'm just a font of knowledge," he said.

And one who's tired of answering questions, thought Melaia. She asked no more.

A strange yip rang out. Jarrod yanked Melaia into a clump of bushes and drew her cloak all the way over her. She peered through a space where the edges overlapped. Jarrod crouched beside her, covered in his own cloak. He was so still it was as if he had disappeared.

A flutter of wings sounded above them. A dry leaf drifted down. Melaia could barely see the tail of a drak on a branch directly overhead. The bird rasped a raucous call that drew a harsh echo from another drak nearby. It flapped its wings, changed its position. Melaia could no longer see it, but she could hear its cry, closer now. Again the strident echo came. It, too, was closer.

The ping of a bowstring sounded from above. Then another. The two draks tumbled to the ground, where they rooted and sprouted into black-barked saplings.

Melaia held tight to her pack. Sylvans scrambled back up into the trees, their bows at the ready. Another leaf drifted down, and the All's-Well warbled through the woodland again.

Jarrod emerged from his cloak. "Let's get back to Wodehall," he said. As they left the grove, he pointed to the new saplings. "Sylvan power. Earthbound. And way beyond me."

◦❦◦

By the third night after reentering the Durenwoods, Melaia was safely back in her bower room at Wodehall. Dreia's book lay before her on the mat where she sat listening to the comforting *shush* of tree-thought. She ran her fingers over the sign of the Tree carved into its cover. A warm *thrum* met her touch. As she eased the book open, she glanced around the room, wondering if the Archae would appear again. But all was still and quiet.

She read again the first line: *For My Child.* Then she turned the page.

> *I am the heart*
> *that makes three one.*

I am freedom,
the curse undone.

Freedom, Melaia thought. Was this Dreia speaking of herself? If so, did her death nullify the saying? Having no answers, she turned to the next page and found:

The Tree will only rise again
by breath of angel, blood of man.

Melaia shivered and murmured, "Me." At least according to Livia. Maybe Livia could help decipher the other sayings as well.

The next page said,

Create and be created.
Consume and be consumed.

The next page:

Fear and courage dwell together.

Slowly Melaia leafed through the pages, scanning each one but finding only proverbs, riddles, prophecies. Enigmas, just as Benasin had said. If he couldn't understand Dreia's sayings, how could she? None told where the third harp was. At least not in a way she could understand.

The last three pages of the book were blank. She stared at them, disappointed, thinking perhaps she was supposed to write on them.

Then she glimpsed a shadowy movement on one page. She blinked to clear her eyes, then squinted at it. A line formed, indistinct and wavering. Another mark joined it. And another. Shapes swam, settled, and sharpened into two figures: the gold-eyed Lord Rejius and Dwin with his dark curls.

They were moving. Talking. Gesturing.

"Impossible," she muttered. Yet there they were as if she were looking through a window at them.

Then Trevin paced into the picture. Melaia's heart wove from anger to disappointment to longing. How could one young man stir up such a riot of feelings?

As she watched, Trevin and Lord Rejius exchanged what were obviously harsh words, though she could hear nothing. Lord Rejius grabbed Dwin by the collar and hauled him out. Trevin rubbed his left hand over his right. Picked up a sword. Turned the blade.

And stared toward her.

Melaia recoiled. Surely Trevin couldn't see her. But how could she see him? She gasped. "The harp!" she whispered. "The harp is the window." The harp was made from the wood of the Tree. So was the book. They were linked. The book showed what the harp saw, and it saw Trevin. No doubt he was guarding the harp.

She turned to the next blank page, which darkened completely. She concluded that if she was seeing through the harp stolen from Dreia, it was covered.

And the third? The lines on the page swayed back and forth, crossing and parting. It made her dizzy to stare at it. She had no idea what it was.

A commotion sounded downstairs, and Melaia heard Pym's voice. She tucked the book into her waist sash and ran down to the common room.

Next to Noll at the brazier stood Pym, clutching his hair at his temples. His cloak was splotched with dirt and gaped open at a rip in the side.

"Curse them!" Jarrod slammed his fist on a table. "And I sent her."

"I summoned her," moaned Pym.

A chill rippled through Melaia. "Where is Livia?"

"Our friends, the talonmasters," said Jarrod. "They've taken Livia."

"And Hanamel," said Pym.

"Hanni?" Melaia sank to the bottom step.

Pym hung his head. "And the priestesses."

Melaia put her head in her hands. "Why? How? Where did they go?"

"They headed for Redcliff," said Pym. "I found Hanamel in Navia and gave her your message. She thought it best to move to a place of safety. Wode-hall, I suggested, and she agreed."

"She agreed to come here?"

"I think Benasin's death shook her," said Pym. "And learning about the Firstborn. Of course, I told her you were here."

Pym studied a cut on his hand. "I thought she might need more protection on the journey than I alone could give her, so I sent for Livia. Soon as she came, we headed for Wodehall. But halfway here, those hellsteeds swooped down on us. They were so fast that we had no hope of escape. Livia told us to run, so we did. Hanamel and the girls were rounded up in no time. I should have turned back and fought. Instead, I kept running. I've proved to be a coward, I have."

"You were in the service of Livia and followed her orders," said Noll. "I'd not call that cowardly. You're lucky to still have your roots connected to your crown."

"But Main Undrian always said if it comes down to obeying orders or doing the right thing, do the right thing. I failed."

"I should have gone in Livia's stead," said Jarrod. "I could have given them a fight to remember."

"You'd have overcome two malevolent talonmasters and their draks with-out endangering a priestess and three girls?" said Noll. "Livia was wise not to battle when the odds were so greatly against her."

Esper wrung her plump hands. "Noll, why would these talonmasters do such a thing? What can priestesses do for them? Why do they want Livia?"

"Lord Rejius wanted Hanni," said Melaia. "He said so in the aerie. Maybe they took the others because they were traveling together." She rose. "I'll go to Redcliff tomorrow and try to gain their release."

"Lady Wisdom!" Jarrod held up his hands in exasperation. "Do you think you can simply saunter into Redcliff and ask the great Lord Rejius to please release your friends?"

Melaia clenched her fists. "At the least I might get the girls out. Lord Rejius doesn't need novice priestesses. I'm certain the priest doesn't want them underfoot, but he's probably playing host to them at the temple. I'll ask there first. He'll no doubt be grateful to let me take charge of them."

"May I remind you that you were hunted in Redcliff?" said Jarrod. "You can't simply walk in and present yourself."

"That's not quite what I had in mind," said Melaia.

"Then what?" Jarrod folded his arms over his chest.

Melaia bit her lip.

Jarrod nodded. "You have no plan. You cannot go to Redcliff—"

"Then who?" Melaia shouted. "You cannot go. Noll cannot go. Esper cannot go. You are all Angelaeon. The malevolents would sense your presence before you could enter the gates. Who else but I?"

"I." Pym rose. "I'll go."

"With me," said Melaia.

"Without you." Pym fingered the hilt of his dagger.

"I have a knife," said Melaia.

Jarrod snorted. "Have you ever used it outside the kitchen?"

She glared at him. "Trevin told me how to use it."

Jarrod's eyebrows rose. "Oh, there's a comfort."

Melaia huffed and turned to Esper. "Can you disguise me?"

"I can make it so you don't know your own self, pipit." Esper chuckled.

"There," Melaia told Jarrod. "I have a plan."

"You're wanted at Redcliff," said Jarrod. "By the Firstborn."

"We can enter by the Door of the Dead," said Melaia. "No one will even suspect we're there."

Jarrod rubbed his forehead. "Work your plan, then. We Angelaeon are not in the habit of thwarting human will." He scowled at her. "I must say yours is one of the most frustrating I've encountered."

⌒✲⌒

Melaia watched from her bower as Pym left for Redcliff early the next morning. He had reminded her that his horse and Benasin's were still at the palace stables, and he was sure the stableboy would be grateful to be paid for their keep. He planned to offer the boy extra coins for information about two women and three girls brought into Redcliff by the talonmasters the previous day.

Melaia prayed Pym would be successful. She had arranged for him to unbolt the Door of the Dead late in the day and wait for her in the catacombs. If he knew where Hanni, Livia, and the girls were, the next step would be trying to reach them. She hoped her disguise would allow her to move around Redcliff unnoticed.

That afternoon, with Esper's help, Melaia donned the tunic, leggings, and sandals of an errand boy, with a turbanlike cap to hold her hair. Noll accompanied her to the edge of the woods. Then, with her journey pack over her shoulder and her knife tucked into her belt, Melaia headed toward the caravan road.

She hid Dreia's book under her tunic in the fold of a wide flaxen sash. She knew Jarrod would have counseled her to leave the book in the Durenwoods, but she wanted it with her in case she needed something of value to exchange for Hanni and the girls. She would barter the book if she had to. But that, she had told no one.

As she approached the caravan road, she concentrated on walking without swaying, which she had practiced under Pym's instruction while Jarrod covered his mouth, trying not to laugh.

She knew Jarrod watched from the woods even now, but a passing wagoner didn't give her so much as a glance. Nor did a man leading a pack donkey. And in the stubbled fields beyond the road, a drover yelled at her to get out of the way of his goats.

Melaia grinned. Did she truly look like a boy? Would Trevin recognize her now? She would love to walk straight past him, steal the harp back, and leave an apricot in its place.

As she crested the hill to the west of Redcliff and crept toward the towering wall, she felt the size of a mouse. And like a mouse, she had to search for the way in. The burial grounds lay ahead, so she knew the Door of the Dead was near, but it was hidden behind a hedge, and it took some time to locate it.

When she did find the door, it was ajar, so she knew Pym had done his part. Her heart pulsed in her ears as she eased the door open and ducked into the pitch-black catacombs.

Gently she closed the door behind her, calling softly, "Pym? Did you bring a lamp?"

A scuffling sound came from across the room, then Pym's half-muffled cry.

Melaia whirled and lunged for the door, but a heavy blow pushed her aside. Her cap tumbled off as she fell onto the edge of Queen Tahn's coffin, crushing the blanket of withered flowers and releasing a pungent scent of dead roses. The mass of dried blooms took the edge off her fall, but she was left fighting for breath.

A torch flared. Shadows danced off the tombstones. A muscular hand grabbed her collar and shoved, pinning her down on the crumbled garlands while her bag was ripped away.

She slipped the knife out of her sash, and as soon as she felt the hand let up, she twisted, intending to bury the blade in her attacker's throat.

She almost did, but he clamped one hand on hers, grabbed her hair with his other hand, and jerked her upright, almost off her feet. She found her own knife at her throat as she stared at Pym, who lay facedown, his hands bound, at the foot of the stairs.

A leather-faced, bulky man stood over him. Melaia recognized him as Vort, the talonmaster who had leered at her when he spoke to Trevin in the courtyard. He did the same now.

"Good of ye to keep yer tryst," he said.

CHAPTER 16

Melaia was prodded forward by her knife as she stumbled up the stairs behind Pym and Vort. Her breath came in short gasps. She silently repeated the words from her mother's book: *Fear and courage dwell together... Fear and courage dwell together.* At the top of the stairs, Vort threw Ordius, the priest, a purse that jangled with coins.

They marched out of the temple and into the courtyard, where Lord Rejius stood barking orders to porters, who bustled around, loading carts and wagons. Vort pushed Pym to his knees before a red-cloaked guard and headed toward the stableboy, who held Vort's black horse.

Melaia, too, was shoved from behind, and she sprawled onto the flagstones at the feet of Lord Rejius. She picked herself up, folded her arms over the book, and glowered at him, hoping to look courageous. She certainly didn't feel bold as the Firstborn looked her up and down, eying her in boy's clothing.

He leaned imperiously on his staff. "You. A spy, aren't you? You and that renegade priest. I'm pleased to have you."

Melaia swallowed dryly. At least he didn't know she was Dreia's daughter.

The younger talonmaster, whose arms were etched in snaking lines, handed her pack to Lord Rejius. The hawkman dumped its contents onto the stones. A hunk of Esper's loaf bread thumped to the ground, wilderberries scattered everywhere, and a clean shift cascaded out.

"Where is the book?" Lord Rejius glared at Melaia.

She tried to look innocent. "What is a book?"

Lord Rejius narrowed his eyes. "Damnation."

He turned and strode to Vort, who was now mounted on his horse at the head of the procession of carts and wagons. A drak flapped down to the talonmaster's gloved hand as they talked.

A covered cart stood just behind Vort. Through its open curtains, Melaia could see a motionless, gray-faced man. King Laetham, she supposed. Beyond him, in the shadows, sat a woman. As the woman shifted, light fell across her face.

"Hanni," whispered Melaia. She took a step toward the cart, but Hanni, almost imperceptibly, shook her head.

Lord Rejius jerked the curtains closed, cutting off Melaia's view of Hanni and the king, and shouted to the driver. The cart lurched out of the courtyard, accompanied by Vort on his sleek horse.

Another covered cart pulled forward, this one carrying the girls. Nuri's freckled face was half-hidden, pressed against Iona, who held Peron in her lap. They silently stared at Melaia, who wanted to cry out to them but dared not put them in more danger. Peron, clutching her doll, began to whimper, and Iona stroked her curls. Their cart, too, clattered out of the yard.

A third cart rolled up with Trevin and Dwin inside. Dwin eyed Melaia through his rakish bangs, but Trevin simply looked away as a porter opened the door for Lord Rejius.

Lord Rejius strode back to Melaia, thrust the tip of his staff under her chin, and raised her head until she stared straight into his piercing gold eyes. "You delay my journey to Qanreef, and I am not a patient man. Where is the book?"

Melaia hardly breathed.

"The book!" Lord Rejius pressed his staff into her throat.

Melaia again said, "What book?" But the words came out broken and hoarse.

Lord Rejius's face twisted as he raised his staff. Melaia shut her eyes and shrank from the oncoming blow.

"Melaia!" yelled Trevin.

A dull whack sounded as the blow hit its mark. But it did not hit Melaia.

She opened her eyes to see Trevin doubled over on the flagstones. The staff hit him again. And again.

Melaia looked away, all her muscles tensed, holding back her impulse to throw herself at Lord Rejius. Then her gaze fell on the object at Dwin's feet. The harp.

Like a loosed arrow, Melaia shot to the cart, scrambled in, and grabbed the harp. Dwin clamped both his hands around her wrists and wrenched her away. As the harp fell with a clang to the bed of the cart, Lord Rejius clutched Melaia's tunic, dragged her out, and twisted her right arm behind her back. She winced and pressed her left arm over the book at her middle.

Trevin lay motionless, facedown, but Melaia knew he would be all right, for his spirit wasn't leaving his body.

Lord Rejius jerked on her as he shouted, "Fein!"

The etched talonmaster stepped up and bowed.

"Take a contingent to the Durenwoods," said Lord Rejius. "Search Wodehall. Burn them out if necessary. I want that book. *And* the priest." His grip on Melaia tightened. "Though now that we've got the girl, he may come to us."

Melaia bit her lip. *Would Jarrod come? Was now the time to bargain the book for the safety of Wodehall?*

As she argued with herself, Fein swept away to his task, and the choice was made.

An angry scream sounded from the palace, and Zastra stormed out, her wiry gray hair in tangles around her wrinkled face, which was as red as her cloak. "My trunks have not yet been loaded," she yelled. "I want porters *now!*"

"Zastra," Lord Rejius crooned at Melaia's ear. "Didn't I tell you? You're not coming to Qanreef."

Zastra's mouth dropped open. "I'm the queen mother," she shrieked. "*I* procured your position for you. I paid dearly, Dandreij. You promised I would reign."

"You'll reign over Redcliff while I'm away," Lord Rejius barked. "I'll leave these three to keep you company, though you'll have to visit them in their cells.

Make sure this one stays alive. My brother seemed to care a good deal for her. I want to show him that she's mine now."

He shoved Melaia down on top of Trevin, who was still doubled up, face-down. He yelped.

"Trevin?" Her voice shook with emotions she couldn't identify. Priestess, chantress—she should know how to help. But she didn't. There would be no help for any of them in the dungeon.

But she had one spark of hope. Lord Rejius intended to show her to Benasin, which meant he was alive. Perhaps he was even in Redcliff.

Lord Rejius climbed into the curtained cart with Dwin, slammed the door, and glared back at Zastra. "Expect my return from Qanreef within one cycle of the moon. See that Redcliff prepares me a royal welcome, for I shall be wearing the crown, and Queen Hanamel will be at my side."

Melaia rose, trembling with anger.

"Queen?!" screeched Zastra. "*I* am to be queen."

"Who says I can't have two queens?" Lord Rejius grinned at Zastra. "After all, I now have three young concubines." He jerked the curtains of the cart shut.

"Beast!" yelled Melaia. She snatched up Esper's loaf bread from the dumped contents of her pack and hurled it at Lord Rejius's window as the cart leaped forward. It hit the back wheel and broke into pieces. "You have no right!" she yelled, darting after the cart.

Two guards, solid as a wall, blocked her and dragged her back while the cart sped through the gate, trailed by loaded wagons. As the rattle of wagons faded and the inner gate scraped closed, Melaia drooped like a cloth doll in the grip of the guards. They dumped her at the queen mother's feet.

Zastra's wrinkled face had gained a stony composure. She shot commands at the guards, directing them to throw Pym and Trevin into the dungeon.

"Zastra." Trevin turned on his side and hugged his ribs, wincing. His eyes went to Melaia as he panted, "Zastra. I beg your mercy. I can be of use to you."

Melaia held his gaze, wondering if he meant his words for her.

"I doubt you will be of use to anyone ever again," said Zastra. "Take them away." She turned and studied Melaia while guards dragged Pym and Trevin down a side street. "Stand up," she snapped.

Melaia rose, rubbing her right arm. It stung as if Lord Rejius had left a taloned imprint.

Zastra strutted around her, fondled her hair, looked her up and down. "I've been looking for you."

Melaia drew back. "For me?"

"We women have our ways, don't we?" crooned Zastra. "I see your wiles. Who would have thought you too were an immortal? But it stands to reason. The Wisdom Tree creates immortals." She chuckled. "Clever, Dreia. Clever to come back as a thin peasant girl. But you made a deadly mistake. You should have changed your eyes. I shall savor the thought of handing you over to Lord Rejius."

Melaia shook her head. "I'm not Dreia."

Zastra stuck her nose in Melaia's face and muttered, "Why did you return? Did you hear about the death of Queen Tahn? She was my daughter, you know. She may be dead, but there is still a queen. *I* am queen."

"But I'm not Dreia."

"And I'm not fool enough to fall for your tricks."

She snatched Melaia's arm and motioned for the guard. He accompanied them into the palace, through a maze of corridors, and up a staircase.

At the top floor, Zastra dragged Melaia into a large bedchamber. Across the room the embers of a dying hearth fire glowed. A regal chair and side table stood in front of the fireplace. The west wall held a tall window with open shutters. Along the east wall was the bed, its posts supporting a crimson canopy. Piles of clothing were strewn on the bed, and two trunks, packed to the top, lay open nearby.

Zastra dismissed the guard and locked the door with a key, which she slipped into her waist sash. Then she dug through the clothing on the bed, muttering, "My maidservant will not look like a goatherd." She pulled out a simple white gown and tossed it to Melaia, along with a red sash. "Wear this." Then she bent over the trunks and rooted through them, mumbling and cursing.

While Zastra was occupied, Melaia slipped off her tunic and pulled on the gown, keeping the book hidden under the flaxen band around her middle. After tying the red sash at her waist, she smoothed the silky gown. Though was a maidservant's, it was nicer than anything she had ever worn. And it might serve to disguise her if she could break free and find a way to Qanreef and Hanni.

The person she hadn't seen in the courtyard was Livia. She wondered if Livia had been in one of the carts or in a cell or...

Melaia went cold and shoved the thought aside. She wouldn't think the worst.

Zastra rose from her crammed trunks, cradling a round-bellied glass jar. "My Eye," she crowed, holding the glass high. She placed the jar on the side table and sat before it. "Bring water for my Eye," she commanded.

Melaia dipped a ladle into the waist-high stone water jar and poured it into Zastra's scrying glass. When it was half-full, Zastra snapped, "Enough!"

Melaia ventured a question. "How powerful is your Eye? Can it show Lord Rejius's brother, Benasin?"

"Is that his name? Lord Rejius just called him traitor. I have no need of a traitor, especially one who's dead and buried in the Dregmoors. I want a king." She waved Melaia toward the trunks. "Put my wardrobe back in order, Dreia."

"I'm not Dreia."

Zastra hissed and swatted at her.

While Melaia folded gowns and shifts, she watched Zastra. The old crone pulled a vial from her pouch, poured a sweet-scented oil into the jar, and swirled it around. Then she studied the patterns it made.

Melaia eyed the door, wondering how she could get the key from Zastra. Maybe she wouldn't need a key. If Zastra sent her on errands, maybe she could simply walk away.

But her first errand was only across the room to light the oil lamps. Then the cook brought supper, and Melaia served the queen mother before eating her own food. At Zastra's directions she readied the leftovers for the jailer to take to Trevin and Pym in the dungeon. When the jailer had left and Zastra had locked the door again, the old crone barked, "Lay us a fire, Dreia."

Melaia sighed and trudged to a stack of logs that rested under the open window. A thick, acrid smell wafted in on the breeze. She glanced out, then caught her breath.

On the western horizon, billows of smoke rose above the Durenwoods, lit by flickering orange flames that licked at the forest.

Melaia could hear the screams of the trees.

⌒☀⌒

All Melaia could think about for the next few days was the fire in the Durenwoods and how it was her fault. She berated herself for not giving up the book. Wodehall. Noll and Esper. The sylvans and their All's-Well signal. The tree at the head of her mother's grave. Was anything left? Or was it all in ashes?

Losing the harp was nothing compared to losing the Durenwoods and her friends. The guilt of it weighed heavier than the trunks of clothing Zastra made her haul from one side of the room to the other. Escape became Melaia's foremost thought.

But thinking about escape was much easier than accomplishing it. She couldn't slip away by night when Zastra was asleep, because the old crone kept her chamber door locked and held the key in her waist sash, even while she slept. By day, Zastra kept Melaia in sight every moment, insisting that she constantly be slave to the tyrant queen's needs. "Comb my hair, Dreia. Bring my sandals, Dreia. Make the bed, Dreia. Mend my gown, Dreia. Rub my feet, Dreia."

The only people who visited Zastra's chamber were the cook, who brought the meals, and the jailer, who picked up the dinner scraps. Zastra left her chamber only to hold court, receiving the ill-informed who had come from some distance only to find themselves bowing to Zastra instead of King Laetham. On those occasions Zastra kept Melaia on a leash attached to a collar around her neck like some wild pet.

At the end of Melaia's first week with the queen mother, the stooped steward brought a crop-haired man lugging a stool to Zastra's chamber.

"My lady." The steward bowed.

"Majesty to you!" snapped Zastra. "I'm your queen."

"I beg your pardon, Majesty." The steward bowed again. "We're offered a dozen of these stools. I brought a sample for you to see. You might like one for your chamber."

Zastra ran her hand across the carving on the stool.

"May I suggest taking it into the light of the window?" said the steward. "I want the craftsman to show you his exquisite work."

"Any design you like, I can carve it," said the craftsman. "M for Majesty. Z for Zastra. A crown for royalty."

Zastra stood tall with a queenly smile and accompanied the craftsman to the window.

The steward turned to Melaia and placed his hand on his heart, three fingers up. "Help me stoke the fire," he said.

Melaia had never been so glad to see the angel greeting, although she abhorred stoking the fire. All she could see in the flames were the Durenwoods and her sylvan friends.

She followed the steward to the hearth and handed him fresh firewood. He thunked it onto the half-burned logs in the fireplace and whispered, "Jarrod works to gain your release. Be ready."

"It's a trap," said Melaia. "He can't come."

"Be ready," said the steward.

"Is there news about the priestess and her girls? About the Durenwoods? Benasin?"

"I'm only a messenger. I've told you nothing today but how to better stoke the fire."

She nodded, disappointed but hopeful. See nothing. Hear nothing. Say nothing. She understood now.

He handed her the poker and spoke in a normal tone. "Now you try. Leave space for air."

As Melaia nudged the logs, Zastra called to the steward. "Order the dozen. Have you any news about the book Lord Rejius wanted? Was it found in the Durenwoods?"

"No, Majesty." The steward bowed, and Zastra walked him to the door.

The craftsman set the stool beside the hearth. "The carvings are good, if I say so myself." He winked at Melaia and followed the steward out.

She knelt by the stool. Its leaf design was formed by scores of three-branched signs of the Tree. She ran her hand over it and smiled. She wasn't forgotten.

Zastra locked the door, then leaned against it, holding out the key. "You know where that book is. Lead me to the book, Dreia, and I'll set you and your friends free."

Before today, Melaia thought, she might have bargained with Zastra. But not now. Not with Jarrod somewhere near.

"I'm not Dreia," she said. "And I know nothing about a book."

She stirred the coals. As the sparks flared, she glimpsed the fleeting figure of Flametender. She thought of the first time she had seen Flametender at the campfire at Caldarius. She had felt so free in that time between Navia and Redcliff. Had Trevin felt the freedom of it too?

She chopped at a coal, sending sparks flying. Thinking of Trevin was like shaking the oil and water in Zastra's jar, except it was the feelings of her heart that got all shaken up. Scoundrel, rogue, ruffian. Deceiver, defender, friend.

Unlike Zastra's oil-water, Melaia's feelings refused to settle into a clear picture.

CHAPTER 17

Night by night, Melaia watched the sky. Lord Rejius had left before the new moon, so as long as the moon waxed toward full, she held the hope of escape. But with each night that passed, she grew more uneasy. Had Jarrod been caught? Had he discovered that the fire in the Durenwoods was her fault and decided she wasn't worth rescuing?

As the moon began to wane, she came to the conclusion that she couldn't wait for Jarrod. She had to get out of Redcliff to see if the sylvans were all right. She had to get to Hanni and the girls.

Zastra, too, watched the moon's phases and grew more distraught every day. She paced and whined. She cajoled and needled Melaia for the book, but Melaia continued to act as though she had never heard of it.

One night Melaia glanced over Zastra's shoulder while she studied her Eye. The oil-water image was small but swiftly grew as the spying drak neared its goal: Caepio and his actors.

Melaia stared as the bird bore down on the wagon. One of the actors swept off his cloak and beat at the drak. The image shrank as the bird rose. Then two riders galloped in. Talonmasters. They searched the actors' trunks and bags, seized a harp, and rode off.

Melaia wondered if Lord Rejius was confiscating any harp he came across. If so, he was grasping at the wind. Caepio's harp wasn't even the right shape.

As the image faded, Melaia leaned closer, enthralled.

"Back!" Zastra elbowed Melaia. The book at Melaia's midriff caught the blow with a thump, and Zastra's eyes grew wide. Melaia stepped back and pressed her hands to the book.

Zastra snapped like a harp string wound too tight. She leaped at Melaia and tore at her gown. Melaia shoved and kicked, but Zastra wrestled her to the bed and fell on her, ripping and tearing until the flaxen sash was exposed. She pried the book out. Melaia grabbed for it, but Zastra yanked it free, returned to her chair, and greedily flung the book open.

An unearthly howl echoed outside the shuttered window. Zastra jerked up her head. "Lock and stay," she commanded the shutters, but they rattled like the stones in the overlord's wagering pouch. Zastra crept toward the window, still holding the book tight, pointing and muttering, "Lock and stay. Keep away." But the more she chanted, the more furiously the shutters shook.

Melaia drew her tattered gown around her, cringing in awe at the force of the rising storm. With a crash the shutters blew open, and in swept a spirit with long white hair. His face was tempest-mad. Zastra shrieked.

"Windweaver!" Melaia gasped, stumbling back as the gale hit her. She ducked behind the bed, watching as the scorching cold wind sliced through the room. It whipped Zastra's skirts and shoved her into the chair by the hearth, where she sat wind-swept and slack-jawed, clutching Dreia's book.

Windweaver snatched up the divining jar and hurled it across the chamber. It shattered against the stone wall. Zastra started to rise, but the wind lashed at her, screaming with fury. It battered the bed drapes. Scoured the stone wall. Spat at the fire until every ember was cold and the room was completely dark. Then Windweaver whirled out the window, slamming the shutters.

Quiet filled the room like drifts of snow. Melaia slipped a gray cloak from the clothing chest and tugged it around her shoulders, shivering. In the darkness she could barely make out Zastra's form, rigid in her chair.

"My Eye," moaned Zastra. "My Eye." She slipped the book down the front of her gown. Then she began to cough in raspy spasms and couldn't seem to stop.

As Melaia listened to the crone's croup, an idea began to form. A tea of herbs would soothe Zastra's cough. Add a few drops of dreamweed, and she would never feel her slave snatch the key and the book. Then, Melaia schemed, when the jailer came for their leftover supper, she would follow him to the dungeon in search of Pym and Livia.

Zastra moaned and coughed all night. When the cook brought breakfast, she unlocked the door and waved it away. "I can't swallow," she croaked. She slammed the door and locked it, then coughed long and hard, squinting her red, watery eyes at Melaia. "You are the cause of all this."

"Lord Rejius is the cause of all this." Melaia slipped on a fresh gown, feeling empty and bare without the book at her midriff.

Zastra scowled. "Buzzard from the Dregmoors. This is the gratitude he shows after I rid him of Laetham's queen."

Melaia tied on a sash, studying Zastra. In the aerie Lord Rejius had told Benasin that Queen Tahn didn't trust him. In the courtyard Zastra claimed she had paid dearly to procure his position for him. "You killed your own daughter," Melaia murmured.

"My own *fool* daughter. King Laetham wasn't interested in me, so I enticed him with Tahn. But she never had the instincts of a queen. Didn't know how to carry power and authority. Fool. I was always better at being queen, and Rejius saw that. He vowed to make me queen once he is king. Riches and youth will be mine." She coughed. "He has promised me his youth potion. Gash."

Melaia recalled Gil mentioning a gash merchant drummed out of Stillwater. "Baize," she said.

"Gash, you dolt."

"Baize is the merchant who sells gash."

Zastra's eyebrows rose. "And you buy it. That's your secret, isn't it, Dreia? Gash." She slowly rose like a snake about to strike, her eyes fixed on Melaia. "I want it." The cough took her again. "Give me some of your gash," she croaked, rubbing her throat.

"If I had some, you'd be the first person I'd give it to." Melaia stood tall, for the first time feeling as though she might be gaining the upper hand. She warned herself to proceed carefully and keep Zastra calm as she mustered her best servant voice. "Majesty, what you need right now is a potion to soothe your throat. I've been trained in remedies. Let me gather herbs from the field and steep a hot drink for you."

Zastra opened her mouth to answer but coughed violently instead. When the fit passed, she glared at Melaia. "We'll go to the fields, but if you think I'll let you out of my sight, you're mistaken."

She slipped the book out of her gown and locked it in a trunk. Melaia noted that she tucked the key into her waist sash.

After a fit of coughing, Zastra fastened the collar around Melaia's neck. "I know my herbs too," she said. "If you dare try to poison me, you'll not live long enough to regret it."

They trudged downstairs. Then, as if she were leading a cow to pasture, Zastra led Melaia out the scullery door. The cook gawked at them, and the palace guards stared as the mad queen and her maidservant left by the postern gate.

On the hill outside the walls, the sun shone, and the air was crisp, but the edge of the Durenwoods looked like a charred fence rimming the horizon. Swaths of ashen ground stretched like giant fingers from the blackened woods toward Redcliff. Melaia wondered just how much her lie about the book had cost the sylvans. Her feet felt heavy as boulders as she plodded downhill and through the fire-swept field toward patches of unscorched grass.

At last Melaia spied saffroot and gathered a handful. She plucked several purple-berried stems of plumwort. But was there no dreamweed?

"Show me what you're gathering," wheezed Zastra.

Melaia held out a palmful of plumwort and saffroot.

"Is that not enough?" Zastra coughed and spat.

"A few more stems." Melaia frantically eyed the ground, then spotted it—a stunted plant but bearing fruit.

"Enough!" Zastra tugged on the leash.

Melaia gasped and snatched up the dreamweed, swiftly tucking it beneath the other herbs in her hand.

⌖

Melaia rebuilt the fire in Zastra's hearth. With her plan under way, she felt as though she herself were full of kindling newly lit. When the flames crackled, she set the kettle on and sifted through the herbs. She hesitated at the dream-weed. Not yet.

Zastra sipped on hot saffroot water most of the day. She ordered Melaia to clean up the shards of her scrying glass, comb her wiry gray hair, and rub her bony feet.

When Melaia reached under Zastra's chair to fetch the crone's slippers, Zastra backhanded her. "Leave them!"

"I thought your feet might be cold."

"Then stoke the fire." Zastra coughed.

Her cheek stinging, Melaia stirred the fire. For a moment she caught sight of Flametender again and took it as a sign of encouragement. But as she stared wistfully into the flames, she wondered, *Is there nothing more the Archon can do?*

At last the cook brought supper. Zastra coughed so hard she found it difficult to eat. "Dreia," she whispered, "fetch me more drink."

Melaia bent over Zastra's goblet again, her heart racing. This time she added the dreamweed. How many drops for a deep sleep? One? Two? She put in three.

Zastra drank. Ate a few bites. Then held out her goblet. "More."

Again Melaia made saffroot water and added dreamweed. Two drops.

Zastra took one gulp. Then another. She blinked slowly and set the goblet aside. Coughed. Murmured. Blinked again. Leaned her head back.

And slept.

Melaia tiptoed to Zastra and slowly reached into her waist sash. Empty. Where were the keys? The jailer locked the door after fetching the scraps. If she had no key, she would have no way out. Besides, she needed to unlock the trunk to get the book.

She patted down Zastra's gown. Nothing. She searched the wall niches. The bed. The jars and basins. Every nook and ledge. Then she searched them all again.

The sun began to set. The scuff of the jailer's sandals echoed in the stairwell. Melaia readied the tray of food and tried to think of a way to convince the jailer to leave the door open.

He unlocked the door, trudged in, and grunted at Melaia.

"Let me help." She held the tray and headed to the door. "I can help you. I can—"

He grabbed the tray from her and trudged out. The door locked.

Melaia wrung her hands and darted back to Zastra to begin the search again. She began with the soothsayer's waist sash. She would never catch up with the jailer now. Zastra would wake, know she had been drugged, and beat her maidservant to within a breath of death.

"Where are the keys?" Melaia wailed as she dropped to her hands and knees, searching all the cracks in the stones around the hearth. Nowhere. Nowhere. Nowhere.

Melaia choked back a frustrated sob, snatched Zastra's slippers one after the other and hurled them at the door.

The keys fell out of the second slipper and clattered to the floor.

Melaia shot to the keys, then dashed to the trunk and opened it. She grabbed the book and shoved it into her waist sash, snatched up a cloak, and ran from the room, pausing only to lock the door behind her.

Melaia could barely hear the jailer tramping down the stairs somewhere below. She followed the sound, groping in the dark, hugging the walls.

At last she saw the light from his torch disappearing around a corner ahead. She quickened her steps, keeping to the shadows, following close enough to see by the torchlight.

Through hallways, down more stairs, she followed the jailer into the underbelly of Redcliff.

CHAPTER 18

At first Melaia tried to keep the path to the dungeon in her memory so she could retrace it, but she soon gave up. It was difficult enough to keep up with the sinewy jailer and be quiet at the same time.

He passed through a room full of barrels tinged with a sickly smell, then descended a narrow flight of stairs. The air turned dank. He kicked a rat out of the way. Melaia drew back for a moment, then moved ahead, praying the rat would stay hidden.

The jailer lifted an iron key ring off a stone ledge. The keys jangled as he unlocked a barred gate. He plodded through, and his steps echoed farther down the passageway.

Melaia started to follow the jailer through the gate, then thought better of it. She dared not risk being trapped behind the bars when he left with the keys.

She heard him talking, followed by a clang. His footsteps came her way. She groped back up the dark stairwell as he shut and locked the main gate and replaced the keys. The light from his torch began bobbing up the stairs.

Melaia quickened her steps, but climbing up was harder than coming down. She could hear the jailer muttering somewhere behind her. A rat scampered across her path. Shuffling aside, she almost fell. She froze and covered her mouth.

"Who's there?" The jailer lifted his torch. Light washed up the stairs only two steps below Melaia and found the foraging rat. "Damned vermin." The jailer lowered his torch.

Melaia reached the storeroom and ducked behind a barrel only a moment before light splashed the walls. The jailer scuffed through the room. Then he was gone, leaving the chamber pitch-dark.

Even after the jailer's footsteps faded into silence, Melaia's heart echoed their beat in double time. She groped her way around the barrels to the stairs, then slowly began to descend again. A faint light outlined the steps ahead. The gate came into view, silhouetted against the glow of the torch wedged into a bracket in the corridor beyond.

With both hands Melaia lifted the key ring from its ledge. It jangled. She clamped it to her chest, tiptoed to the barred entry, and tried the keys one by one in the lock. The fourth key fit, and the bolt slid back with a clank. She pushed on the gate, and it scraped open.

Melaia eased the torch out of its bracket. As she crept down the corridor, a row of barred gates came into view. She strained to see into the shadows of the first cell. Softly she called, "Pym? Livia?"

She heard a shuffling sound. At the third gate two hands grabbed the bars, and a head of disarrayed hair popped into view. "Melaia? Is that you?" Pym peered out, stubble bearded. "Are you alone?"

"I am." Melaia began trying the keys in the lock. "Where is Livia?"

Pym pointed to the next cell. His fingers opened and closed around the bars. "How did you manage to find us? How did you get in?"

Melaia fumbled with the keys. "There will be time to talk when we're away from this rathole."

At last a key fit, and Pym swung the cell door open.

Livia already stood at the door of her cell. Her dusky hair had fallen out of its knot. Her cloak was torn and streaked with dirt. But her gaze was still confident. "So Jarrod broke through at last!" she said.

"Jarrod?" said Melaia. "I never would have escaped if I had waited for Jarrod."

"Well done, then." Livia grinned as her cell opened.

Pym headed farther down the corridor. "I'll check the other cells. The comains may be here."

"Look for Benasin as well," said Melaia.

Livia took the keys and began unlocking the next cell. "Trevin," she explained.

When the door creaked open, Melaia raised the torch. Trevin lay against the far wall, his face unshaven and his chest wrapped in strips of cloth.

He raised his head and gave a weak smile. "I have no apricots," he said, "but I owe you a wagon full."

Melaia wanted to say he was absolved, all was forgiven, but she couldn't. She knew what Jarrod would say, and since he wasn't there to say it, she did. "I don't know if we should release Trevin. He's the son of Lord Rejius."

Livia frowned at him. "You made many confessions across the bars but not this one."

"Because it's not true." Trevin's face was pinched with pain.

"I heard it with my own ears," said Melaia. "Lord Rejius called you *son* in the aerie."

"He said that to hurt me. He's not my father. I swear."

"Then who is?" asked Melaia.

"A laborer. Long dead." Trevin laid his head down and stared at the ceiling.

"Why should I believe you?" All Melaia's anger came boiling back. "You were going to throw me from the king's tower."

"That I confessed to Livia."

"You tricked me into telling you about Dreia's book. You took me and the harp straight to the Firstborn."

"He confessed all that too." Livia helped Trevin sit. "I'll not leave without him. Come. I'll bear him up on one side, you on the other."

Melaia huffed. There was no time to argue. She knelt beside Trevin. With his left arm around her shoulders, his right around Livia, they stood together. Livia had placed Melaia at Trevin's injured side, and he leaned heavily on her. And she liked it.

Melaia gritted her teeth. She didn't want to like it. It wasn't wise.

"I'm grateful," said Trevin. "I'll make it up to you."

"I don't trust your word any farther than I can spit," said Melaia. "You deceived me."

"Melaia—," Livia began.

"I deserve worse." Trevin withdrew his arms and hobbled toward the door, holding his side.

Pym appeared in the corridor, his fingers threaded through the top of his hair. "No comains."

"Benasin?" asked Melaia.

Pym shook his head. "But Lord Beker is down the hall."

"King Laetham's advisor?" asked Melaia. "Gil said he disappeared. Murdered."

"We could all disappear forever down here, we could," said Pym. "Surely that's murder any way you look at it."

Livia settled Trevin against the cell bars to wait for them. Pym led the way to a cell at the far end of the row. A gaunt, blond-bearded man squinted at them as the torchlight hit his eyes.

"Lord Beker," said Livia, "we're here to free you." She tried the keys in the lock.

The man clutched his twisted left hand to his chest and edged deeper into the shadows.

The lock clanked open. Livia stepped in and held out her hand. "We're friends. Come with us."

But Lord Beker drew farther away.

"We support King Laetham," said Melaia. At least she and Livia and Pym did. She didn't know about Trevin.

Livia reached for Lord Beker again, but he hit at her, hissing, "Save yourselves, not a deserter."

"We want to save King Laetham," said Livia. "You could help us."

"No longer," he moaned, curling up in a corner.

Melaia scanned him for signs of his spirit. "He's not dying," she said. "We could carry him out."

"I wager he'd fight us," said Pym. "He'd draw attention to us."

"All right." Livia backed away from Lord Beker. "But I'll leave the doors open. You're free if you leave soon. Before the jailer finds you."

Lord Beker didn't move. Melaia felt as crushed as he looked.

"Let's go." Livia left the cell, slipping the key ring under her sash.

Melaia hesitated, then hurried down the corridor after Livia and Pym. Trevin took Pym's offered arm as they headed out.

"We can't leave by the Door of the Dead," said Melaia. "Ordius the priest isn't trustworthy."

"There's another way." Livia took the torch from Melaia and swept through the gate at the bottom of the stairs. This too she left open.

In silence, everyone climbed the cold stone steps, Trevin leaning on Pym for support. They went as fast as Trevin could manage. When they reached the storeroom, Livia held the torch high and pointed to a low wooden door in the far corner. Shuffling and scraping, they edged around the barrels.

"What's the stench in here?" murmured Pym.

"Gash," said Trevin. "A potion to restore youth."

Melaia thought of Zastra asleep in her chair by the hearth. The old hen would consider these barrels a rich find.

"I've heard of gash," murmured Pym. "Don't the raiders drink the stuff?"

"They do," said Trevin. "Lord Rejius plans to garrison raiders at Redcliff."

"Commanding the raiders, is he?" said Pym. "And providing them with strong drink! I'd sooner swallow tar."

Melaia couldn't help thinking of Trevin in the dead of night, speaking to an outrider, sending the raiders south with the hawkman's signet ring and a red cloak. And she had trusted him. As they were all doing now.

Livia made a quick study of the keys, then unlocked and opened the door and ducked through with the torch.

Melaia stooped to follow and found herself in a narrow tunnel that sloped sharply downward, steeper and narrower than the tunnel at Aubendahl. She took a deep breath and entered, then heard Trevin gasp in pain as he ducked in behind her. Instinctively, she turned. By the flicker of torchlight, she could see his face twisted into a grimace. He pressed his hands to his side. Pym came behind him and closed the door.

"Everyone all right?" asked Livia.

Trevin's lips were clamped in a thin line, and beads of sweat rimmed his brow, but he nodded at Melaia. She turned and nodded to Livia. They crept down toward another door. When Livia opened it, cool night air wafted in from the tunnel's mouth.

Livia paused, her face golden in the light of the torch. A breeze ruffled wisps of her hair. "Empty casks roll out onto carts here. But no cart awaits us—"

"I'd say that's good news," said Pym.

"We'll have to help each other," said Livia.

By Livia's firm look aimed toward her, Melaia knew she meant they needed to help Trevin. She took the torch from Livia.

Livia eased herself over the ledge until only her hands held on. Then she let go, and a soft thud sounded below.

Holding the torch high, Melaia peered over the edge. The cask door was in a recess of Redcliff's outer wall, which loomed up into darkness above them. Below, the rutted dirt was packed rock-hard by the passage of hoofs and wagons. A broken wheel leaned against the wall. Livia rooted around in a dump of old barrels, rolled a large one under the ledge, and motioned for Melaia.

After handing the torch to Trevin, Melaia gripped the edge and eased herself down. Her feet found the barrel. It creaked but held as Livia steadied it. Melaia let go of the ledge with her hands and climbed off the barrel.

Pym held the light for Trevin, who groaned as he edged out of the tunnel. Melaia watched him closely, wondering if his wounds were a ploy. Normally he could have climbed up or down this wall with ease, she was sure, but tonight he couldn't fully straighten his arms. At least it appeared that way.

He slipped. Livia braced him and eased him down from the barrel. He dropped to the ground and doubled up in pain.

Pym tossed the torch down before his descent. When he reached the ground, Livia snuffed the flame, and they all lay on the dirt, panting in uneven rhythms.

Grasses rustled in the chill breeze. Owls hooted in the distance. Melaia placed her hand over the book under her sash and wondered what Zastra would do when she found her slave gone.

She nudged Livia. "We should make our way to Wodehall before we're discovered."

In the darkness Livia, Trevin, and Pym looked like lumps of coal coming to life. "The jailer told us Lord Rejius torched the Durenwoods," said Livia.

"True," said Melaia, "but shouldn't we try to find Esper and Noll?"

"If Wodehall is standing," said Trevin, "you can be sure it's the first place the guards will search for us. I'd feel safer south of the hills."

"I agree," said Livia. "Pym?"

"I'm on the way, I am. Stay close."

Melaia scrambled to her feet. Journeying straight south would indeed be the quickest way to reach Hanni and the girls, but could they trust any suggestion that came from Trevin? He could lead them straight into an encampment of talonmasters. Yet Pym was already heading out, with Livia and Trevin following.

Melaia ran to catch up.

CHAPTER 19

Melaia reckoned the hour to be after midnight when they finally crested the wooded south hills. She sank to the ground and rubbed her sore feet. They had encountered no armed men, no trap. Not yet. She hoped they were safe.

Sssafe, whispered the trees. *Sssafe.*

"Zastra will send a search party," said Pym.

"At least she can't send talonmasters," said Trevin. "They went to Qanreef with Lord Rejius." In the darkness, as he lay flat on his back, he looked like a fallen log.

"What about draks?" said Pym. "And Lord Rejius himself becomes a hawk at will. That leaves me uneasy, it does. Our pursuers may come from the seacoast, not Redcliff."

"Surely Zastra won't tell Lord Rejius we've escaped," said Melaia. "She risks his wrath if she does. Besides, I mixed five drops of dreamweed into her drink. She's still asleep."

Pym chuckled. "Snorts and snores! Five drops! She'll sleep 'til the sun sets on the morrow!"

"Even so," said Livia, "we stay alert. I'll take first watch."

"I have second," said Pym. "Wake me. And if you have one of your terror-dreams tonight, Trevin, just know I'll be stifling your cries so you'll not alert the whole world to our whereabouts."

Trevin had no answer but a soft snore.

"So he truly has terror-dreams?" Melaia remembered the night he had told her to slap him awake if she needed to, but at the time she hadn't known whether he was being truthful or just teasing.

"He often wakes panting and sweating," said Pym. "Sometimes screaming."

"What's his dream?" asked Melaia.

"Some haunting from his past, I think," said Livia.

Melaia lay on her side, her back to Trevin. Even if Lord Rejius wasn't his father, Trevin had served the hawkman, which would give anyone terror-dreams. Trevin had probably screamed in the dungeon, waking everyone, even Lord Beker.

Poor man. She wondered if he was still there.

"Livia?" Melaia could barely see the Erielyon's shadowy form leaning against a tree trunk. "Why would Lord Beker not come with us?"

"When I was first taken to my cell," said Livia, "I heard Lord Rejius and his men trying to persuade Lord Beker to sign papers that certified the king's appointment of Lord Rejius as his heir. They beat him badly." Her voice wavered. "I suspect he signed those papers and now feels too ashamed to take his freedom."

Livia fell silent for a moment. Then she asked, "Melaia, do you sense the presence of angels—the malevolents or the Angelaeon?"

"Before I saw Jarrod in the archives at Aubendahl, I knew he was there. I've sensed the Archae as well."

"Try something for me," said Livia. "Be still, remove all thought from your mind, and concentrate on what your spirit knows. Can you sense me?"

Melaia rolled onto her back, closed her eyes, and tried to ignore the rustle of Trevin turning over.

"Open your eyes." Trevin yawned. "It helps."

Melaia rose on one elbow. "How do you know my eyes are closed?"

"I can see in the dark." He turned over again.

"Try it," said Livia.

Melaia tried, but her mind was a hornet's nest. The night Trevin had climbed in the window at the caravansary he had asked if she could see in the dark. He could. Was he an angel? Or had the Firstborn taught him earth-magery?

"Calm your breathing," said Livia.

Melaia steadied her breath, stared up into the black of the treetops, and tried to empty all thought. Shut out the wind shying through the branches. Push away the murmuring pulse of tree-thought. Sink into spirit.

She sensed a slight movement. Calm. Clear blue. Clean. Like the indoor rain at Wodehall.

"I sense you...I think."

"Stay aware," said Livia. "Anything else?"

Melaia breathed calmly. A rich brown warmth moved south through the woods. Then it curved, gave them wide berth, and headed north. Melaia's heartbeat quickened. "I sense another. Circling us."

"A malevolent?"

"I think not," said Melaia.

"You may sleep easily, then," said Livia. "You've sensed Jarrod keeping watch."

⸙

Dawn's light splotched high boughs and trickled down tree trunks in the early morning chill. Melaia could no longer sense Jarrod's presence as she, Livia, Trevin, and Pym trekked south through the woods.

What she did sense was the sibilant tree sound. *Save us. Save us.* She frowned. This was no echo of her thoughts. Could the trees be expressing their own thoughts? *Save us. Save us.* Could a death-prophet sense the dying of nature? She halted, gazing up at the autumn-bare, interlaced branches. Was nature waiting for Dreia's daughter to take her mother's place as Archon?

"Melaia?" Livia called from the top of a hill. "I can see Gil's stead from here."

Melaia stroked a gnarled tree trunk, then ran to catch up. Pym and Trevin waited just over the rise. Together they all walked a cow path downhill toward a road that skirted a pond.

As they neared the road, a rig rattled around the bend, driven by a big-eared, bush-bearded dwarf. The rig clattered to a stop in front of them, and Gil grinned, holding three fingers to his chest. "Climb in, friends, and I'll carry you to *my* palace! Jarrod said you'd be coming. Said there'd been trouble."

Melaia glanced at Trevin, clamped her jaw, and climbed in. His eyes met hers, and he looked sheepish as he eased into the bed of the wagon.

"We've seen a great deal of trouble." Livia gracefully settled herself beside Melaia. "We'll tell you about it as soon as we're safe."

"You're in no danger here," said Gil as Pym took a seat beside him. "Least-ways, nothing has periled us yet."

"I may *bring* you trouble," said Melaia. "It seems to follow me these days."

"Better to face trouble with friends than without, eh?" Gil circled the wagon around and headed back down the road.

Melaia looked away. Facing trouble with friends was one thing. *Bringing* trouble to friends was another matter altogether.

Gil and Pym talked, low and friendly, as they rambled down the road past stubbled fields and low stone fences. Livia gazed behind them, deep in thought. Trevin rubbed his right hand, tensely silent, now and then glancing at the sky. For draks, Melaia thought. Did he want draks to show up or not?

"Eyes sharp now," Gil said, "and you'll see my stead."

Off the road ahead lay a long, low shed. Two cart wheels and a wagon tongue leaned against the wall, and an upturned wagon lay nearby. As Gil drove around the far side of the shed, a whitewashed house with windows made of wagon wheels came into view. Its domed roof reminded Melaia of the temple in Navia, but it was much smaller. A white dog with brown patches bounded over a stone fence and raced to greet them.

"Behold Bram, master of the family." Gil laughed. Bram trotted alongside them, his tongue lolling out in a dog grin, all the way to the front of the house.

"Is this Stillwater?" asked Melaia.

"Thinking of the signpost at Omen Crossing?" Gil helped her down from the wagon. "Stillwater's a bit south of here." He angled his bushy head toward Trevin. "But I see your omen came true." He chuckled and headed to unharness his horse.

Melaia glanced at Trevin, climbing down from the wagon with Pym's help. *Whatever you spy first at the crossing is the omen for your journey.* She wondered when her journey would be over. She wondered if she wanted it to be.

The smell of fresh wheat cakes drifted from Gil's door and drew them all inside to a table laid with a bowl of blackberries, a jar of cream, and a dish of butter. At the end of the table sat Jarrod, popping berries into his mouth.

"Welcome," he said. "I trust you had safe passage from Redcliff." He flipped his horse tail of hair over his shoulder.

"We did." Livia chose a stool. As everyone settled around the table, Gil's aproned wife, Gerda, marched in with hot wheat cakes, her fair, red-cheeked face broadening in a smile.

Jarrod shot a stern look at Melaia. "I told you not to go to Redcliff, didn't I? I told you it was unwise."

Melaia scowled at him. "Good morning to you too." She took some berries. "I happen to have discovered where Hanni and the girls are. And I rescued Livia. *You* didn't do that." She bit into one of the tart, seedy fruits.

"Because *you* didn't wait for me."

"*You* never came," said Melaia. "We all could have withered away and died in Redcliff."

Jarrod snorted. "I did come. As it happens, I fought fire and its aftermath in the Durenwoods, then—"

"Wodehall." Melaia sat alert. "Did it burn?"

"The trunk's blackened," said Jarrod. "The odor of smoke is suffocating. Otherwise the tree is whole, and the woods will recover. Esper and Noll were more distressed for you than for Wodehall."

"Thank the Most High." Melaia took the wheat cake Gerda passed to her.

"Back to my tale," said Jarrod. "I learned that the harp was on its way to Qanreef—perhaps both harps. And, yes, the priestesses too. So when I found out you were all right—"

"All right?" Melaia gaped at him. "It's all right that I was hounded day and night by Zastra, that crazy crone, not knowing whether I would ever be free again?"

Jarrod calmly buttered a wheat cake. "I discovered from acquaintances in Redcliff that you were all right. So I went to Qanreef to take advantage of the fact that the harp was being moved. Thinking it might not be as carefully watched, I hoped to find a chance to get it back."

"What about Hanni?" asked Melaia.

"I was looking for harps," said Jarrod. "But I imagine the priestesses are all right."

"Harps are more important to you than priestesses?" asked Melaia.

Jarrod glanced up at her and took a bite of wheat cake.

"Did you get the harp, then?" Livia asked him.

Melaia stared at Livia. Were the harps more important to her as well? Didn't these angels realize the trouble Hanni and the girls were in? Didn't they have hearts?

"Couldn't get near the harp," said Jarrod. "Lord Rejius swept it into the palace under a double guard of malevolents and hid it under some kind of enchantment. But he's not hiding the fact that he has the harps. 'Mage-harps,' he calls them. That rumor has traveled far and wide."

"To excite people, no doubt," said Pym. "Awe them so they don't whine when he takes the throne."

"Needless to say, I'm not awed." Jarrod dabbed a cloth to his mouth. "When I realized I was of no use in Qanreef, I journeyed north, fought a malevolent to get into Redcliff, and worked my way to the tower room. Only to find the queen mother snoring in her chair."

"You must have arrived shortly after we left," said Livia.

"Must have," said Jarrod. "I ranged wide of Redcliff and finally sensed you heading south."

Livia laughed. "You must admit Melaia is quite resourceful, getting us out on her own."

A hint of a smile played around Jarrod's eyes. "It was a clean piece of work, lady. Well done. You still have the book?"

"I do." Melaia glanced at Trevin, who was helping himself to wheat cakes at the other end of the table. She suspected the spy in him noted every word they said.

Jarrod studied him. "Have I seen you before, sir?"

"I told you about Trevin as we left Aubendahl," said Melaia.

"I remember. You also said he taught you to use a knife." Jarrod raised an eyebrow at Melaia.

She reddened and looked away from Trevin's roguish smile, the same smile he had given her on the road to Redcliff.

Gil, finished with his horse, pulled up a stool and took a stack of wheat cakes.

Jarrod wagged a finger at Trevin. "I remember you now. I was priest at Redcliff before Lord Rejius banished me. You were his lackey. You and your brother."

Everyone stopped eating. All was quiet, as though they had come to a long rest in a song. Gil's bushy eyebrows met in a frown, and Gerda paused, her pitcher poised over his empty cup. Livia shot a look of caution at Jarrod. Pym stopped chewing and eyed Trevin. Melaia glanced back and forth between priest and kingsman.

Trevin sat straight and noble as if he were blameless. "I've fallen out of Lord Rejius's favor."

"Gil," said Jarrod, "didn't you say you had some planks to plane?"

"Out in the wagon shed." Gil dusted crumbs from his beard.

"Good." Jarrod nodded at Trevin. "Let's you and I put our hands to good use for our host."

"Trevin has a wounded side," said Livia.

"Then maybe he'll tell me how he was wounded." Jarrod ushered Trevin outdoors.

The whole room seemed to let out its breath slowly. Gerda refilled their cups.

"Jarrod's a wise one, eh?" said Gil. "He'll sort out the pegs from the pebbles."

"It's time someone sorted it out," said Melaia. "Trevin is a betrayer." She took her last bite of wheat cake. It was thick and dry and had a bitter edge.

Livia took a sip of cider. "In the dungeon Pym and I learned that Trevin's father died of an illness when Trevin was nine and Dwin was four. Their mother was with child at the time, but both she and the baby died in the birthing, leaving Trevin to find food and shelter for himself and his younger brother."

"Which they found," said Melaia, "when Lord Rejius took on the role of father."

"That, I don't believe," said Livia. "Hear the full story before you pass judgment, Chantress."

"Trevin was caught stealing food," said Pym. "I've helped Main Undrian bring thieves to justice, I have, and I can tell you, thieves are always hanged. Even young ones."

Melaia cringed at the thought of a child being hanged.

"As it happened," said Livia, "Lord Rejius caught Trevin. He gave him a choice: be hanged or come to the palace as a spy and thief in the hawkman's service."

"Not much of a choice, eh?" Gil shook his head.

"We think either his mother or father was Angelaeon," said Livia.

"That makes his tale true?" Melaia asked. "I happen to know he's quite a good liar."

Livia raised her eyebrows. "He had no reason to lie to us. Besides, I heard truth in his voice."

"He'll betray us," said Melaia, irked that Livia could discern truth in Trevin's voice when she herself was so gullible she couldn't tell his truth from his lies. "He's probably spying for Lord Rejius even now."

"How did Trevin end up in the dungeon?" asked Pym, running his fingers through his hair. "Tell me that."

Melaia shrugged. "Lord Rejius was angry at him. But don't you see? Trevin could easily get back into the hawkman's good graces by bringing him a certain book. Or an entire company of Angelaeon, including Dreia's daughter."

Livia held her cup of cider in both hands, swirled it around, and stared into the steam that drifted from its surface. "The way Trevin tells it, he didn't want to involve you. Or to purchase a harp, for that matter."

"Then why did he?" Melaia crushed a blackberry under her thumb in her wooden bowl, then tried to mop up the juice with wheat cake before it stained.

"Lord Rejius makes it terribly hard to refuse orders," said Livia. "What would you do if he threatened to turn your younger brother into a drak if you didn't do his bidding?"

Melaia folded her arms and scowled at the blackberries as if it were their thorns that pricked her. She knew Livia was right. She was ready to give up Dreia's book to save Hanni and the girls.

Pym dumped berries into his bowl and poured on cream. "If I saw it right," he said, "Trevin was trying to save *you* when Lord Rejius raised his staff to strike. Trevin took your blows."

"I don't deny that," said Melaia, "but don't you see? It's just as Livia said. Lord Rejius still holds Trevin's brother, Dwin. So where do you think Trevin's loyalty lies? You may be able accept him, but I can't. The risk is too great."

Livia's eyebrows arched. "What risk? The risk that you may realize Trevin cares for you…and you care for him?"

"I don't…" Melaia gaped at Livia. "I *can't*!" She stood, her hands in fists, her voice rising. "You don't understand. I *saw* Trevin in the service of Lord Rejius, bearing his signet ring, wearing the red cloak. Trevin used me, almost killed me, almost had me turned into a drak." Her anger boiled over at these angels who didn't see the real tragedy unfolding in Qanreef: helpless priestesses in the vindictive hands of the Firstborn. "Hanni was right," she said, gruffer than she intended, but she barreled on. "Angels can take care of themselves and their own affairs. You have no hearts."

But you are one of them, a voice in her head whispered.

She swatted it away and stormed out of the house.

CHAPTER 20

Melaia stomped down the road toward Stillwater, trying to walk off her anger. She intended to go only a short distance, just to a place where she could think without the presence of angels to sway her.

With every footfall she was free, free, free. Except she wasn't. She was still Dreia's breath of angel, blood of man. Hanni and the girls were still captives. And Trevin. What to do about Trevin? Melaia's feelings built up within her like thunderheads on a stormy day.

Shameful, she thought, and heard the trees echo, *shhhame,* as if to confirm it. She hadn't meant to speak to Livia and Pym so harshly. She knew she wasn't being reasonable, and she hated herself for it, but she didn't know where her heart lay anymore.

"I do *not* care for Trevin." She picked up a rock and squeezed it in her fist. "I do *not* have to join the Angelaeon. If they admire Trevin so much, they can let *him* find the harps and restore the Tree." But she knew that was stupid and made no sense.

Stupid senssse, shuddered the trees.

Melaia hurled the rock down the road, hitting a tree trunk. A small drak fluttered up from the branches and slowly circled.

"Confound you!" she muttered, ducking into the shade. Instinctively, she looked for a second drak, for she had always seen them in pairs, but there seemed to be just the one, and it flapped away south. She wondered if Zastra was trying to find her.

Then Bram bounded up.

"Go home," Melaia ordered. The dog ran a few paces away, then frolicked back with that silly grin on his face. She pointed north and yelled, "Go home! Now!"

Bram again ran a few paces away, then pranced straight back.

Melaia sighed and walked on. Angels didn't interfere with human will, so she wouldn't interfere with dog will.

"Please yourself," she told Bram. "But it's not my fault if you get lost." It occurred to her that Jarrod might have thought the same when she bucked him and went to Redcliff against his counsel.

A drover of donkeys passed, heading south toward Stillwater. A peddler in a cart entered the road from a side path and disappeared over a rise. And Melaia walked on.

At midday she came to a fork in the road. The right branch headed through fields. The left curved at a grove.

"It doesn't matter which," she mumbled. Her anger was spent. She wanted only to sit and rest and think. Then she would go back to Gil's stead like a dog with its tail between its legs. She hadn't much choice. She had left her pack behind, and her cloak, although the book was still snug beneath the band around her middle.

She hiked to the grove and discovered wild blackberry vines twining around the thicket. But while there were plenty of thorns, there were few berries. She picked what she could find and munched the tart fruit. The thorny thicket was like her heart, she decided. Plenty of prickly dilemmas but few answers. As with the berries, though, she'd take what she could find. The one obvious need was to get Hanni and the girls away from the hawkman.

Melaia popped the last berry into her mouth, cleaned her stained fingers on the grass, then rose to head back to Gil's stead.

Bram waited at the edge of the road, wagging his tail.

"All right," said Melaia. "Time to go back. Lead the way."

Instead of turning and trotting up the road, Bram growled and stood his ground.

Melaia put her hands on her hips. "I thought you wanted to go back."

Bram bared his teeth and snarled.

Everything went black.

⁌❦⁍

Melaia woke with her head throbbing. She lay on her side in the darkness of the woods, her hands bound behind her, her feet tethered to the trunk of a sapling.

A stone's throw away, three hulking men with broad mouths and small eyes squatted around a fire, talking in low, garbled voices. Dregmoorians, no doubt. Stringy dark hair trailed down their backs. By their smooth, dun-colored skin, Melaia could tell they were gash drinkers, but they were not yet as far gone as the man at Drover's Well. She wondered if they were raiders.

Each of Melaia's heartbeats rattled her stiff body and pounded at the pain in the back of her head. She was afraid to move. Afraid to breathe. She wondered how long she had been there. She couldn't see Bram anywhere, and she was cold.

Losssst, the trees whispered. *Lossssst.*

Panic snaked through her. The book! She concentrated on the sash around her middle. It went tight, then slack as she breathed in and out. She could still feel the book.

Her relief was short-lived. One of the raiders rose and headed toward her. She quickly shut her eyes and tried to still her spirit.

Heavy footfalls crunched on dry leaves and stopped nearby. The man nudged her side with his toe. She dared not move. He muttered something that sounded like a curse. Another raider laughed.

As the footsteps plodded away, Melaia barely opened her eyes. The raider made his way to a companion with shorter hair and cuffed him on the side of the head. The man with short hair shot up with a gruff yell and pushed the other man back. The third, the stoutest of the three, pointed at them and barked an order. They backed away from each other, grumbling, then lay down on opposite sides of the fire.

Now that the raiders had fallen silent, Melaia was sure any movement, any sound she made would draw their attention. But the more she thought about not moving, the more she felt she had to move, to scream, to fight. Her wrists ached from her bonds.

Then she heard a whisper: "Melaia."

She held her breath and eyed the trees. They had never called her name before. The stout raider took a swig from a flask, then leaned against a tree trunk. His eyes blinked heavily. He seemed to have heard nothing.

"I'm behind you."

She startled as a firm hand clasped her arm, a hand missing a finger.

"Don't move until I tell you to."

"Trevin?" she whispered.

"Shhh." He sawed at the cords that bound her hands.

As the cords fell away, Melaia wiggled her fingers and stretched her arms as much as she dared. The ropes around her ankles moved slightly. She squeezed her eyes closed. What was taking so long? She could have sung three slow ballads by now.

Beyond the campfire, tree branches swayed. A rustling sound echoed through the woods. The guard went to take a look.

"Roll back slowly."

As Melaia eased herself onto her back, Trevin slipped over her, their bodies brushing past each other, his breath skimming her ear. Then Trevin melted into the place where she had lain, his feet next to the tree trunk, his hands behind his back.

The next moment Livia was at Melaia's side, drawing her away through the grove. Melaia stumbled, her feet still regaining feeling, her head aching. Livia picked her up and carried her, weaving in and out among the trees. At last they came to a road where Jarrod waited in a horse cart. He hauled Melaia into the back, then took the driver's seat. As soon as Livia had climbed in, Jarrod snapped the reins, and they sped away as fast as the horse could gallop over the moonlit road.

Livia drew Melaia into her arms but said nothing.

"Livia," Melaia asked, "what will happen to Trevin?"

Livia smoothed Melaia's hair but remained silent. The rumble of the wheels was so loud that Melaia thought Livia hadn't heard her. "Livia? What—"

"Why do you care what happens to Trevin?"

Melaia shifted uneasily. *Why indeed?* "How did you find me?"

"We saw Bram follow you, so we let you go. We didn't expect you to walk farther than the edge of the stead. When you and Bram were not back by midday, we grew anxious and began searching for you."

"Then Bram led you to me."

"Trevin led us to you."

"Trevin?" Melaia rubbed her tingling wrists.

"For some odd reason, while Jarrod and I can't sense your presence, Trevin can."

Melaia grew dizzy trying to comprehend it. She remembered the first time she saw him at the overlord's villa in Navia, the way his eyes had seemed to read her soul. Had he sensed her even then? "Does that mean he's Angelaeon?"

"We can't sense him, so no. But somehow his gifts seem greater than most Nephili."

"Even mine."

"That remains to be seen."

Melaia leaned her head on Livia's shoulder. "Where are Gil and Pym?"

"They went to rouse Stillwater. If all goes as planned, by the time Trevin is discovered, the raiders will be surrounded by townsfolk, who will dispose of them as they please."

"And if all does not go as planned?"

"Then, most likely, you'll have your wish. You'll not see Trevin again."

Melaia covered her mouth. The thought curdled her stomach.

Bram pranced around the rig when it rattled into Gil's yard. Gerda scurried out of the house, dusting her hands on her apron. "You found her!" she cried. Then she frowned. "Where is my Gil? And Pym?"

"Chasing raiders." Jarrod helped Melaia out of the cart.

Melaia pressed a hand to the back of her head where a dull pain lingered. "They must have hit me with a rock." She swayed and reached for Livia.

Gerda shook her head. "You've led us all into a patch of trouble, young lady."

Jarrod scooped up Melaia, carried her into the house, and laid her on a low bed in a side room. "You're just like Dreia," he muttered. "Impatient. Defiant."

Melaia raised her head to protest, but her skull throbbed. She dropped back onto the pillow.

"It's one thing to be determined and steadfast. It's another to be bullheaded and willful. That's what got Dreia killed." Jarrod brushed back long strands of hair that had escaped the thong at the back of his neck. His robe was dusty, his face weary and stern. "Have you ever worked with ramble roses?" he asked.

She wanted to tell Jarrod that she was picking a blossom from the ramble rose on the temple wall when Livia's son, Sergai, arrived and the hawk attacked. But her head pounded, so she simply said, "In Navia."

"Then you know that the ramble-rose vine overruns all other plants and chokes them out if it's not trained to a wall or trellis," said Jarrod. "Your destiny is beginning to bloom, Melaia, but you've got to train your will. If you let it go wild, it will overrun you and everyone around you."

"I'll never be free of Dreia's task, will I?"

"Free of your destiny?" Jarrod shook his head as if she were crazed. "Why would you want to be free of your destiny? Nothing else will satisfy. As for freedom, that's a matter of the heart. Pursue your destiny, and you'll find your freedom along the way."

Melaia thought Jarrod sounded a lot like the proverbs in Dreia's bewildering book. But it occurred to her that, like Livia, she could hear truth in his voice. It was Jarrod's voice, to be sure, but it gave her hope that she would some-day be able to discern truth in Trevin's voice as well.

She wanted to assure Jarrod that she had heard him, but her head hurt so much, all she did was groan.

Jarrod trudged out, rubbing his forehead, and Gerda bustled in. Melaia winced as Gerda gently lifted her head and pressed a warm spice-scented poultice in place.

"Where's Livia?" Melaia whispered.

"Resting." Gerda drew a blanket over her, then tiptoed out of the room.

Melaia's wound pulsed painfully with the pressure of the poultice. She thought about her destiny as Dreia's daughter. Restore the Tree. Simple enough to remember, but how would it be accomplished? And who would be part of that destiny?

A tingling sensation spread through Melaia's scalp, and the pain began to ease. She blinked sleepily at a beam that crossed the ceiling. A painted spring green vine curled along it. Here and there it blossomed with red ramble roses.

⟨✾⟩

For a day and a night, Melaia lay in bed, her mind churning over how to get to Hanni and the girls. By the morning of the second day, when Livia came to check on her, she was able to sit up without getting dizzy.

"I have a plan," Melaia announced.

Livia placed a cool hand on Melaia's forehead. "What kind of plan?"

"A plan to get into the palace at Qanreef. I rode partway to Redcliff in a wagon with a troupe of actors."

"Indeed?" said Livia. "I saw them enter Redcliff the day I met you at the temple."

"Their leader, Caepio, said they would be going to Qanreef. If we can find the troupe, we might ride into the city with them. We could pass as actors, couldn't we?"

"We?"

Melaia felt her face grow warm. "I was wrong to yell at you and Pym. I'm sorry. I need your help."

"We've saddled you with a great deal of responsibility in a very short time, I'm afraid."

"Did Pym and Gil return?"

"They did," said Livia.

Melaia glanced at the painted ramble roses. "Trevin?"

"He returned as well." Livia stroked Melaia's hair. "May I suggest tempering your impulses with wisdom, my lady?"

Melaia sighed. "I'll try. Does my plan sound wise?"

"It sounds possible. I'll think on it."

❧

At midday Livia brought Melaia a cup of hot barley broth and a clean gown. "Gerda says when you finish this broth, you can join the rest of us." She began combing Melaia's hair.

Melaia sipped on the salty brew and gazed out the round bedside window. In the distance Jarrod and Trevin talked as they sat on the ground, leaning against a large wagon wheel that rested on a pile of planks. "They're not toiling much out there," she said.

"On the contrary, I think there's a great deal of work going on. It's hard to heal a wounded heart."

Melaia's cheeks warmed. "If you're speaking of Trevin's heart, I have good reason to be wary of him."

"I'll grant you that." Livia tugged at a tangle. "But long-held anger ferments into poison, the same kind that infected the Firstborn. I hate to see it seeping into you. You remember Lord Beker? Like him, a bitter heart often refuses to be set free, even though the cell door is open." She looked Melaia full in the face. "What would it cost you to free both yourself and Trevin? Just a word or two. Sometimes one word sways the balance between bondage and freedom, pain and wholeness, death and life."

For a long time after Livia left, Melaia stared out the window at Trevin, who handed Jarrod tools as they worked on the side of a wagon. "Feel free to shake me," Trevin had said of his terror-dreams. "Slap me if you need to." She felt Livia's words—and Jarrod's too—as a slap to wake her from viewing the world in temple-tight rules.

She had wanted Trevin to be one thing or the other, good or bad, trustworthy or not. The same with Livia and Jarrod and the rest of the world. The same with herself. She wanted certainty.

But life was not certain. Temple rules, the easy dos and don'ts, had masked that fact. Wake up, Melaia told herself. Life had never been certain. It wasn't certain now, and it never would be.

Trevin bent down so fast Melaia thought he was fainting. Then she saw two draks flying over the field. Jarrod stepped between the draks and Trevin, shielding him from view. The draks flew low above them. She wondered if Lord Rejius was searching for Trevin.

It occurred to Melaia that she could make her own search. She slipped Dreia's book out from under the bedcovers and turned to the blank pages at the back. As she suspected, the dark page was still dark. The other page was quick to form lines that crossed and swayed, nothing else.

But on the page that had previously shown images, lines sharpened to reveal a man lying on a bed. Or a bier. His spirit outlined his body. A woman knelt at his side, but Melaia could see only her back. The woman placed something at the man's lips, then whirled around in alarm.

Melaia clapped the book shut. The dying man was King Laetham. The woman was Hanni.

CHAPTER 21

Melaia dashed into the common room. "I've seen Hanni! In the book!" She thrust Dreia's book into Livia's hands. "Hanni is with the king. He's dying."

"How can you see such a thing?" Gerda dumped peas from her apron into a bubbling pot on the hearth.

"The book shows what the harps see," said Melaia. "That means Hanni is wherever the harp is. Surely the girls are nearby. I must leave for Qanreef *now*." She looked at Livia. "*We* must leave for Qanreef. I've wasted our time grandly, but perhaps there's still a chance—"

"You can't go yet." Gerda wiped the back of her hand across her red cheeks. "Pym and my Gil have gone to find Caepio. That was your plan, wasn't it?"

"But—"

"Pym knows our time is short," said Livia. "With or without the actors, Pym and Gil will return."

"When?" asked Melaia.

"Soon as they can." Gerda handed her the spoon. "Your turn to stir."

Melaia swished the spoon in the thick stew, which steamed a rich, golden aroma.

Jarrod and Trevin tramped in, sweaty and grinning. Jarrod settled himself on a bench by the wall and began combing sawdust out of his hair. Trevin's glance met Melaia's for only a moment. He quickly looked away, then stretched out flat on the floor and closed his eyes.

Melaia gripped the spoon tighter, took a deep breath, and said, "Trevin, thank you for rescuing me from the raiders. I'm sorry I put you in danger. You too, Jarrod."

Jarrod nodded. Trevin opened one eye and peered at her. "If I remember correctly, you rescued *me* once." He closed his eye again.

So that's why you took my place, thought Melaia. *This for that. Even the score.*

She stirred so hard that splashes of stew spattered out of the pot and sizzled in the fire. One drop landed on her arm. She quickly licked it off, taking it as a warning to hold her impulsive spirit in check. She recalled the ramble roses. *Train yourself,* she thought. *Train your stubborn self.*

Jarrod suddenly straightened, his head cocked. Livia rose at the same time. Melaia stopped stirring and watched the warning that flashed between them. Melaia sensed it herself, a dark threat edging around her spirit.

"Malevolents!" said Jarrod. "Approaching."

"And fast." Livia handed the book back to Melaia. "They must be on horses."

"Talonmasters?" Melaia stuffed the book into her waist sash, every muscle tensed.

"Blast!" said Trevin. "The draks must have seen me. And I have no sword, no dagger."

"Gil has a blade in a trunk by our bed," said Gerda.

Trevin hurried out of the room, holding his side again.

"Keep the blade out of sight," Gerda called after him. "My Gil says not to provoke a ruffian."

Bram began to bark furiously in the yard.

Gerda peeked through a crack in the shuttered window. Her red cheeks paled. "Two riders down the road. Pausing now. Releasing their draks."

"Livia and I can take them," said Jarrod.

"No fighting unless you absolutely must." Gerda shoved Jarrod toward the back door. "Get out before they sense you. You too, Livia. You'll best serve us all by getting Melaia well away from the house until I get rid of them."

"And how will you do that?" Trevin stepped in, slipping the dagger under his belt.

"I'll be the only one here." Gerda wrung her apron. "Go! Go! There's a back door. Use it."

Jarrod growled, but he took Livia by one arm and Melaia by the other. "I hope this works."

"I stay," said Trevin. "They may have come for me anyway. I'm sure by now they know I'm out of my cell."

"Will they take you back?" Melaia asked, but Jarrod steered her and Livia through the cookroom before she could get an answer.

"According to Livia, you believe Trevin is a good liar." Jarrod trotted them out the back door. "Maybe he can talk his way out of it."

"How far must you be from malevolents to remain hidden?" Melaia asked.

"If we're still, we can sometimes be quite near," said Livia. "And in this case, Gerda's presence will be a distraction."

"We can hide in the shed, then," said Melaia.

"Too obvious." Jarrod hesitated. "But we risk being seen if we cross the field to the woods."

Livia pointed to the upturned wagon. They dashed to it and crawled underneath. There they crouched, peering through chinks in the sideboards and listening to Bram bark. Livia and Jarrod were soon as still as stone. Melaia tried to draw a sense of calm from Jarrod's hand on her shoulder and Livia's grasp on her arm, but when the back door of the house banged open, she startled.

Gerda scurried out, followed by Fein, the younger talonmaster. The etchings on his muscled arm squirmed as he shoved her along. Bram barked and nipped at Fein's heels.

"I tell you," said Gerda, "the girl isn't here. Search the shed if you like, but you'll find no one."

"I'll do that." Fein kicked at Bram, who dodged and went to Gerda's outstretched hand.

Trevin stepped out of the house with Vort, the leather-faced talonmaster, who held Gil's dagger. "You taught me the birds," said Trevin. "I mended the wing of your best. You can believe me. I've been after the girl for a long time. Just because I traced her here before you did is no reason to take your wrath out on me."

Vort tossed Gil's dagger from one hand to the other as if weighing it. He seemed to be weighing Trevin's story as well. Clangs and crashes came from where Fein searched in the shed. Bram barked.

"You saw me through the draks, no doubt." Trevin chuckled. "From Qanreef?"

"From Redcliff," said Vort. "Dwin had been askin' about ye."

Trevin frowned. "Is he all right?"

"Lord Rejius keeps him supplied with what he needs to stay servile."

"Not gash, I hope." Trevin rubbed his left hand over his right.

"Barley beer and wine are easier to come by." Vort laughed. "Anyway, Lord Rejius sent us to Redcliff to see if ye'd cooled yer heels long enough." Vort shook the tip of the dagger at Trevin. "Turns out, ye're gone with the whole lot of 'em, and the jailer's in one of his own cells. Zastra's run as well."

Trevin laughed. "No doubt Lord Rejius will say good riddance to that."

Bram barked at Vort.

"Quiet yer dog, Gran, or we do it fer ye," said Vort.

Gerda snapped at Bram. He sat as Vort and Trevin disappeared into the shed. Gerda wrung her apron, and Bram padded to the upturned wagon, where he began sniffing.

"Begone!" whispered Livia.

"That doesn't work with Bram," said Melaia.

"I'll strangle him with my bare hands if he gives us away," said Jarrod.

Gerda called to Bram, and he bounded to her as Trevin and the talonmasters came out of the shed. Fein held a coil of rope.

"Mayhap Gran knows more'n she's lettin' on," said Vort. "Mayhap she needs help remembering. We'll show ye how it's done, Tree-vun boy." He motioned to Fein. "That rope'll go 'round Gran's neck."

The color drained from Gerda's cheeks as she stepped back, her eyes wide. "You'd not dare hang an old woman."

"Ye're right there, Gran." Vort held her while Fein slipped the rope around her neck.

Trevin leaned against a wagon wheel, an amused look on his face. Melaia couldn't tell whose side he was on.

Bram snarled, and Fein kicked the dog in the ribs. With a whine Bram retreated a few paces but crouched, glaring.

"Ever run behind a horse, Gran?" Vort pulled the rope snug. "Let's see how fast ye trot." He nodded at Fein. "Bring us yer horse."

Fein handed the end of the rope to Trevin and headed for the front yard and his horse. Trevin gave the rope a jerk, causing Gerda to stagger forward.

Melaia thumped her fist on her leg and whispered, "I can't sit by and allow—"

Jarrod squeezed her shoulder and murmured, "Gerda is expendable. You are not."

"Wait!" called Gerda. "I'll tell you. I'll tell you true. The girl was here, sure enough. She and a woman friend spent the night. But the girl got angry and left. I heard raiders nabbed her somewhere on Branch Road, east of Stillwater. The woman's gone now too. I don't know where. That's the truth of it."

"Raiders?" Vort snorted. "That'll please the high lord. He'll find her easy enough among the raiders." He turned to Trevin. "Ye think Gran's telling the truth?"

"She's told you more than she told me." Trevin toyed with the end of the rope.

Vort poked his finger at Gerda's nose. "We'll see about yer story, Gran. If ye've lied to us, we'll be back in the night, and this place'll be ashes." He turned on his heel and punched Trevin in the stomach.

Melaia gasped. Livia's grip on her tightened, as did Jarrod's. Trevin fell to the ground, fighting for breath.

"That's my mercy to ye, boy, and fair warnin' to hie yerself west and stay there," said Vort. "It's better'n what ye'll git if ye show yer face to Lord Rejius after fleein' yer cell."

Fein led his horse around the corner of the cottage, but Vort motioned him back. Within moments the talonmasters galloped toward the south road, and Bram snuffled under the edges of the wagon again.

⟡

Melaia smoothed Gerda's menthia ointment on Trevin's belly as he lay outstretched by the hearth in the common room. She told herself she was simply a healer at the moment.

He winced. "Is that supposed to make me feel better?"

"After it stops burning."

Trevin caught her hand. "And when will it stop burning, lady?" His dark eyes searched hers. "Have you ever felt something so cold it burns? That's what I feel from you. I'm sorry I deceived you. I said I would make it up to you, and I will."

"I think you have."

"Not until I get your harp back."

Melaia withdrew her hand. She wanted to warm to him, but she was galled by the ease with which he had spoken to the talonmasters. Still, they had given him reason not to rejoin Lord Rejius. She smoothed more ointment on his bruise. "The harp isn't truly mine, but I'll not stand in the way if you want to support the Angelaeon."

"I vowed my allegiance to them in the dungeon."

"Then Livia told you who I am, our mission…everything?"

"As far as I know." One eyebrow rose as he smiled. "You know, you were right. It stopped burning." He eyed her. "Melaia, I vowed myself to the Angelaeon because for the first time I saw another way. I felt hope. I felt it the moment I first saw you."

"At the overlord's villa?"

"You played the harp, and something stirred in me—a strange yearning for something pure and right and good. It seems you carry it within you, for I've felt it each time you're near. I promise, lady, I'll never deceive you again."

Melaia's face went hot red, and she looked away, cleaning ointment from her fingers. She wanted to believe him, to be able to speak freely and easily with him, to look into his eyes without suspicion. Yet the fact that she wanted it so much made her wary. It was her own self she mistrusted, her own judgment.

Bram barked in the yard, and Melaia grabbed a fire poker. Livia stepped into the room with a pry bar. Gerda snatched a kitchen knife. Melaia handed Trevin Gil's dagger, which Vort had tossed aside as he and Fein rode away that afternoon. Had they returned?

"Jarrod?" Gerda called.

Jarrod was outside, standing guard with an ax. He cracked the door and leaned in. "Gil and Pym are back."

Gil tromped inside, and Pym popped in behind him. Gil's bushy eyebrows met in a frown. "Brandishing weapons, are you now?"

Gerda ran to Gil, and soon they all sat around the table, even Trevin, who claimed he felt much better. As they shared food and drink, the day's story was told on both sides. Gerda led in the report of the unwelcome visitors. Gil told how he and Pym had found Caepio and the actors camped between Stillwater and Navia.

"Caepio's glad to lend his aid," said Gil. "He says he has a score to settle with the malevolents."

"It's on account of his brother," said Pym. "Vardamis. One of the comains that's disappeared. I met him when I was serving with Main Undrian. Vardamis was a good man, he was."

"All the high-ranking kingsmen were worthy." Jarrod nodded at Pym. "Their men-at-arms too."

Gerda refilled the mugs. Livia bound Trevin's ribs again in spite of his protests. Talk lulled as the hearth fire burned low. The order of night watch was set, and everyone trundled off to sleep.

Except for Trevin, under Gerda's orders to lie still by the fire, and Melaia, who had spent the last few days in bed. She didn't think she could sleep. Not just yet.

She didn't want Trevin to think she was so cold she burned. Besides, sitting by the fire with him reminded her of their camps at Drover's Well and Caldarius, when she was excited about the world. And Trevin. She wanted to sit with that feeling a bit longer.

She eyed Trevin, who stared into the fire. "Who are you?" she asked.

"Another question." He grinned. "I missed your questions in the dungeon."

"Truly?"

"See. There's another one."

"Do you have any answers for me tonight?"

"Who am I?" Trevin took her hand. "The plain truth is I don't know anymore."

Melaia folded her hand around the spot where his small finger had once been. He was telling the truth. She heard it in his voice.

CHAPTER 22

A yellow-pink dawn spread across the sky the next morning as Melaia and her friends said good-bye to Gil, Gerda, and Bram and rumbled south in a borrowed wagon. Both Melaia and Trevin were well hidden by the hoods of their cloaks as a precaution against spy-birds.

Pym glanced over his shoulder from his place in the driver's seat. "Jarrod, tell your strange news from Qanreef."

"Does it involve Lord Rejius?" asked Trevin.

"Some say it does," said Jarrod. "There's no wind. Not a breeze. Not a breath."

"How do the ships sail?" Trevin eyed the sky.

"They don't," said Jarrod. "The only boats that go out are those that can be rowed."

"Windweaver is keeping his distance," mused Livia. "Would you know why?"

Jarrod shrugged. "The Archae are inscrutable, Livia. You know that."

Melaia hugged her journey pack. No wind. No Windweaver. It seemed a bad omen for anyone headed toward the hawk's nest.

❧

Midafternoon, Melaia spotted Caepio waving from the roadside ahead. He directed their wagon to turn. Swaying and creaking, they bumped off the main highway onto a path that led into the woods. Caepio guided them to a clearing where his wagon stood. As Melaia and her friends disembarked, the actors called out greetings.

After a flurry of introductions, Caepio directed them to a circle of boxes and bundles that served as seats around the coals of the campfire. When everyone was arranged, except Jarrod, who paced the perimeter of the clearing, Caepio clapped his hands, and they all fell silent.

"Lords and ladies, news of our coming goes before us to Qanreef," he said. "Even now, the townspeople eagerly anticipate our arrival, for we sent news of ourselves ahead with several of the court."

"In that case my plan may not work," said Melaia. "I hoped to slip into the city with your actors unannounced."

"She's right," Jarrod said as he strode around them. "We'd be on display as soon as we reached the gates."

Caepio stepped onto a stump. "We're aware of the dire situation. But herein lies the genius of our plan: your company, Chantress, will trade places with our troupe. As we near Qanreef, you will all don masks and ride in our wagon, which I will drive. My fellow players will follow in your old rig as worthy rustics." He motioned toward the troupe, who posed in a pitiful mimicry of peasants. "Or unworthy rustics, as the case may be."

"That may get us through the city gates," said Melaia, "but how do we enter the palace?"

Caepio spread his arms wide. "Envision the scene we shall play. We enter the city announcing the coming entertainment. But before we bring the full pageant to the common folk, it will be our privilege to give a private performance for the court, who so greatly enjoyed our show at Redcliff. When the time comes, it will be you who enter the palace masked."

"We perform?" Jarrod stopped in his tracks. "That seems unwise."

"Extremely unwise. And unnecessary." Caepio tapped the spot of beard in the center of his chin. "You see, we require a crew to help us set a stage. Thus my worthy rustics. Once we're all inside the palace, my troupe will again take their position as performers. What you do at that point is up to you. Our job, as I understand it, is simply to get you within the walls."

"When do we make the journey?" asked Melaia.

"First thing in the morn," said Caepio. "If all goes well, we'll reach Qanreef by early afternoon on our second day of travel and announce our arrival with a grand procession through the city."

"You mean to invite people to watch us tramp through the city?" asked Jarrod.

"Clever, isn't it?" said Caepio. "Guards expect subversives to sneak in on the sly. You will prance in, attracting all kinds of attention, yet remain undetected."

"Clever if it's successful," said Jarrod. "A fool's wager if it's not."

ᴄᴔᴖ

As afternoon turned to evening, Melaia sat by the campfire and munched on a tart apple, watching Pym and Caepio in swordplay. Practice, Pym called it. Rehearsal, insisted Caepio.

"You mean to tell me *all* the comains have gone missing?" Pym asked Caepio. "Solivius and Brevian too?"

"Disappeared about the same time as my brother, Vardamis." Caepio drew his sword, returned it to its sheath, drew it again. "My fellows and I have traveled the kingdom hither and yon, and all I know is that the comains' shields were collected and hung in the great hall at Qanreef to honor their memory."

Pym ran a callous hand through his hair. "A sorry state of affairs, it is. A sorry state."

Trevin sat down by Melaia, holding a cup of cider in one hand and two stems of dreamweed in the other. "Livia thinks I should have something to help me sleep tonight. How much should I take?"

Melaia took the stems from him and plucked the orange berries.

Trevin raised one eyebrow. "Not as much as you gave Zastra."

"You don't want to sleep through tomorrow?" Even as Melaia teased, she saw the wisdom in holding back a few berries in case she decided to ensure that Trevin was not awake to betray them when the time came. It was the fact that Lord Rejius still held Dwin that bothered her. She had seen the worry in Trevin's eyes when the talonmaster mentioned Dwin. Since she knew she would do anything to free Hanni and the girls, she had to assume Trevin felt the same about his brother. She put all the berries but one into her waist pouch, then squeezed a single drop into Trevin's cup.

He saluted her with his cider before downing it in one long draft. "How long will it take to put me to sleep?"

Melaia remembered the night Jarrod had put dreamweed in her peal-melon. "Not long."

"Time enough for you to smear some of Gerda's ointment on me? She sent a jar of it with explicit directions that you administer the healing."

"She said that?"

"Mmm," said Trevin. "I'll get the jar. Then I'd better lie down before I fall down."

Melaia put her hands on her hips and watched Trevin trudge toward his journey pack. She shook her head and followed. She'd have to have a word with Gerda one of these days.

❧

That night Melaia lay on a mat, her cloak drawn up against a chill breeze that bore the sharp scent of smoke from the campfire. An owl cooed its deep, round night song. Hundreds of stars sailed the sky, keeping silent watch. Melaia took note of all she could see and hear and smell, then tried to clear her mind and sink into the reaches of her spirit.

She sensed the clear water blue of Livia and the rich, warm brown of Jarrod as they leaned against tree trunks nearby, talking softly. But beyond them, she sensed colors of all kinds in waves that shifted and flowed in a broad stream southward.

Jarrod rose and strode toward the campfire.

"Livia?" said Melaia. "Are the Angelaeon gathering here?"

"You've sensed them? They pass us tonight and will encircle Qanreef. But they'll remain a certain distance from the city. If they move too close, Lord Rejius will sense them and may call in more malevolents. The Angelaeon wish to avoid a battle." She stretched out on the grass near Melaia and gazed into the sky. "There are worlds upon worlds out there. Each with its own Wisdom Tree and stairway to heaven."

"Where the Angelaeon are free to come and go," mused Melaia. "Where there's no blight, no need to raid, no need to war."

"We only wish it," said Livia. "Worlds have a way of blighting themselves, stairway or no."

"Jarrod showed me the stargazers' hill at Aubendahl."

"And he told you about the beltway of stars coming into alignment?"

"He told me the stargazers say we may have a year, but no more than two, before our beltway is open to receive the stairway to heaven."

"Before that happens, the Wisdom Tree will have to be restored," said Livia.

"For the stairway's protection?" asked Melaia.

"Exactly."

Exactly, exactly, exactly, echoed the trees.

A rustle among fallen leaves on the forest floor announced the presence of a small creature scurrying home, and Melaia pulled her cloak around her tensing shoulders. She could no longer still her spirit enough to sense the angels' colors. Instead, she could think only that her chance of finding the harps and restoring the Tree in time was as remote as the most distant star.

❧

The heat of the seacoast became more oppressive the farther south the wagons traveled. Before they reached Qanreef, Caepio directed the rigs off the road and into a whispering grove of eucalpa trees, where everyone disembarked to prepare to enter the city.

Melaia placed her hand on the white flaky bark of a tree. *We die. We die. We die.* She withdrew her hand and stared up at the leafless tree. Was it truly dying? Perhaps with their guardian gone, the trees were falling to the blight.

She wove her way to Livia. "Is it true that the blight is greatest in the south?"

Livia tied a wide gold sash around her waist. "I've heard that the blight began south and east of the Dregmoors and slowly expands northwest."

"Then there's more damage here and in Qanreef than in Navia or Redcliff."

"True. The farther north, the less the land is affected by the blight. Thus far."

"Chantress," called Caepio. "Your mask."

He helped her don the face of a lioness. Pym was masked as a frog, Trevin as an eagle. Livia slipped on a smiling white face, and Jarrod wore its frowning twin.

So it was that in the early afternoon a pageant wagon full of masked players, drawn by four prancing horses, emerged from the eucalpa grove and made its way to Qanreef road. Not long afterward, a smaller wagon carrying a band of bedraggled peasants rambled out of the same grove and took to the same highway.

From the almond eyes of the lioness, Melaia watched the countryside change. Dried grasses replaced woodlands. The ground became sandy. Long-legged coastal birds tiptoed in jerky motions through marsh meadows baking in the sun, and a lone dark bird rode the currents high above.

But while Melaia stared at the surroundings, other travelers on the road stared at her and her companions. People shouted greetings. Carts that normally would have passed them trailed them instead. Caepio saluted the onlookers, sang, and quoted lines from plays. Once in a while he reminded Melaia and her friends to wave and nod and generally act like actors. Melaia found it hard to remember, for she was distracted by a growing awareness of the cordon of Angelaeon around them as well as the rising hope of finding Hanni and the girls.

In the heat of the afternoon, the pageant wagon approached the gates of the stone wall that encircled Qanreef. "Halt!" called a guard. "Unmask yourselves."

"This is my celebrated troupe of actors," said Caepio. "We travel in character, entertaining as we go."

The guard eyed them. "I've heard of your coming. But actors or no, you'll have to let us search the wagon." He motioned for two soldiers to climb in as Melaia and the others climbed out.

"We carry only our costumes and props," said Caepio. "And swords, of course. Swordplay is one of our entertainments."

"Any instruments?"

"Timbrel. Sistrum. Reed pipe. Lute."

"No harps?"

"None."

Melaia could see Caepio's jaw clenching as the guards rummaged through first one trunk, then another, just as they had when she'd spied them through Zastra's Eye.

Meanwhile, a crowd gathered. From his pouch Caepio pulled a reed pipe. As he played, the crowd pressed in. The actor-peasants clapped and cheered from their wagon, and the people began to clamor for a performance then and there.

"Back! All of you!" yelled the guard. He barked at Caepio. "Get your actors in the wagon and be on your way before you start a riot."

Melaia climbed back in. Her mask was moist, sticking to her skin. Her own breath added to the heat on her face. She wondered if there was any hope for a cool breeze.

Then they were through the gates, and for the first time she saw Qanreef and the brilliant blue Southern Sea. Melaia marveled at the splendor of the silky water stretched out in the afternoon sun like a bolt of cloth displayed at a bazaar.

The city sprawled all the way to the coast. A massive white gated palace commanded the eastern side of the city from atop a chalk bluff, which rose out of the sea like a giant hand offering the citadel to the sky.

"Alta-Qan." Trevin pointed to the castle. "The heights of Qanreef."

Melaia stared at the square towers, her mind on Hanni and the girls, who even now might be peering from the latticed windows. An urgency surged within her, tugging her straight to the palace. She had to remind herself of

Livia's counsel to temper her impulses with wisdom. Waiting was wise. She groaned. It was also agonizing.

With effort Melaia turned her eyes from the towers. From the foot of Alta-Qan to the shore, flat-roofed houses, their white paint chipped and peeling, descended in rows like great stairs. Wilted, graying ramble-rose vines webbed over their boxy walls. Beyond the buildings stood the wharves.

Jarrod had been right. There was no wind. Ships sat moored at the docks, their sails limp in the sultry heat that blanketed the city.

The actors' arrival, however, stirred the town from its stupor. Women leaned out their windows, and children tugged at their parents' arms and pointed. Men on street corners stopped their conversations and stared.

"Ladies and gents!" Caepio called. "The Pageant Players have arrived! Tell your friends! Tell your neighbors! Tell the beggars! Tell the king! The players have come to town!" He eased the wagon to a stop and turned to his masked players. "A small show just to gain a following. Anyone know a dance?"

"I'm too bowlegged," said Pym.

"I've stones for feet," mumbled Jarrod.

"The Tantelais." The eagle Trevin stood, then extended a hand to Melaia. "Lioness, do you know the dance?"

"You're still recovering from your wounds," she muttered.

"It's an easy dance," said Trevin. "I can do it if you can."

Melaia huffed. He had chosen a dance so easy that she and the girls had taught it to themselves at the temple. She had done it dozens of times.

The crowd clapped and whistled. Melaia rose, placed her right palm on Trevin's, then bowed her head toward him. He did the same toward her, and Caepio began a tune on the lute.

Melaia and Trevin walked in a circle. Their eyes met and held. Melaia was glad her mask hid her blush. They moved apart, turned, and came together again. Their fingertips touched, their palms pressed together. She concentrated on not trembling. They circled again. Dark, friendly eyes circling her heart. Steady... Steady... Bow.

She was sweaty, she was hot, but she would have danced with the eagle again at the next street corner. And the next.

Cheers splashed on them like a wave, and when the wagon rolled again, scores of people young and old followed, forming a procession that trailed them all the way to the wharf.

"With a crowd like this, news of our arrival will travel to the palace before we're halfway down the street," said Caepio.

Sweat trickled down Melaia's neck, and she wondered if there was a cool spot anywhere in this town. Then she saw a wrinkled woman with tangled, wiry gray hair clinging to a stocky merchant who was hawking jars of drink from a cart. One customer tasted the drink, but the merchant was losing his other customers to the crowd following the actors.

Melaia tugged on Trevin's sleeve. "Zastra."

"Great seas," said Trevin. "Who's she with?"

"That's Baize," said Pym. "Sells gash. I've run into him more than once in my travels."

"Zastra found him, then," said Melaia. "She has what she wants." But she didn't really, and Melaia felt truly sorry for her.

Caepio drew the pageant wagon to a stop in front of an inn with a ship painted on its sign and the words "Full Sail" carved above the door. The clamoring crowd pressed around the wagon.

"When's the next show?" called a walleyed man.

"A show won't fill yer stomach," grouched an old woman.

A thin woman craned her neck to see into the wagon. "Who can afford it?"

"Could be it's free!" called a little boy.

"Is the show free?" a girl yelled to Caepio.

"Which of the women is free?" asked a snaggle-toothed man. "That'll take my mind off my hunger."

"That *is* your hunger." A sharp-nosed woman punched his arm. He pushed her back, and she bumped another woman, who jostled a skinny boy.

"Hey! Watch it!" someone called. The crowd began elbowing each other.

"If they get any rowdier, we'll be arrested for causing a public disturbance," Caepio muttered. He stood and held up his hands. "Ladies and gentlemen, we are delighted at your attentions. We shall send a herald to announce future performances. Then come, one and all, and we'll treat you to grand entertainment."

Melaia straightened. She sensed a presence, wavering and rusty orange. She looked at the eye slits in Livia's mask. Livia nodded and motioned toward the inn.

Out of the shadows, beyond the open door, swaggered a heavyset innkeep with a closely trimmed black beard. His shirt was open halfway to his belly, showing a chest covered with curly black hair. He scowled at the crowd and mopped his brow with a cloth. But when he saw Caepio, he threw his arms wide, and a broad, toothy grin spread across his face.

"Welcome, friend!" he cried. Over his shoulder he called, "To the kettle, cook! It's Caepio at the inn now! He's brought a whole troupe with him. Lay a feast. He's likely to eat us out of lard and larder!"

"When have I done that, Paullus?" asked Caepio, laughing.

"When haven't you, now?" asked the innkeep.

As the crowd dwindled, Trevin offered Melaia a hand to help her down from the wagon. She gladly took it, wondering why it was easier to be lioness and eagle together. Why was it so hard to sort out her feelings when the masks came off?

Paullus charged a servant boy to look after the wagon and horse, then led the actors through the tavern room, where customers lolled around tables.

A bony man lifted his mug. "It's the players come to town!"

"Give us a show!" shouted a mop-haired sailor.

Paullus strutted across the room, his chest out. "They'll be doing plenty of performing soon. For now, they need a rest from this infernal heat."

That set the drinkers to muttering about the steamy weather. Meanwhile,

Paullus marched the troupe around a corner, down a stairway, and into a wide cellar.

Dim light drifted through a window high on the wall above a bench. Kegs lined one side of the room. On the other, strips of smoked meat hung from the ceiling. Jugs of oil crowded one corner. And it was relatively cool.

"At last," murmured Melaia, fanning her skirt to stir a breeze.

"Ah! This is fine, Paullus, just fine," said Caepio.

Paullus filled a mug with ale from a keg and said, "For a performer you've got bad timing, Caepio."

Melaia plopped down on a bench and pulled off her mask.

Caepio took her mask and began fanning her with it. "Don't faint on us, now." He looked back at Paullus. "Why is my timing bad?"

"All Qanreef holds its breath, waiting for the flag to change at Alta-Qan." He handed Caepio the mug.

"It's of no great consequence to us," said Jarrod. "We'll play for whoever happens to be at court."

"Your sights are set on Lord Rejius, then." Paullus held three fingers close to his hairy chest and raised his curly black eyebrows at Caepio.

Caepio made the sign of the Tree. Paullus scanned the room. Melaia held up three fingers, as did the others.

Paullus nodded. "You should know, then, that Lord Rejius's men keep an eye on me. That crowd you brought to my doorstep helped not a whit."

"Lord Rejius allows you your freedom?" asked Melaia. "Doesn't he sense your presence?"

"He knows I'm not fully committed to the Angelaeon," said Paullus. "Nor am I fully committed to his kind. The lordly Rejius is completely wary of me."

"Do you think he'll send his men here, then?" asked Melaia.

"No doubt," said Paullus. "The question is whether they'll invite you or arrest you."

CHAPTER 23

Before sunset, Paullus and Caepio were summoned to Alta-Qan. They did not return that night.

By midmorning the next day, the mood in the tavern cellar was as tense as a bowstring holding an arrow taut. Jarrod, his hair hanging over one shoulder, leaned motionless against a column beside the stairs and gazed out the high window on the opposite wall. Livia, too, sat still, her eyes closed. Trevin inspected a dagger Paullus had loaned him. Pym lugged in a jug of water.

Melaia slipped Dreia's book out of a waist pouch Caepio had given her and flipped it open to the blank pages. The first, as she expected, was still dark. The page with the swaying lines still swayed. But it was the page with the wavering shadows that she wanted, and it didn't disappoint her.

As she stared, lines sharpened, and she saw the back of a man looking out a window. A sword hung at his side. A guard, she decided. She wondered if this was another part of the room in which she had seen Hanni. Melaia exhaled slowly. Even if they made it into the palace, how would she ever locate that room?

She thumbed backward through the pages and stopped at what appeared to be a poem.

> Three from one and one from three.
> Music of the living tree.
> One sleeps in stone, one touches skies,
> One in the hands of mortals lies.
> One shall wake, one shall shake.
> Three shall light the way.

The harps. The whisper came clear and near, as if someone stood at her side. *The harps.*

Melaia looked up. Beside her, Pym splashed his face with water from a basin. A small woman with pale blue skin and frothy white hair twirled in the shower of droplets as if she were dancing in a waterfall: Seaspinner.

The harps, whispered Seaspinner, fading. *The harps.*

Melaia leaned closer and was splashed. Pym laughed and handed her a wet washcloth. She thanked him and mopped her face as she turned back to the poem.

The living tree had to be the Wisdom Tree. The music, then, was from harps made of its wood. Three harps. Was this the riddle that told where Dreia had hidden them? "One shall wake." The runes on Benasin's harp spelled *Awaken.* But awaken what? Or who?

Paullus and Caepio tromped down the stairs, their voices tense.

Melaia clapped the book shut. "What happened? Did you see Hanni? The girls?"

"The harps?" asked Livia.

"We spent the night under lock and key and saw very little," said Paullus.

"Fortunately, my actor-peasants have been spreading generous reports about the new entertainers in town," said Caepio, "so we ranked better than dungeon dwellers."

"We were held in the stewards' quarters," said Paullus. "And questioned."

"But you weren't arrested," said Trevin.

"On the contrary," said Caepio, "we were invited. We perform tomorrow."

"Then I have to reach Hanni and the girls tonight," said Melaia. "I have to warn them."

"We can't risk it," said Jarrod.

"Wait," Livia said. "We'll be pressed for time tomorrow, and we may be watched closely. We have no notion of where the harps are held. Wouldn't it be to our advantage for someone inside the palace to know our plans and stand ready to help?"

"Not at the cost of our entire mission," said Jarrod.

"The person inside would have to be trustworthy, they would," said Pym.

"Who better than Hanni and the girls?" Melaia asked.

Jarrod huffed. "And how do you propose to send a message to them? They're no doubt under guard."

"I'll go myself and find out." Melaia hungered to see Iona and Nuri and Peron to prove to herself that they were all right.

"Pardon my memory," said Jarrod, "but the last time you headed off to rescue your friends, it was a disaster."

"I'll go with her," said Trevin. "I know the palace."

"Every servant from Redcliff knows you by sight," said Jarrod. "You'd be no more hidden than an uncloaked Erielyon."

Paullus eyed Melaia. "I can get you in." He scratched his hairy chest. "I'd not go with you, understand, but I can send you with a message for my friend Cilla. I usually send a boy, but you'll do, I wager."

"Unbind your hair," said Livia. "We'll make you look as unlike yourself as possible."

"I've costumes in the trunks." Caepio rubbed his hands together eagerly. "Something like a street woman, you think?"

"Some face color?" suggested Trevin.

Melaia scowled at him. "I'm a priestess."

"Do you want to enter the palace or not?" asked Livia. "It was your notion."

Caepio headed upstairs. "I'll bring a choice of clothing."

"I don't like it," said Jarrod. "I don't like it at all."

❧

Midafternoon, Melaia arrived at Alta-Qan's side gate disguised as a tavern maid, her red brown hair loosely hanging to the waist of a plain sea green gown that fit more snugly than Melaia liked and showed more skin than she had ever dreamed of showing. The gatekeeper questioned her, but when she told him she carried a message from Paullus to Cilla, he looked her up and down, winked, and sent her in.

She followed Paullus's directions to the handmaids' quarters, a boxy white-washed building near the back wall behind the palace. There she snagged the first maid she saw. The girl's close-set eyes barely peeped over the pile of garments in her arms.

"I've come with a message for Cilla." Melaia held up a coin as Paullus had instructed.

The maid rolled her eyes. "And if it's not the busiest days he's wont to ask for her," she mumbled. "With the wedding and this, that, and the other."

"Whose wedding? When?"

"Lord Rejius, of course." The maid narrowed her eyes. "Where've you been that you've not heard? Day after the morrow. We're all of us like to be driven to madness afore it's over, with all the preparations."

"I simply bring the message," said Melaia. "Will you call for Cilla, or shall I find someone else?"

The maid eyed the coin. "Cilla, she'll be lucky if she can get free. But she can tell you with her own mouth if you want."

Melaia tucked the coin into the maid's waist sash, and off the girl waddled.

"Lord Rejius's wedding." Melaia clenched her jaw. He meant to keep his promise to return to Redcliff with Hanni as his queen. But so soon? She sighed. At least a bride would not be held in the dungeon.

Melaia turned her attention to the palace, a big box itself, three levels high. Taller towers rose at each corner. She saw few guards, but as she stilled herself, she sensed a sickly color, a dirty dun shade coiling around the guard at the postern gate. Two draks glided high above one tower, while one lone drak drifted down to the dome of the temple.

She felt the impulse to duck into the shadows, but she stood her ground, trusting her disguise to protect her from whoever might be watching. And Livia had said angels couldn't sense Nephili, so she should be safe from the malevolents. She hoped Livia was right.

A buxom woman with a head of brown curls bobbed down an outer stair-way of the palace. Melaia recognized her from Paullus's description. She wore a gown of pale rose, not as fine as that of nobility, but of higher rank than a washmaid. And Melaia sensed her as an angel, muted yellow. Very muted. No doubt she could work here because she, like Paullus, gave allegiance to neither the Angelaeon nor the malevolents.

Melaia stepped toward her. "Cilla?"

"That's me." Cilla flipped back her curls as she glanced around the yard.

"A message from Paullus," said Melaia.

"I heard. But it's a hard time for me to be leaving, and he should know that."

Melaia lowered her voice. "Paullus's message was a way to get me into the palace. I'm a priestess, and I must see Hanamel and the three girls Lord Rejius brought here."

Cilla put her hands on her broad hips. "Then Paullus *doesn't* want to see me? The dolt."

"Of course he wants to see you. He hopes I'll bring you back with me. After I see—"

Cilla took Melaia by the elbow and led her quickly up the stairway. "Three girls, you say? I've seen only two. But you may play servant and help me fit their wedding clothes. As for Lady Hanamel, we may be in luck. It's she who must give me leave to go into the city. Whether she'll let me go or not, I can't say."

Melaia wiped sweat from her forehead as she entered the palace behind Cilla. She knew better than to engage the woman in conversation, but she was frantic to know why Cilla had seen only two girls. Which two?

In a wide-windowed, sunny room where two maids toiled with needles and thread over a sheer red cloth, Cilla scooped up three soft-flowing gowns, one a deep purple and two lavender. She draped them over Melaia's arms. None were small enough to fit Peron, Melaia noticed, but she breathed more freely, for that gave her an easy explanation. Peron was too young to be part of the wedding.

At the end of the corridor stood an arched doorway, where they passed a guard, who simply nodded at them. A malevolent. Melaia sensed him as a dull stain, but she was too agitated to pick out the color. Past him lay a stairway.

They climbed three floors up and entered a chamber with two beds by a window on one side and a table beneath the window on the opposite wall, where Iona and Nuri sat threading shells onto red cord. Iona's waist-long dark hair was unbraided. Dimpled Nuri looked older, thin and solemn.

As Cilla stepped into the room, Iona glanced up, red eyed, and sighed. Nuri mumbled something but did not look up at all. Melaia wanted to toss the clothes aside and run to the girls, but the heaviness of their mood held her back.

"Your wedding clothes are sewn," Cilla chirped. "You must try them on to see if they fit properly." She took the dresses from Melaia.

Iona stared out the window, where the sea stretched to the horizon. A drak sailed past.

"It doesn't matter to me whether they fit or not," said Nuri.

"Shall I tell you a story while you try them on?" asked Melaia.

Iona and Nuri turned, their eyes wide. Then they leaped at Melaia and hugged her so tightly she thought she might smother.

"Where's Peron?" asked Melaia. "Staying with Hanni?"

Iona pulled back, a trembling hand over her mouth. Nuri clamped her arms around Iona.

Sweat ran down Melaia's back, but she felt cold. "Where's Peron?" she whispered.

"He sent her to the Dregmoors." Nuri blinked back tears. "She wouldn't stop crying, and she wouldn't do what she was told, and he sent her to the Dregmoors—"

Cilla stood open-mouthed, the gowns hugged to her bosom.

"Fiend!" Melaia paced to the far side of the room and back, her fists clenched. A drak settled on the windowsill between the beds. She snatched a shell and hurled it at the bird.

"Stop!" Nuri dashed to the window. The shell had missed, but the drak darted away.

Iona grabbed Melaia. "That was Peron."

Melaia felt the blood drain from her face. "Peron?" she whispered. Curly-haired, dancing Peron who fed the chee-dees, babied her cloth doll, told stories. The room blurred, grayed, crowded in on Melaia like a tunnel. She sank to her knees, her throat too tight to utter its swollen wail.

Iona knelt beside her. "She homes to us, Mellie. The hawkman meant it as a threat to us, but at least Peron is free to come and go."

"I've frightened her," Melaia murmured. "I've scared her away."

"She'll return," said Iona.

"We shooed her off too when we first saw her," said Nuri. "It wasn't until we noticed her hands—"

"Enough!" snapped Cilla. "This is not the ladies' gab-gathering. We'll all be draks if we're discovered." She handed Iona and Nuri their gowns. "Try these, and be quick about it. We'll return shortly to make sure of the fit." She tugged Melaia to her feet. "No time to wallow."

Melaia felt numb as she followed Cilla out of the room. But she knew Cilla was right. She would have to work around the pain.

She sniffed, squared her shoulders, and let Cilla lead her to the top room of the square tower. It was sumptuously furnished with everything a queen could want: a wide, sculpted hearth, a bed canopied in gold-trimmed red silk, ornate brass lamps, a window-sized polished steel mirror, and fresh-scented rush mats.

But none of it fit the high priestess who sat on a plain bench, gazing out the window toward the sea. Hanni's fawn brown hair was laced with tiny diamonds. A larger one graced her neck. A goldsmith displayed jewelry on a black cloth before her.

"None of them," said Hanni.

Melaia swallowed the lump in her throat. Her eyes blurred with tears.

"You've hardly looked," whined the goldsmith.

"I don't need to look to know," said Hanni.

Melaia half smiled. The high priestess hadn't changed.

"Something simple, then." The goldsmith held up a large silver disk dangling on a gold chain. "Might this one be suitable?"

Cilla put her hands on her hips. "Give her some time to think about it. Lady Hanamel may know better once she tries on her gown."

"Of course. I'll return later." The goldsmith bowed himself out of the room.

Hanni continued to stare out the window. "Must I try the gown now?"

Cilla handed the purple gown to Melaia, who carried it to Hanni. "If you try it now," said Melaia, "we might have a few moments to talk."

Hanni rose so fast that Melaia almost fell backward. "What are you doing here?" she whispered, glancing between Melaia and Cilla. Her face was pale and drawn.

Melaia wiped her eyes. "I expected a warmer greeting."

"You're not here against your will?" Hanni studied Melaia. "You look like—"

"It's to get me in here so I can help you get out," said Melaia.

"Knowing you're free has been my one comfort," said Hanni. "Please don't put yourself in danger."

"It's a mite too late for that advice," said Cilla. "I'm going to check on the girls, but I'll be back. Try on that gown." She headed downstairs.

As Hanni changed into her gown, Melaia told her about the plans to enter the palace and asked where the harps might be.

"I did see a harp once," said Hanni, "but it was moved. I've no idea where it is now." She scowled at the snug drape of the gown. "I know only that I'm to marry Lord Rejius two days from now. He thinks that by marrying me, he's hurting Benasin."

"Is he?" asked Melaia.

Hanni shot a severe look at Melaia as if they were still chantress and high priestess. Then she sighed. "Yes. Yes, he is."

"Do you know where Benasin is?"

"Somewhere in the Dregmoors."

"Then he'll be no help to us tomorrow," said Melaia. "I'll try to come for you myself. Be ready."

"I'll not endanger Iona and Nuri," said Hanni. "Already Peron—"

"I know. It's a terror. But if you can make your escape—"

Hanni gripped Melaia's arm. "Lord Rejius is immortal, Mellie. You know that, don't you?"

"Did you know Benasin is his brother? The Second-born?"

Hanni sank to the bench. "He told me the last night he was in Navia. He told me all he knew—and all he suspected. I understand your need for the harps." She took Melaia's hands in hers. "I'm sorry I chose not to teach you about angels, Mellie. I was afraid. Perhaps all of this is my fault."

"It's not your fault," said Melaia. "I know why you were afraid."

Hanni drew Melaia down to the bench beside her. "Only Benasin knows that Rejius was the 'dark angel' who overpowered me in the Durenwoods."

"The Firstborn!" Melaia's flesh crawled. "No!" She searched Hanni's eyes, expecting to see terror. But she saw only sad resignation. "At Navia," said Melaia, "the hawkman said he had unfinished business with you."

"Doubly so since Benasin befriended me. But you've more important matters to think about, for you have a far greater calling than high priestess. It's my understanding that the Firstborn will be defeated only when the Tree and its stairway are restored." She looked Melaia firmly in the eyes. "Hear me, Mellie: you must not put your duty at risk for me or the girls."

"My duty," Melaia echoed. Coming from Hanni, it sounded like a priestly mandate, as binding as a vow. She gazed out the window, squeezing Hanni's hands. Seaspinner strode toward the shore on the gentle waves of the tide. Angelaeon surrounded the city. Livia and Jarrod and Trevin waited for her back at the Full Sail. And all their hopes were bound up in Dreia's daughter. "But how can I bear to leave you and the girls with Lord Rejius?"

"You'll do what your duty requires of you," said Hanni. "We'll do what's required of us."

Cilla bobbed into the room, and Hanni walked Melaia to the door. "Cilla will finish with my gown. Go back to the girls."

"I'll see you again. I promise." Melaia kissed Hanni on the cheek, made her way back to Iona and Nuri, and told them the plans.

"A tower," said Nuri. "The harps are held in a tower, I heard."

Iona nodded. "And many here would gladly oppose Lord Rejius if they thought they could survive it. So if it comes to a fight…" She shrugged.

"We might have help if we appear to be winning," said Melaia.

Cilla bustled in and gathered up the fitted gowns. "We've no more time." She stepped to the door and glanced down the stairs.

"One more question," Melaia murmured to the girls. "Do you know who spies through Peron's eyes?"

Both girls shook their heads. Melaia wondered if it was Lord Rejius himself.

She hugged Iona and Nuri, then hurried downstairs with Cilla. After leaving the gowns with the seamstresses, they went back to the handmaids' quarters. Cilla instructed Melaia to wait for her there. Not only had Hanni granted Cilla's request to leave for the evening, but she had insisted on it, ordering her to get Melaia safely back to the Full Sail.

In late afternoon a flurry of drumbeats sounded from the rooftops. Melaia frowned. It was not yet time for the gates to close.

She stepped into the courtyard, where the servants, frozen in their steps, gazed upward. She looked up as well and watched as the white lion flag of the king was lowered. Three long blasts of a trumpet swelled the air. Then came a slow, rolling cadence of drums that grew louder and louder and stopped with a sudden pop. A flag of red emblazoned with a black hawk in flight slid up the flagpole and hung there, limp in the still air. The servants shuffled back to their tasks, and Melaia returned to Cilla's quarters.

As the room fell into shadows, Cilla scurried in. She grabbed a pack, pinched Melaia's cheeks, and fluffed her hair around her shoulders. "Follow me. And forget you're a priestess."

Melaia trailed Cilla across the courtyard. The nearer they came to the postern gate, the more Cilla swished her hips. Melaia tried it but felt she looked like a duck mincing through mud.

Once more the drums sounded, this time for the closing of the gates. Cilla stepped up to the postern guard as he swung the gate around. He smirked and left an opening barely wide enough for them to sidle through, then gave Cilla a parting pinch and a salty word of advice. Melaia was grateful the shadows hid her reddening face.

The narrow street skirted the palace walls, then descended past the boxy houses, now purple in the twilight. Two men entered the roadway ahead. Melaia halted as they approached, but Cilla darted into the arms of one of them. Melaia squinted at the other, who stepped closer. Trevin. He held out his hand.

Melaia let out her breath. "Forgive me for not recognizing you. I can't see in the dark."

"I know." Trevin took her hand and drew her close. "Would you care to make this look real? To aid in the deception, of course."

"Of course." *Deception is his gift,* a thought warned, yet his embrace was gentle, the hand holding hers warm. *Would I care to make it look real?* She cared so much it frightened her. She dared not risk it. Yet she found herself stroking his hand where he was missing his small finger.

"An injury from long ago." Trevin chuckled. "So long ago I don't remember it."

"Maybe that's for the best." Melaia leaned her head on his shoulder. To aid in the deception, she told herself. "Tell me about draks," she said.

"At a time like this?" asked Trevin. "Besides, I thought the spy-birds disgusted you."

"Who do they home to?"

She felt him tense. "Anyone they feel strongly tied to." He shuddered. "I'm trying to forget it."

"Don't," said Melaia. "I need you to teach me how to call one."

CHAPTER 24

Melaia made herself eat the bread and saltfish Paullus had laid out for breakfast. She had not slept well for thinking of Peron. Trevin said draks sometimes homed between the people they loved and the one who did the scrying, if the scry-master held a possession valued by the one who was now a drak. A ring, a sandal, even a lock of hair. *Or a doll,* thought Melaia. Still, with all Trevin knew about draks, he hadn't been able to answer her most pressing question. Could the birds be given back their human form?

As Melaia chewed on her breakfast, she eyed Trevin. The news of Peron had so shaken him last night that he had asked for dreamweed to help him sleep. Now he seemed sullen and distracted. She thought maybe he was thinking about Dwin, wondering whether his brother was now a drak.

Trevin wasn't the only one tense. Everyone seemed ill at ease as they waited for Paullus to return from escorting Cilla to Alta-Qan and for Caepio to get back from staying the night where the true actors were quartered. When footsteps sounded on the cellar stairs, they all looked up expectantly.

"If I dared, I would back out even now." Caepio trudged down the steps, puffy eyed and scowling.

Paullus came right on his heels. "You said you'd not be choosy."

"That was before," said Caepio.

"Is there a problem?" asked Livia.

"You've surely heard that the king met his end," said Caepio.

"The whole of Qanreef knows," said Livia.

"Yet the king's body is not cold before celebrations start for the crowning of King Rejius," said Caepio. "Such disrespect is outrageous!"

Pym ran his hand through his hair. "All the comains gone. Now the king. Is there to be no time of mourning?"

"Not when there's so much to celebrate," Caepio mocked, his face an angry red. "So says Lord Rejius. Tomorrow he is crowned. The next day he is wed. On the third day he journeys back to Redcliff. And it is *we* who are to begin the festivities!"

"Lord Rejius accepted only what you offered," said Jarrod.

"I admit that," said Caepio. "But wouldn't you think he could postpone his own celebration until after the traditional time of mourning?"

Trevin looked at Melaia. "I'm sorry about your father."

For a moment Melaia didn't realize Trevin was speaking to her. She frowned at him.

"I truly hoped he would recover," said Trevin. "Since I supported Lord Rejius against him, I feel I had a hand in his death."

Melaia shot a questioning look at Livia, who exchanged glances with Jarrod. Jarrod rubbed his forehead.

"King Laetham was her father?" asked Caepio.

Melaia's mind reeled from Hanni to Benasin to the aerie. The sylvans. Dreia's grave. The scriptory. King Laetham in his stupor in the curtained cart.

She felt Livia's hand on her arm. Melaia shook it off and glared at her. "You knew."

Trevin stiffened. "And you didn't?"

Livia knelt in front of Melaia. "For hundreds of years, angels have watched kings rise and fall, live and die. Restoring the Tree is of the utmost importance, no matter who is king."

"So the king is expendable." Melaia turned her glare to Jarrod.

He inclined his head. "Your task is already so great that we hoped not to burden you with worries about the king."

"And Hanni? And the girls?" Melaia clenched her fists. "Are they expendable as well?"

Trevin leaned back against the wall and stared at the ceiling. "I've complicated matters."

"Not greatly." Paullus scratched his hairy chest. "The king has died. I mean no disrespect, but doesn't that simplify your task? You'll have no qualms about ignoring the king. Get the harps. Restore the Tree. Simple."

"He's right," said Pym. "The best way to save your kingdom, Melaia, is to restore the Tree."

"My kingdom?" said Melaia.

"You're the rightful heir," said Pym.

Jarrod sighed. "*That* complicates matters."

Melaia glanced around the cellar. All eyes were on her. She bent her head into her hands, wishing she were alone with the feelings that whirled within her like a windstorm.

At last Caepio strode to the stairs. "I don't know the thoughts of angels, but I do know that I have a performance to oversee. I'll draw the wagon to the front of the inn. If anyone wants to bow out, do it now." He headed up the stairs, taking them two at a time.

"If you two angels go, I'll go as well," said Paullus. "My presence may serve to mask yours, as will Cilla's. Now that I've involved her, I'd like to see that she gets out if the tide turns against us."

The tide is already against us, thought Melaia. She looked around. When no one made a move to leave, she realized they were waiting for her. No one would overrule her will.

She took a deep breath, then slipped on her mask.

                        ⚬✤⚬

Caepio drove straight through the marketplace. People clapped and laughed, and children squealed at the sight of the masked players. Melaia waved, as did Trevin and Pym, but Livia and Jarrod, the frozen smile and the stiff frown, merely posed near Paullus so his presence might cover theirs. The closer the wagon came to Alta-Qan, the more still the angels grew. Melaia knew they were trying to sense malevolents as well as avoid being sensed themselves.

The jubilant crowd escorted them all the way to the Alta-Qan main gate, where the real actors met them, arriving as a cartload of peasants.

Caepio pointed them out and spoke to the portal guards. "These I've hired to set up our stage." The guards waved both rigs through.

At the entrance to the palace, Caepio halted the wagons and clapped his hands. "My fellow actors, the steward shall escort you to a private chamber where you'll ready yourselves and rehearse without interference. I shall join you there shortly. Remember: we must give our best today, as we shall be performing for the Honorable Lord Rejius."

"Overacting, isn't he?" Jarrod mumbled.

Caepio ordered the real actors to haul this trunk, carry that canvas, while Melaia and her silent, masked friends followed the steward into the palace and up a flight of wide stairs. There he stopped and swept his arm toward an arched doorway flanked by columns. "This is where you are to perform this afternoon. While you set up, guests will gather for drinks in the garden."

Livia and Jarrod stood beside Paullus, as still as the columns, eying the great hall. Melaia stepped into the room, which was larger than the banquet hall at Redcliff. Both the north and south walls held four tall windows, all wide open. Above the north windows, a high gallery ran the length of the hall.

Along the east wall, opposite the entrance, a dais held the king's long table and gilded chair. Melaia stared at it, trying to grasp the fact that it was her father who had sat in that chair. If events had been different, she would have sat beside him.

Behind the table six shields hung on the wall, each painted with a different image. Pym pointed to one that bore the picture of a bear. "Main Undrian's shield," he said. "The ram is Gremel's. Brevian held the rock badger. The partridge belonged to Solivius, Vardamis had the osprey, and Catellus the white stag."

Melaia nodded. The shields were a terrible reminder of the trouble plaguing the kingdom. No doubt that situation too was woven into the outcome of this day. She turned away, her task pressing like a heavy weight on her shoulders. She feared that if she thought on it too long, she might race out the door, never to return.

Two of the actors lugged a wooden platform into the hall. Another trudged in with a rolled-up drape over his shoulder. Servants moved benches and tables aside. Melaia noticed that Livia and Jarrod had slipped away. She rubbed her moist palms on her skirt and wondered if Caepio and his troupe could truly hold Lord Rejius's attention long enough for the rest of them to find the harps. Might she also have time to find the king, simply to look at the man she should have called father?

She pulled Caepio aside. "Do you know who has seen the king dead?"

"The steward for one. He said he saw the body laid out."

"Where?"

"That he didn't say." Caepio wagged a finger at one of the servants and called out, "That bench will have to be moved. Set the framework closer to the wall."

Melaia followed Trevin and Pym down the corridor to where Paullus stood outside a door. He waved them into the chamber where the actors' costume trunks had been placed. Jarrod and Livia were already there, quiet and still, standing sentry at the two open windows, which let in only thick, storm-brewing air. Paullus remained in the corridor and closed the door behind Melaia. Everyone pulled off their masks.

"Flustrations! That's all I want of being an actor." Pym wrinkled his nose as if trying to get his face back into shape.

Melaia slipped the book out of her waist pouch and held it close, hoping its warm thrum would calm her.

"This feels too easy," said Livia. "I expected to sense a stronger presence of malevolents."

Jarrod stroked his chin. "The talonmasters are here. That's two."

"One malevolent guards Hanni and the girls," said Melaia. "One guarded the postern gate yesterday."

"Four, then," said Jarrod. "And I would guess one or two more. Probably bodyguards for the Firstborn, stationed near his quarters."

"A confrontation would outweigh the two of us, then," said Livia. "Three if Paullus fights."

"Four, counting Cilla," said Melaia.

"That depends on whose side Paullus and Cilla join," said Jarrod. "If they join at all."

The room fell into an uneasy silence. Melaia opened Dreia's book and turned to the blank pages. Again, one was dark. The other formed swaying streaks. But on the third, the shadows soon settled into lines, some vertical, some horizontal, beyond which stood a window like those in Hanni's room, showing a rooftop beyond. And no one in sight.

"I visited Dreia here. It's where I met my husband." Livia strode to the door. "I know my way around the palace. I'll visit the servants' quarters and find a gossip willing to say where the harps are being held."

Melaia closed the book. "One is in a tower room, I think."

"But which tower?" asked Livia. "I hesitate to send us out in all directions. It's much too risky. Wait for my return."

"And if you don't return?" Melaia tucked the book back into her waist pouch.

"I'll take Paullus to mask my color," said Livia. "I'll return." She slipped out the door.

"Paullus," muttered Jarrod. "I'm not comforted."

Melaia paced to the window and gazed out at the courtyard. The two wagons that had brought them were nowhere to be seen. Instead, guests dressed in fine tunics and loose, flowing gowns approached the castle. Some were accompanied by servants stirring the air with wide feathered fans. Melaia felt certain that some of them would meet Lord Rejius for the first time today, and she wondered if they were as unsuspecting as she had been upon entering the palace at Redcliff.

She turned to Jarrod, who sat near the door, his arms folded, his eyes closed. Listening, she supposed. "Jarrod," she said, "you were a priest at Redcliff."

His eyes eased open as if his mind was returning from far away. "Priest at court. Yes."

"Where would a king's body be laid out?" she asked.

His eyes opened fully, and his eyebrows arched. "Are you simply curious?"

"He's my father. I want to see him before he's buried."

"A foolish distraction," said Jarrod.

"I never saw my mother. I just want to get near enough to see—"

"He wasn't worthy of your mother." Jarrod rose, his face red. "She wanted a child with human will and chose her mate from the highest rank, but he was never worthy of her. I tried to warn her, guard her, protect her, but she wouldn't listen. She was always running ahead of wisdom. So are you. But you're twice as hard to protect, for I can't sense you."

Melaia's eyes widened. "You loved Dreia."

"Of course I loved her. She was my mother." Jarrod's face was hard with pain.

"Your mother?" Melaia gaped at him. "Then *you* are Dreia's child. Can't you restore the Tree? Why should I be involved?"

"I don't make the kyparis wood leaf out—evidently because I have no mortal, human blood. Believe me, my father and mother both explained in no uncertain terms that my father was immortal long before I was born."

Melaia frowned. "I don't understand."

"My father is Benasin. His blood runs with the life of the Tree."

Melaia covered her mouth and stared. Jarrod was her half brother. Dreia's son. And Benasin's. Of course. She saw it now. He was very much like Benasin.

Jarrod's face softened into a sad smile. "I told you Dreia ran ahead of wisdom."

Melaia dropped her hand. "Why didn't you tell me before?"

"And risk your hatred?"

"Why would I hate you?"

"Because I should have protected Dreia. I was at Aubendahl when Dreia came to get the harp she had hidden there. I was completing a volume of the histories and asked her to wait for three days so I could accompany her. Three short days. But she set out without my knowledge. She was always leaving and going who knows where. I was so exasperated with her that I stayed at Aubendahl, debating whether I should follow her or not. Then the Erielyon came for help. By the time I got there…" He turned away. "I failed her. I failed you."

"You don't know that," said Melaia. "You could have been killed with the rest of them."

"I should have been."

Melaia hardly breathed, wondering what to do next.

Trevin's touch on her arm startled her. "To answer your earlier question," he said, "a king would normally be laid out in the courtyard or in the great hall for viewing and mourning. Right, Pym?"

"Normally," said Pym. "But this turn of events is far from normal."

"Maybe my father is on a bier in the temple." She headed for the door.

Jarrod blocked her way. "We have no time."

"I agree." Melaia ducked around him. "We have no time to argue. And frankly, I'm glad you weren't killed. I could use your protection right now." She opened the door and sauntered out, smiling over her shoulder. "Brothers can be such a thorn in the foot."

Jarrod grumbled, but he led her a roundabout way, skirting the presence of malevolents, to the temple. They found easy access, for the priest was attending the celebration, but the king's body was not on a bier in the altar room.

"Surely they've not buried him already," said Melaia. "Where are the stairs to the catacombs?"

Jarrod turned and swept down the corridor. Melaia followed on his heels. After a few moments he yanked her aside. "A guard," he whispered.

"Malevolent?"

"No, but his presence means there's something to guard, doesn't it?" He shook a finger in her face. "I'll do the talking, and you'll be quick about paying your respects." He bowed his head, folded his hands, and stepped solemnly down the hall, chanting softly all the way. Melaia followed. When he reached the glum guard, Jarrod bowed. His priestly hair slipped over his shoulder. "This chantress has been sent to administer death rites since your priest is occupied with more urgent matters."

The guard jerked his thumb toward the stairs, and Melaia descended behind Jarrod into a burial chamber much like the one at Redcliff. On the far wall, beyond biers and death masks, one torch burned in a bracket. Below it, on a stone slab, lay the body of the king. At his feet a coffin-sized recess in the wall gaped hungrily. A broad stone stood nearby for sealing the tomb.

"Go ahead," said Jarrod. "Take your look. I'll keep the guard occupied."

As Melaia made her way to the king, she heard Jarrod trudge up the stairs. "Ah, what a shame," he said to the guard. "Such a terrible, wasting disease that caused the king's death."

Melaia tiptoed toward the king's body, then froze. His spirit floated like a fog around him, wavering and struggling in a horrible death dance. But he was alive. Her father was alive.

She stroked his face. High cheekbones. Long, narrow nose. Dark hair, graying on top and on his beard. He didn't appear as old as he had seemed from a distance.

Melaia touched her own face, felt her cheekbones and nose. Then she pressed her hand to his chest. His heartbeat was almost imperceptible. Hers pounded in her ears: *do something, do something, do something.* But what would bring back a king so nearly dead?

Her fingers tingled. "A harp," she whispered. "A harp with runes that say *awaken.*" *One shall wake.* She cupped his face in her hands. "I'll return...,

Father." The word sounded foreign on her tongue, but when she said it, she sensed something in his spirit shift. Was it recognition? Hope? Or regret?

Melaia had to will herself not to dash up the stairs. Halfway to the top, she was glad she had slowed, for she spied the guard's flask lying on the top step. The guard's back was toward her, Jarrod holding him in conversation, so she plucked two orange berries from her waist pouch, crept up, and squeezed dreamweed juice into the flask.

She completed her climb and nodded to Jarrod and the guard. "He'll rest in peace now," she said.

"I pray that the king's disease is not a plague," Jarrod told the guard. "May the Most High have mercy on your health, sir."

The guard took up his flask, saluted Jarrod, and swilled his drink.

CHAPTER 25

Melaia didn't feel free to speak until Jarrod had brought her safely back to their quarters. Even then, she had to hold her tongue, for she was besieged by Caepio and the other actors eagerly asking how they looked with this hat or that sash, this cloak or that pendant.

At last she pulled away and wormed through the fuss to Jarrod. But Pym held his attention.

"Livia and Paullus haven't returned, and it's almost time for the performance." Pym ran his hand through his hair. "What now?"

"I say we spread out and search for the harps on our own," said Trevin.

"The guard at the catacombs spoke of a protective spell," said Jarrod.

"Listen!" hissed Melaia. "King Laetham is alive."

Jarrod rubbed his forehead. "Are you certain?"

A knock sounded at the door. "Lord Rejius calls for entertainment," said the steward.

"Then let the performance begin!" Caepio strode out of the room with a flourish. His actors danced out behind him.

At the same moment Livia swept in, her cheeks flushed. "We have friends here," she said. "Throughout the city, people blame the poor sailing weather on Lord Rejius, for the wind stopped blowing the day he arrived."

"What about the harps?" asked Jarrod.

"Only one has been seen," said Livia. "In the northeast tower."

"The king is not dead." Melaia grabbed Livia's arm. "I saw him myself."

"How did you—" Livia eyed Jarrod.

"She was determined to go without me."

"He'll be buried alive if we don't save him," said Melaia.

"We must have the harps," said Jarrod. "With or without the king."

"With or without the king?" snapped Melaia. "With or without Hanni and the girls? Is that all that matters to you—saving *your* people? What about mine?"

Trevin cleared his throat. "You should know that I intend to get my brother, Dwin, out of Qanreef."

Livia pressed her fingers to the bridge of her nose. "Most High, help us!"

"I can wake the king with the harp. I'm sure of it." Melaia paced to the window. The courtyard was almost deserted now. Only a few servants scurried across, intent on their tasks.

"Harps first then," said Jarrod. "But neither Livia nor I can get to the harp."

"Paullus could go with one of us," offered Livia.

Jarrod shook his head. "Paullus distracts malevolents. He doesn't blind them. The northeast tower is on the far side of the palace from us. If we're discovered, we compromise the entire mission."

"I'll go," said Melaia. "I'll meet you in the catacombs with the harp. Livia, can you find Hanni?"

"I was able to send word to her." Livia checked the dagger beneath her cloak. "By now she'll be seated beside Lord Rejius in the great hall. The girls too, if I'm not mistaken."

Melaia nodded, but her throat tightened. Would she truly have to leave Hanni and the girls behind? She hoped Cilla could get them out somehow, but it was a thin hope. "Can we have the wagons waiting for us outside the catacombs?" she asked.

"I'll see to it," said Pym.

"Well and good," said Livia, "but I don't want Melaia going alone to the tower."

"I'll go." Trevin looked at Melaia. "My vow was to see the harp returned."

"But Dwin…," said Melaia.

"No doubt Dwin is in the great hall supporting Lord Rejius at the moment," said Trevin. "I'll help you get the harps and see you to the temple. But I'll not ride away with you. Perhaps Dwin and I can join you later."

Melaia took a deep breath and nodded, wondering if she would ever see Trevin again. But as Cilla had said, there was no time to wallow. "One more thing." She glanced at each of them. "Don't tell the king I'm his daughter."

"Why?" asked Livia.

"Because it will change everything." She blushed as her eyes met Trevin's. She quickly looked away. "I can't see myself on a throne."

"No promises," said Jarrod. "We don't even know if the king is still alive."

Melaia scowled at him, then turned to Trevin. "Show me to the tower."

As they slipped into the corridor, Livia pulled Melaia close. "If you can't reach the harp, come straight to the temple. We'll decide what to do from there."

Livia, Jarrod, and Pym stole away in one direction, and Melaia followed Trevin in the other. They slipped downstairs to the storerooms, crossed under the great hall, climbed back up to the main floor, and entered a narrow corridor. Halfway down on the left stood an arched doorway. "Through that arch and up the stairway," said Trevin. "We're almost there."

They picked up their pace and were nearing the doorway when a young guard with dark, curly hair strode out of a passageway beyond. He paused for only a moment before he drew his sword and cried, "Halt!"

"Dwin!" Trevin linked his arm in Melaia's and strode forward. Under his breath he said, "When we get to the stairs, go up. I'll divert Dwin."

"I said halt!" commanded Dwin, heading toward them.

"Lucky I found you," Trevin called, picking up his pace. Melaia matched his stride, her heart racing.

"No one is to be in this hallway," snarled Dwin. "Not even you. Don't force my hand."

The archway was only a few steps ahead. Trevin broke into a trot and gently shoved Melaia through the door as he passed.

Melaia entered a blanket of thick darkness and total quiet. She froze, straining her senses for something, anything. She couldn't even hear Trevin and Dwin, only a few feet behind her, to know whether they were talking or fighting. All she heard was her own heartbeat thudding in her ears. It was if she had been swallowed into nothingness. She choked back a frantic cry.

For a fleeting moment she thought of turning back, but a needle-sharp fear pricked her. What if Trevin had closed the door behind her? Was Dwin even now congratulating him for trapping the chantress? She shook off the thought. Told herself to calm down. Breathe deep.

Then she noticed a warm, woodsy scent drifting around her, like the smell of Wodehall. And though she could see nothing, her foot met the first stair. She began to climb. One step, two, she felt her way up. Tentatively she reached out to touch the wall. Smooth, polished, but not marble. Wood. She stroked it. The stone stairwell had been paneled. In kyparis wood?

On the fifth step a stinging stench filled her nose and made her eyes water. With one hand she covered her lips against the bitterness that welled in her mouth. She pressed her other hand against the wall for balance, stepping up where she thought a step must be. So palpable was the darkness, she felt as if she were slogging through odorous sap, ascending the inside of a tree, its walls closing in on her the higher she climbed. She wondered if she should turn around.

Shhhould shhhee? Shhhould shhhee? came the echo.

Then she felt sap oozing around her ankles, rising rapidly from below, blocking her retreat. It engulfed her feet like quicksand, and panic choked her. She ran up the stairs. But there were no stairs. The ooze seeped over her ankles, lapped at her calves. She lunged for the wall but found nothing. The sap bore her higher even as it sucked her in up to her waist. She fought at the void as it swirled around her shoulders and crept up, up, and over her head. She gulped for air.

"You can't have me," she yelled. Her words dissolved in a cacophony of sounds throbbing around her. The screams of the Erielyon in the temple yard, the cries of Peron, the rasping breath of the gash-drunk, the screech of draks, the cough of Zastra, the shattering of her Eye, the sough of the trees. *Shameful. Shameful. Stupid. Save ussssss!*

"Stop!" Melaia yelled, covering her ears. But the sounds were inside her head, memories pulsing louder and louder, and above it all came Trevin's voice, hissing, *You're wise not to trust me.* Melaia fought and ran, and ran and fought, faster and faster through a thick nothing that pressed closer and closer in an ever-narrowing tunnel. Up and up and up.

And then, in a breath, it was gone.

The muck beneath her became stone, rising step by step. Melaia stood for a moment, panting, sweating, her hand on the kyparis wall. *Shhhh,* it said. *Shhhh.*

The darkness had lightened. At the top of the stairs, through an open door she saw a large cage that held a harp.

Melaia flew up the stairs and into the room, knelt beside the cage, and read the familiar runes. *Dedroumakei.* "Awaken!" She ran her hand along the bars, searching for a latch. Then, out of the corner of her eye, she saw a movement. She turned and gasped.

Across the room, in a guard's tunic, sword at his side, stood Yareth, the moon-pale son of Navia's overlord. He had gained some muscle, but his eyes still held the same sly menace.

Melaia rose slowly, feeling as if she had been knifed in the gut. Trevin had betrayed her after all. Had led her to the trap and sent her up alone.

In his uneven gait Yareth strutted across the aerie, past empty cages, until he blocked the doorway.

"You." Melaia tried to gather her wits. "Your father sent you to Lord Rejius after all. And this is the high position you were promised? Guarding a tower?"

"For *King* Rejius," said Yareth. "I'm sure to be promoted soon. You see, I've trapped a thief. Interesting that it's you." He eased toward Melaia, and she stepped back. "As it turns out," he said, "King Rejius has been waiting for you."

Melaia backed up to the cage, and Yareth pressed close, his hot breath seething over her face as he reached around her and flicked the latch open. Then he ran his hand up her back and clutched her braid at the nape of her neck. She shoved at his chest, but he was immovable.

"Too bad," he breathed into her ear. "Too bad I have to throw you to the hawk."

A sharp pain wrenched Melaia's neck as Yareth twisted her down and pushed her into the cage. He snapped the latch closed.

She rubbed the back of her neck. At least she had the harp, she thought bitterly. And the book was still in her waist pouch. Dreia's harp. Dreia's book. Dreia's daughter.

Dreia's fate?

She hugged the harp and felt it pulsing in time with her own rapid heartbeat.

Yareth leaned out a wide window and shouted to someone below. The cage began to rise and sway on a rope that held it to a long wooden arm. Melaia scrambled to balance herself and the harp as Yareth pushed the wooden arm and the cage swung to the window. One more push, and it cleared the ledge.

Melaia gasped. The cage hung high above the courtyard where only the day before she had stood looking up. Her stomach felt as if it were in her throat. Yareth smacked the wooden arm and the cage lurched wildly. Melaia let go of the harp and clutched the bars. Below, two guards let their end of the rope play out. The cage lowered toward the ground.

Melaia looked to the horizon. A small drak circled just beyond the city wall. She felt helpless, shriveled inside. She had risked, and she had lost, and she was no good to anyone now. She only hoped her friends could get away, but even that seemed an impossibility. If Trevin had trapped her, he had trapped them as well.

When the cage thudded to the ground, the guards thrust poles through the top and carried it like a low-slung litter across the yard. Melaia wondered if Trevin was watching, and a tingle of defiance ran through her.

She would not let him get the best of her. She would not shrivel. She would not cower. She was a priestess and Dreia's daughter, and her last breath would not be a whimper but a shout.

CHAPTER 26

Melaia was hauled up the front steps of the palace and past two expressionless guards. Servants blinked with surprise, then quickly looked away as her handlers took her cage straight to the door of the great hall, where the two talonmasters stood. They, too, eyed the cage but promptly turned their attention back to the grand gathering inside. Melaia supposed they were intent on quelling opposition and knew it would not come from a caged harper.

But there was no opposition. The only movement in the great hall came from Lord Rejius, who strutted across the room, reading aloud from a scroll. Even the colorful pennants, which should have been fluttering gaily in a sea breeze, hung motionless from the lower edge of the gallery.

Melaia sat in her cage outside the door, flanked by the talonmasters and her guards, scanning what she could see of the hall. Hanni, finely dressed but unsmiling, sat at the head table. Iona and Nuri sat stiffly to her left. Cilla stood against the wall behind Hanni. The guard behind the girls was the malevolent Melaia had seen guarding their stairway. She tried to discern the presence of other malevolents, but her spirit was far from still and would not focus.

From the serving door, Dwin drifted in, eying the room through his rakish curls. Melaia expected to see Trevin follow. When he didn't, her hands balled into fists. He was no doubt rounding up Livia, Jarrod, and Pym. She vowed that if she survived, she would never look at another apricot again.

Lord Rejius smugly strode to the center of the hall, a sheer scarlet train flowing from his shoulders. Around his neck hung a gold chain inset with rubies, regally displayed against the layered black feathers of his sleek sleeveless tunic. Jeweled rings adorned his bony fingers.

He held the scroll high, and his voice rang out. "You have heard the reading of the document. Lord Beker, trusted advisor, oversees Redcliff in our absence. He encouraged me to assume the kingship in these dark days. To that end he has witnessed this declaration, which appoints me monarch of Camrithia upon the death of King Laetham. So be it."

As sporadic applause echoed through the hall, Caepio began a lofty melody on his lute, and his players joined him with reed pipe, sistrum, and timbrel. Lord Rejius made his way to the lords and ladies seated at tables along the north wall. Each of them rose in turn, kissed his hand, and bowed. Paullus was first and made no protest. Melaia's heart sank. Cilla would follow his lead.

Caepio bobbed to his music. When he looked toward the doorway where Melaia sat caged, his puffy eyes widened. She glanced away. She dared not act as if she knew him for fear of drawing him and his players into trouble. Nothing had gone as planned, and it was her fault. All she could do now was avoid feeding anyone else to the hawkman.

As Caepio drew his song to a close, he called out, "I now introduce to you the finest harper in the land: chantress of Navia!" He swept his arm toward the entrance.

Melaia stared at him, her eyebrows raised in a question. Surely he could see that the plan had melted. He didn't know Livia, Jarrod, and Pym were probably in a cell by now, with Trevin holding the keys, but he could certainly see her plight. What was he trying to do?

Lord Rejius turned to her, his mouth twisted into an amused smirk. He motioned to the guards, who carried her barred litter to the center of the great hall to the fanfare of reed pipe and lute. Melaia tensed like a cornered rabbit.

Lord Rejius strode toward the cage and unlatched it. "The little chantress, is it?" he murmured. "I'm pleased you took my bait and came for the harp. Did you enjoy the enchantments of the kyparis stairway? Designed just for Dreia's child. No one else could have survived it."

A chill snaked through Melaia, and she held tight to the harp. Rejius's fingers curled around her wrist, and though she cringed at his touch, he drew her out of the cage. Maybe this was what Caepio intended, wagering that his announcement would set her free from the cage. She'd felt safer with bars separating her from the hawkman.

"Ah, but you are a pleasant surprise," Lord Rejius crooned in her ear. "I expected Dreia's son." He held her at arm's length and eyed her. "Shall we see how enchanted the chantress is?" He turned to his guests, and the cage was removed and set near the hall's entrance.

"It's well-known that I have two mage-harps," Rejius said. "I've had my harper bring one of them for this occasion." He strutted around Melaia. "A powerful prize for a powerful ruler who will build a powerful kingdom and reward his followers well! Entertain us now, Chantress."

"Not until you release the priestesses." Melaia set her jaw and hugged the harp, glaring into his unblinking gold eyes. Her stomach knotted. She felt as if she were back in Navia, defying him at the temple. But this time they had an audience, and she doubted he would want to begin his reign by strangling a chantress in public. Or would he? She braced herself.

A fierce look of vengeance flitted across Lord Rejius's face. Then his smug smile returned, and he rubbed his hands together as if preparing to taste a delicacy. "My harper suggests that I release my personal priestesses to dance." He waved his hand toward Hanni and the girls. "Come, come. Dance for us while my harper plays."

Iona turned white as the moon. Nuri's mouth fell open. They both glanced at Hanni, who shook her head, stern faced. The entire room sweated.

"Perhaps another day." Lord Rejius laughed, moving behind Melaia. He placed his taloned hands on her shoulders. She tried to breathe normally. "I'll release the younger two. As draks," he hissed. "And you will be their food. If you don't obey me. Play. Now." He pressed her down, his talons pricking her shoulders through her gown.

Melaia winced and sank to the floor, wondering how far she would go to get the priestesses released. Would she hand over the book? The Angelaeon? Promise him the third harp when she found it? How could she blame Trevin for returning to Lord Rejius for Dwin's sake if she was willing to do *anything* to save Iona and Nuri?

She shoved the thought aside and settled the harp, which had grown several leaves at its base, in her lap. She closed her eyes in an effort to compose herself. The pulse of the harp met her like a faithful friend, and she realized her fingers were hungry for its strings, her heart thirsty for its voice. She began plucking a song about friends, one that Peron had always liked. She played with all the feeling she could, as a tribute to Peron.

Halfway through the song, Melaia became aware of a fresh breath of wind ruffling her hair. She glanced up, her fingers still dancing on the strings. The pennants hanging from the gallery swayed in the breeze. "Windweaver?" she murmured, grasping at a breath of hope.

"Behold the power of my mage-harp!" crowed Lord Rejius. "Even the wind is at my command!"

Melaia clenched her teeth, glared at him, and intensified her song. Notes showered the air like the spray of a fountain. Guests rose and elbowed each other to get to a place where they could stand in the breeze. Only two guests, a steely-eyed man and a sharp-nosed woman, remained at the side table, one at each end. As they rose, Melaia caught a faint sense of their colors, oily brown and a blood-streaked gray. Malevolents. They placed their hands on the hilts of their daggers.

Then Pym entered the hall from the serving door and stood beside Dwin. Melaia's heart jumped. How was Pym free? Why would he stand beside Dwin? What about Livia and Jarrod? Before she could sort it out, Jarrod and Trevin appeared, supporting King Laetham between them.

Melaia stared, her fingers slowing on the strings. Trevin? He hadn't betrayed her? He hadn't! And the king was alive!

Relief and joy and hope flooded through her like the fresh air through the windows. She began to play a wild tune of welcome to spring. It was autumn, she knew, but she felt like spring. A spring that would wake the king.

Pym leaped onto the table and thrust his sword into the air. "King Lae-tham lives!" he shouted. "The king is here! Long live King Laetham!"

The guests gaped, gasped, pointed. A wave of murmurs swept the hall. The king was pale and still in a stupor, but he was definitely alive. Livia swept in behind him, her dagger drawn. Hanni and the girls rose.

"This is not your king." Lord Rejius forced a laugh. "The king is dead. I saw his body with my own eyes." He pointed a sharp-nailed finger at King Laetham. "This man is an impostor."

The king cocked his head, blinked his eyes, parted his lips. Jarrod held a goblet for him, and he sipped some wine. A stiff wind stirred the king's hair. He raised his hands to his temples and tried to speak, but his eyes stared straight ahead as if he were blind.

Melaia poured herself into the music. To wake the king.

Lord Rejius whirled, his hawk eyes fixed on Melaia, his smile gone. "It's the harp," he seethed. In two strides he was grabbing her wrists, yanking her hands away from the harp, and twisting her arms behind her.

Trevin drew a dagger. Caepio and the actors snatched swords from among their props as Pym leaped down from the table with his blade. In response, the malevolents slid out their swords. The talonmasters blocked the entrance, while guests and servants retreated toward the walls. Wind whipped the pennants, and everyone waited for an advantage.

Melaia seized the silence. "Here's the impostor," she yelled to the guests. "Lord Rejius tried to murder your king."

A taloned hand clapped over her mouth, and the hawkman dragged her toward the gallery stairs, leaving the harp standing silent in the center of the hall. All the anger stuffed inside Melaia for weeks past came flaming back. The Firstborn was the betrayer. She tried to wrench out of his grip. He was the destroyer. She kicked at his shins. Once for Peron. Once for Iona. Once for Nuri.

He shook her until her teeth rattled. "I'm done with you," he growled in her ear.

Trevin sprinted toward them from the dais, Caepio from the stage. But the two malevolents at the guest table darted out and blocked their way as Lord Rejius tugged Melaia up the gallery stairs.

She fought him at every step, but his grip was like iron, and by the time they were in the gallery, she was limp and panting. He walked her to the edge, where the pennants flapped in the gusting wind. There he held her like a trophy.

Pain throbbed in her arms, her legs, her neck, her back. But the sharpest pain was the grief that sliced through her as she resigned herself to the fact that the Firstborn would never let her leave the great hall alive. Which meant she couldn't wake the king with the harp. She'd never know what would happen to Iona and Nuri and Hanni, and she'd never know what might have come of her friendship with Trevin.

She bowed her head, and Lord Rejius removed his hand from her mouth. "Say farewell to your friends," he hissed.

In the hall below there was a movement, slow and deliberate. Melaia blinked to clear the teary blur from her eyes and saw Livia strolling halfway down the opposite wall, holding her thin cloak closed against the wind that streamed through the north windows and swept out the south. Her gaze was locked on the hawkman like a cat eying a mouse. The entire hall was poised, a wave about to break, except for the king, who stood as rigid as stone, unseeing, unhearing. Melaia swallowed hard.

Lord Rejius leaned her over the gallery edge. Her knees felt as weak as water. She glanced at her friends one last time, then turned her eyes to the king, remembering her pledge not to go out with a whimper but a shout.

"Father!" she yelled.

The king's body jerked. Jarrod steadied him as his gaze drifted toward Melaia. His arms reached out.

Lord Rejius crowed. "The king is your father? You want him?" Keeping an unearthly hold on Melaia's right wrist, he pushed her over the edge.

She screamed. Her heart throbbed in her throat and pain knifed through her arm as he dangled her high above the floor of the hall. With her free hand, she grabbed desperately toward the gallery, the pennants, even the hawkman.

A small drak dived through the window and shot like an arrow toward Lord Rejius. He swatted at it with one hand, then screeched at the king. "You want your daughter? Take her."

The grip on her wrist relaxed, and Melaia plummeted toward the floor of the great hall. She clutched at empty air, the breath stolen from her lungs, and tumbled into a white presence that swept her upward. She gasped and found herself clinging to Livia as her broad white wings rode the wind, circled the great hall, and descended toward the harp.

And the wave broke.

Lord Rejius shouted commands. Two draks swooped in through the windows, and Pym and the actors rushed to block the talonmasters. Fein, the etched one, tossed Paullus a sword. He caught it, whirled around, and in one stroke slashed through Fein's torso. Livia ran Vort through as he turned from cutting down two of the actors.

Cilla pulled a knife from her bodice and opened the neck of the guard behind Hanni. The high priestess grabbed the girls and ducked under the head table. Dwin positioned himself over them, while Jarrod left the king with Cilla and dashed to where Trevin and Caepio held off the remaining malevolents. Paullus shot to their side as the small drak darted back to harry the hawkman. Livia took to the air to deflect the large draks.

And Melaia played. Her right wrist throbbed, and pain shot into her fingers, but she forced herself to pluck the strings. Amid the shouts and crashes and screams and blood, she played. One more tune before they all died here, every last one of them.

Then she noticed the king staring at her with life in his eyes. With Cilla's aid he began to walk toward her.

A giddy, lightheaded laugh bubbled in Melaia. She thought she was surely as crazed as Zastra, but her heart still beat. The harp still thrummed. She was alive. Her father was alive. Trevin had not betrayed her. She laughed.

A charge of thunderlight struck the harp, which deflected the blazing bolt, shattering it into sparks and jolting Melaia to her senses. As she blinked away the glare, she realized the king was near now, and she wondered if she dared stop the music.

Then she glimpsed Lord Rejius raising both his arms. They shriveled and twisted sideways as black feathers spread across his skin. His face contorted, a beak emerged, his gold eyes glared like live coals in charred wood. For a moment the hawk balanced on the edge of the gallery as the horrified onlookers stood stunned. Then with a deafening screech, he shot from the ledge, razor talons extended, a gold-eyed stare locked onto the king.

Melaia leaped to her feet. As the hawk grabbed for the king, she swung the harp with all her might. The blow sent the bird tumbling to the floor. Melaia dived on top of the hawk and pressed the harp down across its chest and angled head. Down, down, down.

A hiss spewed into the air, smoke curled up, a singed stench roiled around Melaia, and she was engulfed in the hot fumes of Lord Rejius's spirit as it left the hawk's body. It writhed around her like a vine, constricting tighter and tighter.

Unable to move, Melaia felt her body sink, heavy as stone. She couldn't draw a breath. Her eyesight dimmed, and sounds blurred. With weighted hands she groped for her pouch and wrapped her fingers around Dreia's wooden book.

A hot pulse shot through her like flames racing across a dry branch. Her spirit surged with new strength, and she sensed the alarm of the Firstborn at the power of the Tree. For a moment they grappled, each spirit locked in the other's grip, breath of angel against Firstborn immortal, the Tree their bond. Melaia could feel the hawkman's fear, but instead of fighting, she calmed her spirit and allowed the Tree's force to flow through her. At last the Firstborn's spirit released its choke hold and whirled away.

Melaia lay panting on top of the harp and a pile of feathers. As her eyesight cleared, she saw a large tattered drak fly out a south window, bearing the spirit of the Firstborn on its back. A second drak lay dead on the floor nearby, while a third, smaller one sat on Melaia's arm, preening herself.

Iona scooped up the small drak, and Nuri stroked it while Hanni helped Melaia rise. Bedraggled actors, servants, and guests surveyed the damage, tended their wounds, and took deep breaths of the fresh breeze that gusted in from the sea.

Melaia stared at the distorted body of the hawk beneath the harp. She would have the body burned. Every bit of it. But she knew it would make no difference. Rejius was immortal, and, like Benasin, he would have even his ashen body back.

"Melaia?"

She didn't recognize the hoarse voice, but as she looked up, the people around her parted and bowed.

"Melaia." King Laetham steadied himself with a hand on Jarrod's shoulder.

Melaia dropped to her knees. "My king."

CHAPTER 27

Melaia shifted from foot to foot, eying the great wooden door of King Laetham's private apartment. Last evening when the king approached her in the crowd, it had felt so natural. He had beamed at her, and she had smiled back, and they had watched the rush of activity around the great hall. The king had spoken few words, for the exertion of walking and speaking for the first time in months had drained him. Melaia, too, had found herself exhausted, so they had parted for the night.

But this morning before breakfast, the king had called for Melaia, which had set a flurry of tasks in motion. Now here she stood, wearing a new silk gown. She exhaled slowly as Hanni adjusted her sash. Visiting the king in his apartment didn't feel as natural. Already she missed the breakfast of barley bread broken with friends around a morning fire.

She rubbed the bandage around her right wrist, which still ached from the hawkman's grip. "I can't do this, Hanni."

"Of course you can."

"He's the king."

"He's your father. Very much human. He just happens to wear a crown."

"What do I say?"

"That, Mellie, is something only you will know."

"Can't you go with me?"

Hanni put her hands on her hips and scowled. "You are a priestess. Daughter of Dreia. You carry authority with you. Remember, he loved Dreia."

"Did he? Then why—"

The door lumbered open, and Hanni stepped back, leaving Melaia feeling small and alone and vulnerable. But she recognized the blond-bearded man who bowed to her, his twisted left hand at his chest. She had last seen him in the dungeon at Redcliff. She felt the impulse to bow to him in return. In her estimation he certainly deserved it, but the bow was reserved for the king. Such was the world of cumbersome formality.

She stood tall and nodded. "Lord Beker."

As Lord Beker rose from his bow, the smile in his eyes told her he recognized her as one of those who had set him free. "Your father will receive you now," he said.

Melaia took a deep breath and allowed Lord Beker to usher her inside. The sitting room was high ceilinged, its windows letting in a fresh sea breeze with the morning light. On the walls hung shields, round, square, oval, and tricornered, of leather, wood, copper, and gold. Beside a thick-legged table stood a generously padded chair, and in the chair sat the frail king, his eyes lively, obviously enjoying her awe. He held out his hands. She clasped them as she bowed.

When she rose, he grinned at her. He pointed to the shields. "You see the past." He gazed into her eyes. "I see the future."

Lord Beker directed a servant carrying a stark wooden chair to set it at an angle to the king's. He said, "We'll have a more comfortable chair made for you, my lady. For now, perhaps this will do."

Melaia sat down as Lord Beker retired. She hadn't wanted to be in this position, but in one afternoon everything had turned on its head. She folded her hands. Her palms were clammy.

"My father was the last in a long line of warrior kings who collected the shields of those they conquered," said King Laetham. "Even tribes who bargained for peace without war sent shields as part of the price. These shields now remind me that we are a kingdom of peace. I am no warrior, and I wish to have no enemies. My entire purpose is to rule in peace and prosperity."

Melaia found herself fascinated with the king as he talked. His demeanor was regal, even though his thinness accentuated his high cheekbones and narrow nose, giving him a gaunt look. His beard and full, dark hair, sprinkled with gray, were newly trimmed. She could see why her mother had found him handsome, but she found his words baffling. Was he under the impression that he had no enemies?

"That is my story," he concluded. "The simple story of a simple, single-minded man." He paused and studied Melaia. "I've done all the talking. Surely you have something to say. I perceive you as a very brave woman."

Melaia felt her face redden. "I must confess that I'm a bit overwhelmed. I learned only yesterday that you're my father."

"As I learned only yesterday that you're my daughter. So perhaps we can be overwhelmed together." He leaned over and gingerly took her bandaged hand. "I learned all I could about you last night."

Melaia raised her eyebrows. "So you're sure I'm Dreia's daughter?"

"I'm sure. You have her eyes."

"So I've been told." Melaia felt the pulse of his hand on hers and tried to frame her next words respectfully. She cleared her throat. "Would you be willing to tell me about my mother?"

The king set her hand back on her lap and smiled sadly. "I think your mother has overwhelmed us both." He sank back into his chair. "I suppose it's my turn to confess. I've been a fool, and I've paid the price." He motioned to a servant who stood nearby.

The man took up two silver pitchers, one in each hand. Into each of two goblets, he poured wine and citrus water, the two streams mingling as they flowed into the cups.

When the king had his goblet and Melaia hers, he waved the servant out of the room. Although they were now alone, the king spoke in a low voice. Melaia sipped the tangy wine and leaned forward to hear him.

"I was young when I became king. I married an island princess to seal a peace treaty with the southern isles. But she was very young and very homesick and couldn't seem to carry a child all the way to birth. She died trying to give me an heir, and I was grieved. For many years, in spite of counsel otherwise, I remained unmarried. Then came Dreia. You might say she wooed me out of my melancholy."

Indeed she did, thought Melaia. Dreia had chosen well. Melaia could see it: a handsome man, strong, well schooled, with resources at his disposal, guards and comains at his beck and call.

"I enjoyed Dreia. She was the colorful, creative, energetic partner to my staid, stubborn, retreating nature. I clung to her, annoyed that she seemed so flighty. But the more I held to her, the more restless she became. She took extended trips into the countryside when, as queen, she should have sat beside me on the throne. It angered me."

"Maybe it was her disposition," said Melaia, hoping King Laetham would affirm that Dreia was Angelaeon. "Maybe she found her inspiration in the wide, free world of nature rather than in the confined walls of the city."

"That was the cause of the trouble. Exactly." He swirled his wine, staring into it as intently as Zastra had gazed into her oil-water. "Rumors began to circulate that Dreia journeyed hither and yon to meet a lover. Lady Zastra claimed she had seen them together. So when Dreia told me she was with child, I refused to believe the child was mine. Lady Zastra confirmed my suspicions, so I banished Dreia. I missed her so much I turned to strong drink. Not this watered stuff." He saluted Melaia with his goblet.

After a moment Melaia said, "I've been told Dreia was the angel guardian of the Wisdom Tree."

The king snorted. "Is that story still going around? Part of her creative imagining. She was a good storyteller. Some people truly believed the tale."

"Did Zastra—"

"A schemer, that woman. Wormed her way to the top. Zastra and her daughter Tahn took it upon themselves to soothe me in my distress. I was a fool not to stop them, but I was disinterested in everything. How patiently they wove their web. 'A king must have an heir. A king must have an heir. A king must have an heir,' they droned. They were as relentless as water dripping on stone. Eventually I married Tahn. Eventually I got her with child. Meantime, Zastra brought a new physician to court, one who claimed to have a healing potion for the melancholy that often besets me."

"Rejius."

"You know of him? Of course." He gazed at her bandaged wrist. "It turns out his healing potion not only numbed my melancholy; it also numbed my mind. Privately, Tahn was against Rejius and said so. She advised me to send him away. I was awaiting Lord Beker's return from a journey, to get his advice on the matter, when Tahn was trapped in a fire in one of our outbuildings. She died with our unborn child."

"I'm sorry," whispered Melaia, appalled at the pain her father had suffered.

"Lord Beker exploded, to put it mildly. He's a friend from my childhood, a wise and soft-spoken man, but he yelled at me for the first time. Accused me of destroying my heirs and the future of Camrithia. 'Dreia was faithful,' he shouted. 'Her child was yours.' He wanted me to search for the child—for you—but it was too late. I was too numb." He set his cup on the table. "The rest you know better than I. But I was a fool." He slid out of his chair and dropped to his knees before Melaia. "I don't deserve you."

She gasped. Surely this was not proper. "Your Majesty... Sire... My Lord..."

He looked her in the eye. "Father. I want to be the father I should have been. If you'll have me."

Melaia blinked at him. If she would have him? Here was her chance to back out, but looking at his hopeful, beseeching face, she couldn't do it. Besides, she had already confessed to being his daughter in front of witnesses in the great hall. She had made her decision then.

Emotions swirled in her heart like wine and citrus water. Holding her goblet in her left hand, she took the king's hands with her right, although it pained her wrist. She stood, raising him to his feet.

He took her goblet and set it beside his, then turned to her, his eyebrows raised.

"Father," she said and smiled. She would worry about the rest of the world later. Right now, the word was joy on her tongue. "Father."

He laughed, warm, soft, and strong. Then she was in his arms, and he was stroking her hair. "Can we make up for the lost time?" he asked.

"We can try," she said.

"We can try," he echoed. "We can try."

And try they did. Bereft of his physician, King Laetham rapidly regained his strength. Within the week he arranged for Melaia's coronation and gave her the queen's apartment at the palace. Every day he took Melaia out in his carriage and showed her the sights of Qanreef. She had seen much of it already but didn't say so, for she enjoyed his delight in showing her his favorite city. She suspected he was also proving to the people that he was alive and well and that their future was secure.

But while the king's face reflected joy and hope, Lord Beker's revealed concern. Melaia watched the advisor nudge her father toward serious discussions about the state of affairs in Camrithia. "After the coronation," the king would say. Or, "Give me some time to heal."

Melaia concluded that her father was a stubborn man. Delightful but stubborn. She wondered if he might say the same of her someday, for though he was her father, Dreia was her mother, and she had no intention of abandoning her task of restoring the Tree.

⌐✦¬

On coronation day Melaia gazed out the south tower window at Seaspinner's misty form, which danced for a moment on the crest of a breaking wave. Ships coursed their way to the open sea, their sails billowing in the wind.

"Let me unwrap your bandage before I go," said Livia. "I want to know that I leave you healed." She sat beside the north window with her feathered white wings peeking in a curve over her shoulders. She had come to say farewell while Hanni and the girls dressed in the room downstairs.

Melaia examined her wrapped wrist as she trudged across the room.

"Is there anything you want to discuss before I go?" asked Livia.

"One thing I've wondered: why didn't the Firstborn take the harps long ago? Why now?"

"At first he wasn't aware that the harps existed."

"How did he find out?" Melaia held out her wrist.

Livia gently unbound it. "Probably through Benasin. The Second-born has loved Dreia since he first met her at the Tree. They kept up with each other."

Melaia laughed. "Enough to have a child. Jarrod."

"But they had to stay on the run, because Rejius was constantly hounding Benasin." Livia felt Melaia's wrist. "Healed." She folded her arms.

"Why would Benasin tell the Firstborn about the harps?"

"Do you think Lord Rejius is above torturing his own brother for information?"

Melaia rubbed her wrist. "Is the Firstborn's daughter like him?"

"Stalia. She was a skillful warrior. Fought in the angel wars. I hear she's fierce, but that's all I know. She lives in the Dregmoors. I imagine the Firstborn keeps her under his thumb."

"So somehow the Firstborn made Benasin tell him about the harps, but he didn't learn where the harps were hidden."

"I don't think Benasin knew. Dreia hid them very well, just as she hid you. There's still one harp that no one has found. Isn't it interesting? All the harps stayed hidden until you were of age. I assume that was Dreia's plan."

"So Lord Rejius has one harp, which he stole from Dreia. And I have one. And there's one more hidden somewhere. I have a great deal of work to do before we can unite them."

"Then you *do* intend to carry on."

"Of course." Melaia flexed her hand. "But can't you stay to help?"

"I've already overstayed," said Livia. "By the law of the earthbound Erielyon, when we commit to serve someone, we restrict the use of our wings to saving life or returning home. Once we've flown, we must then go home. Such a law protects our race. I broke the rule after I flew to Navia to help Pym protect Hanni and her priestesses, but I had little choice then. Now I'm not needed."

"But you are. I don't know my next steps. How do I find two more kyparis harps and restore the Tree while learning to oversee a court and a kingdom as my father expects me to do?"

"Melaia." Livia looked her firmly in the eye. "You know more than you think. Trust yourself to do what's right. I promise you'll have a great deal of help." Livia hoisted herself onto the window ledge and drew her knees to her chest. For a moment she gazed out, fully framed by the window. Then she looked at Melaia and smiled. "Until we meet again, may the wind blow your way."

As Livia leaped out, her wings spread, and she rose into the air.

Melaia felt her own heart pulsing to Livia's wingbeats as she headed north, rising higher and higher, getting smaller and smaller, until she was out of sight. And free.

Melaia sat on the ledge and stared after her, feeling empty. Tiny and tired and empty.

"I thought Livia was helping you get ready." Hanni stepped into the room, wearing her gold-trimmed, priestly blue cloak.

"Livia had to go home."

"Before your coronation?"

"The law of the Erielyon."

"Ah." Hanni smoothed her hair back. "I came to tell you it's time. Your father is waiting."

Melaia squared her shoulders, took up her harp, and went with Hanni to the girls' room. They greeted her, twirling in the gowns they would have worn at Hanni's wedding. Hanni had agreed to allow them to wear the soft-flowing gowns this once.

A drak skittered up from a bench to the windowsill.

"Stay close, Peron," said Melaia. "I promise you'll get to wear a gown at least once before Hanni cloaks you in blue again." But her voice cracked on the last words. She had no idea whether Peron would ever be whole again.

As Peron fluttered out, Melaia led Hanni and the girls downstairs. Pym met them at the bottom step. One of his arms was in a sling, but he wore a new sword, presented to him by the king for his valor.

"Charms and chantments, ladies! You all look comely this day." He blushed. "Not that you haven't looked comely before, you understand, but—" He unsettled his hair with his fingers.

The girls giggled. Melaia laughed. "You look quite noble yourself," she said as he stepped into his bandy-legged stride beside her.

Together they descended the broad front staircase and strolled out into the sunshine. Melaia was amazed by the crowd in the courtyard. Tables of food and drink lined the perimeter of the grounds, and everyone was in a festive mood. As soon as they noticed Melaia, a cheer went up. It was like a grand hug, and it grew louder as she approached the raised platform, where banners flapped in the breeze.

King Laetham rose from his gilded throne to receive her. He wore a purple robe with a necklace of linked golden medallions, each inset with an amethyst. A gold crown graced his dark, gray-tipped hair. The warm, natural color had returned to his face, and although he was still thin, his movements were strong and steady, as was his gaze.

Melaia took her place beside her father. The crowd grew silent, and he addressed them. "As you know, my daughter found me and brought me back to life. She is to be an advisor to me now and will inherit the throne when the time comes."

Melaia's insides twisted, but she told herself that "when the time came," she would worry about the throne.

"I hereby give her all the rights, privileges, and responsibilities of her position," said the king. "And you will give her the allegiance, respect, and service she deserves."

Lord Beker stepped onto the platform holding a velvet bag from which the king withdrew a circlet of gold. He motioned for Melaia to sit. As he placed the crown on her head, the cheering began anew.

From the steps of the palace, Caepio struck up a lively song on his lute. He had lost two of his actors to a talonmaster in the great hall but had already found two others to take their places.

Pym approached, carrying a bowl brimming with apricots. "I'm to tell you it's a gift."

"Our thanks," said the king.

Melaia reached for one, but the king drew back her hand. "Patience," he said.

A pinch-faced man, the king's taster, took an apricot and nibbled on it.

Melaia spotted Trevin sitting on the steps to the palace, his shoulder bandaged. During the fight in the great hall, a large drak had chased a small one, swift on her tail. Trevin had stepped between the draks to protect Peron and had taken the talons of the large drak in his shoulder. The wound would heal, but it would take some time.

"Safe," said the taster, holding the bowl out to Melaia.

She picked a plump fruit and bit into it. When she looked back at Trevin, he smiled. She saluted him with the apricot. Absolved forevermore.

She wondered if the gap between the ranks of kingsman and princess was an impassable gulf. Did having royal blood mean that some dreams were destined to remain unfulfilled forever? Would she truly be free only in her heart?

The king cleared his throat. "Did Trevin tell you I asked him to train as a comain?"

Melaia blushed. Were her thoughts about Trevin that obvious? "Did he agree?"

"On one condition. He wants Pym to be his armsman." The king laughed. "When Undrian returns, they'll have to fight over who gets Pym's services. By then maybe Trevin will be a match for Undrian." He clasped her hand. "You've inherited your mother's giftings. I can tell. Now that you're at my side, I'm confident the blight will lift."

Melaia smiled as best she could. Now was not the time to tell him that in order to defeat the blight, she had to restore the Tree. She wondered if he would allow her to leave to search for the harps. Perhaps not now. Maybe in time. But how much time did she have? How long would it be before Lord Rejius found the third harp himself?

Yet it did seem as if the blight had been dispelled, if only for a day. People milled around, ate, laughed, danced. Paullus, with Cilla's help, filled mugs of foaming ale from enormous kegs. Gil and Gerda served honeyed cakes. Hanni, Iona, and Jarrod conversed as they strolled toward the tables of food, and Dwin tried to teach Nuri a new dance. Melaia purposed to keep an eye on Dwin. Trevin said his brother had renounced Lord Rejius, but Dwin would have to prove himself, just as his brother had.

A young woman approached the platform, the fresh breeze tossing her golden red hair and rippling the light cloak she wore around her broad shoulders. She looked familiar, but Melaia couldn't place her.

The young woman inclined her head. "I'm Serai," she said. "My mother asked me to give this to you." She held out a white feather.

Melaia took the feather and stared at the young woman whose green-flecked eyes held a direct gaze. "Livia?"

"My mother."

"Then you're Sergai's twin."

"I am," said Serai. "I wanted to serve the lady my brother gave his life for." Melaia's throat tightened.

"Mother said to tell you she would be honored if you would allow it." Serai's eyebrows arched expectantly.

Melaia held the feather to her heart. "I'm the one who would be honored."

Serai grinned, made her way onto the platform, and gracefully knelt beside Melaia.

The wind gusted and shook the dry, bare branches of the ramble-rose vines that webbed the courtyard walls. The presence of angels was strong, but somewhere beyond the Angelaeon coiled the taint of malevolents.

Melaia fingered the white feather and turned her face to the wind. High above, riding the currents, was a lone small drak.

An excerpt from

ANGELAEON CIRCLE
BOOK TWO

EYE
OF THE
SWORD

Coming in spring 2012

As Trevin stepped into the seedy tavern at Drywell, his hand instinctively slid toward his dagger. Not that he was daft enough to challenge the three well-muscled strangers who had cornered his younger brother. Nor did Dwin look as if he wanted to be rescued. He laughed like a madman, his dark curls matted to his forehead, his hands around a mug. One of the three men pushed another mug his way.

A stringy-haired tavern maid sidled up to Trevin. He shook his head and watched her swish away. Maybe he was the mad one, tracking Dwin to Drywell when he should be at Redcliff preparing for the banquet being given in his honor. He fought the urge to throttle his little brother.

Melaia's name blurted from Dwin's mouth. His shoulders bounced as he chuckled.

"Dwin!" barked Trevin, striding to the table. His brother spewed barley beer, guffawing as if "Dwin" were the funniest name he had ever heard.

The three strangers eyed Trevin with expressions ranging from amusement to disdain. They appeared to be his age, maybe a few years older. One had a crooked nose. Another was wiry with a scar across his temple. The third wore a close-cut beard, dark as charred wood. A crimson band spanned his forehead and disappeared beneath wavy locks.

At first Trevin thought they might be malevolent angels, but he sensed no aura, pure or impure. By their appearance they were Dregmoorian. Raiders and refugees entered Camrithia from the Dregmoors these days, but the men sitting with Dwin fit neither description. They were too richly dressed. Merchants? Or spies passing themselves off as merchants?

Dwin saluted Trevin with his mug. "My eshteemed brother," he slurred.

Trevin deliberately moved his hand away from his dagger. "Let's go, Dwin."

"I was just getting shhtarted." Dwin grinned.

"It's time you finished," said Trevin.

"I believe the young man wishes to stay," said the Dregmoorian with wavy hair. His eyes were as black as stag beetles. "Join us." He signaled to the tavern maid. "More beer!"

Trevin was tempted. The midsummer day was warm, he was sweaty, and the stone-walled tavern was cool. Drink was at hand. But he didn't want to drink with Dregmoorians. Besides, he hoped to get to the great hall early and perhaps spend some time with Melaia before the banquet started. He relished the thought of seeing her dressed in her royal best. Even in her priestess's garb, she was beautiful, but seeing her in a gown stole his breath and rushed his pulse.

Trevin started for the door. "Let's go, Dwin."

Dwin stood, wobbling. The three Dregmoorians smugly rose to let him out. If they were spies, Trevin could only guess what information they had floated out of Dwin, who would tell anything to keep the drink coming and the air jovial.

Dwin swayed toward Trevin. "I musht show you the gash pits. Gash spits. Pits spits." He doubled over in laughter. "Gashpitspits."

"Show me, then." Trevin offered a hand to his brother, who shook it off and weaved toward the door. Benches scraped back up to the table behind him.

"Gash pits. Spits," murmured Dwin, stepping outside. He squinted in the bright afternoon light, then pointed to a path leading through the woods. "That way."

"Show me the pits another time," said Trevin. "Where's your mount?" He eyed the tethered horses that stood beside his borrowed roan. The three finely groomed and blanketed mounts no doubt belonged to the Dregmoorians.

"Follow me." Dwin wobbled down the path.

"Your mount?"

"At the gash pits. They stink. You'll see." He giggled. "No, you'll smell." He pinched his nose and weaved ahead.

Trevin followed to a clearing, barren except for Dwin's gray donkey, Persephone, and the dry well from which the village took its name. He frowned at the well. Steam writhed out of it, along with a burbling sound.

"Obviously no longer dry," he muttered.

"You think the town'll change its name?" asked Dwin. "Mistwell. Fogwell. Hellwell." He chortled.

Trevin peered over the crumbling rim of rock. At the bottom of the shaft, a dun-colored muck belched bubbles of hot vapor, its stench not unlike eggs gone to rot.

"You're right," he murmured. "It's gash." The stuff was touted as a drink to restore youth, but it was dangerous. He had seen gash-drunks, youthful but foggy eyed and dull minded, dying from their addiction.

"Over here." Dwin crouched beyond the well. Muck oozed from a rift, and steam curled into the air.

"Looks like the Under-Realm is vomiting its own bile," said Trevin.

Already a greenish hue, Dwin turned away and lost his stomachful of beer.

Trevin shook his head in disgust and knelt to examine the rift, which was about as wide as his thumb. Its length he couldn't judge, for it snaked into the woods east of the clearing.

"It's a landgash, Dwin. Lord Beker sent a dispatch about them, but I thought landgashes were closer to the Dregmoors. The blight must be growing worse." Killing crops and parching rivers, the blight that had started in the Dregmoors was slowly creeping across Camrithia. Stinking rifts would not help matters.

Hoofbeats sounded behind them. Trevin rose. Dwin turned, lost his balance, and sat hard on his rump.

The three Dregmoorians reined their mounts to a halt four paces away, followed by a tan wolf-dog with one black leg and gray eyes.

At the edge of the clearing, Dwin's donkey backed into the shadows, pulling her tethering rope taut, her ears laid back.

The man with wavy hair and the crimson band across his forehead, clearly their leader, nodded at Dwin. "You said you're a friend of the court and can get us into Redcliff. Or was that a child's boast?"

"It doesn't always pay to listen to my brother," said Trevin.

"It could pay today." The man rattled a coin purse at his belt. "We're looking for a forerunner. Someone to ease the way."

"You're best advised to go back to where you came from," said Trevin.

The man with the crooked nose studied the tip of his dagger. "I fancy your tongue as a souvenir, comely boy." He turned to their leader. "What do you think, Varic? We could add *that* to our gifts for Redcliff."

"Not today, Hesel." Varic laughed. "I wish to impress the princess, and I hear Camrithian ladies turn their heads at the sight of blood."

Trevin clenched his jaw. Why did this reptile wish to impress Melaia?

"Let's try again." Varic eyed Dwin and fingered the free end of his waist sash, a fine silver mesh. "You promised to introduce us to Redcliff. Do you mean to go back on your word?"

Dwin rose, pale.

Trevin folded his arms. "What's your business at Redcliff?"

"Are you the gatekeeper?" asked Varic. "The constable?"

"He's a dung digger." The wiry one wrinkled his nose. "Can't you smell him?"

"Ah, Fornian, always a good judge of character." Varic grinned at Trevin. "Ever tried gash?" He tossed a gourd ladle at Trevin's feet. "Drink some. It's free."

Gash merchants, Trevin thought as he picked up the gourd. No doubt they had an eye on the profit to be made from newfound rifts and a tavern nearby. He turned the gourd around in his hands, admiring the delicate black designs etched into it. "If you and your friends drink gash, you've less wit than your dog."

Varic narrowed his eyes and pointed to the ladle. "Drink up."

"We always let guests go first." Trevin tossed the gourd back to Varic.

Obviously startled by the gourd's return, Varic was slow to the catch. It struck his knuckles with a loud crack. "Scum," he snarled.

The wolf-dog bared his teeth. Hesel and Fornian dismounted and drew their daggers.

Trevin tensed. He had expected Varic to catch the ladle and respond to the sarcasm with a few choice words of his own. He shot Dwin a glare, warning him to keep quiet. Dwin's tongue could be sharper than his own. As long as the daggers were not aimed his direction or Dwin's, the threats were self-puffery. Let the bullies strut and swagger, and then they'd be on their way.

Trevin drew his own blade but kept the tip up, unmenacing, warily watching the Dregmoorians' movements.

"A cripple's grip," Hesel crowed. "The dung digger is missing a finger."

Varic rubbed his knuckles, his stare boring into Trevin. "Which one?"

"Little one."

"He can handle a dagger better than you," Dwin barked.

Trevin groaned inwardly. Out of the corner of his eye, he saw Fornian edge closer to Dwin. Trevin hoped his brother had his knife with him—and that he was sober enough to use it.

"What's your name, dung digger?" Varic leaned forward in his saddle, studying Trevin. "Where do you come from? How did you lose your finger?"

Trevin glared. "You tell me your business, and I may tell you mine."

"My business?" Varic gave a sharp laugh. "We hear your king is short of royal defenders—comains, I believe you call them—so we've come to help clean up the Camrithian countryside. I think we'll start by giving a couple of dung diggers a much-needed bath. Nice and warm. In gash. Off with your sandals, boys."

Trevin seethed. Now twenty-one, he had lost his boyhood long ago. Daggers, swords, fists—one on one he could take this reptile. His muscles burned with coiled energy. He locked eyes with Hesel, who pointed his dagger at Trevin's feet.

"I'll have your sandals, boy," said Hesel.

Trevin raised his dagger. "And I'll have your crooked nose."

Each eased into a fighter's stance, assessing the other. Trevin knew he had the advantage of height and reach, but Hesel was all muscle and would be a goring bull if he found an opening. Fornian's dagger was a concern as well. Trevin glanced at Dwin, who was clutching his knife but unsteady on his feet.

Swift as a snake, Hesel struck, slashing toward Trevin's face and growling, "*Your* nose, lowlife."

Trevin ducked and cut toward Hesel's shins.

Hesel dodged, and their daggers met with a clang.

Back and forth they attacked and parried, Trevin trying to prevent Hesel from slipping in close enough to lunge at him. At the same time, he was trying to keep track of Fornian and Dwin, who were circling warily but had not engaged.

Trevin evaded a cut and struck back, scoring Hesel's left arm. Hesel lashed out in retaliation. As Trevin jumped back, he saw Dwin twist away from Fornian, throwing the wiry man off balance.

Fornian stumbled, Varic whistled, and the wolf-dog charged Dwin.

Trevin swerved from Hesel and dived in front of his brother.

At Varic's sharp command the dog froze, his fangs a handbreadth from Trevin's wrist. Fornian bounded up and knocked away Dwin's knife. Hesel grabbed Trevin's dagger.

"You want into Redcliff, I'll get you in," said Dwin.

"You will not," Trevin huffed.

The dog growled.

"Get up!" snapped Varic.

Trevin edged away from the dog and stood, panting.

Hesel pointed his dagger at Trevin's feet. "I'll have your sandals."

Trevin removed his sandals. At least Hesel wasn't demanding his nose.

"Tunics too," ordered Varic as the wolf-dog ambled back to his side.

"I can't get you into Redcliff if I look like a beggar," said Dwin.

"Keep your tunic then," said Varic. "You'll get us in."

"Not as long as I have a say in it," said Trevin.

Dwin clenched his jaw and glowered at him.

At sword point Trevin and Dwin stripped to their leggings.

"Now into the well," said Varic.

"You're mad," said Trevin as Hesel prodded him toward the steaming pit.

"Salaciously sane," said Varic. "In fact, I feel like doing you a favor. You lack balance. It's the missing finger. Make his hands match, Hesel. A small finger is just the token I need to impress a certain lady."

As Hesel came toward him, Trevin grabbed his wrist and knocked his dagger hand on the ragged edge of the well. As the blade tumbled into the darkness, Trevin hooked his leg behind the man's knees. The brawny Dregmoorian hit the ground, and Trevin laid into him, fast and furious. Hesel was strong, but Trevin was enraged. He punched and pummeled, twisted and turned until he had Hesel pinned.

Varic applauded. Trevin looked up to see the wolf-dog crouched, poised to leap at him, and Fornian holding his dagger at Dwin's throat.

"I would recruit you for my guard, dung digger," said Varic, "but you have more courage than common sense. One word from me, my dog is on you, and your brother will be something the country folk will gawk at for years to come." He stroked his mesh sash. "But I'll be fair. You release my man, and I release your brother."

Trevin slowly loosed his grip on Hesel and stood, his back to the well, watching Fornian. He wanted to tell Dwin to take the blasted devils to Redcliff and be done with their bullying, but the oath he would take on the morrow loomed over him. A comain pledged to defend king and kingdom dared not provide a way for no-goods like these to enter the royal city.

Hesel rose, wiping his bloody mouth. But Fornian kept his dagger at Dwin's throat.

Trevin flexed his fists and growled, "Release my brother."

"Now!" commanded Varic. The wolf-dog shot toward Trevin.

Fangs rushing him, the well at his back, Trevin didn't hesitate. Before the dog could leap, Trevin grabbed the sharp, crumbling ledge of the well and hurdled over it, hoping to find the inner wall with the balls of his feet. He heard the mongrel claw at the ledge, and he lowered himself, grabbing at chinks in the stone, trying to hug the wall, but it was slick with slime. Before he could gain a hold, he slid within an arm's length of the bubbling ooze.

Trevin heard Varic's whistle and Dwin's strained voice talking fast. He wedged his feet and hands into the widest cracks he could find and felt his way around until he straddled the well, bracing himself to take the full force of Dwin's weight. His eyes stung from the steam, and he swallowed to keep from retching at the stench.

Hesel peered down, one eye swollen. "How long can you hold on, dung digger?"

Dirt and rocks, leaves and sticks showered down. Trevin turned his head, closed his eyes, and clenched his teeth. Moments later hoofbeats faded into the woods.

Trevin listened for Dwin, then called to him. No answer. He shook the dirt and twigs from his hair and studied the shaft above him. He had scaled walls before, but with hooks, never barehanded. The crevices that pocked the sides of the well might serve as handholds if they were not too slick. He reached up and grabbed at a protruding rock with his right hand.

As the rock touched the place where his small finger was missing, a mist descended over his mind. He blinked back the image of a cloaked figure. His terror-dream. Never had he fallen into his dream in the daytime. Gripping the rock, he fought back the image, ignored the flashing pain in his hand, swallowed the screams.

A stinging sensation on his feet brought him fully back to the danger of his situation. Hot muck spat on him with each thick belch of gash below.

"Climb," Trevin muttered to himself. "Climb or boil."

About the Author

Karyn Henley grew up on myths, fairy tales, and spiritual stories and began writing because she loved to read. She is now an award-winning author with more than one hundred titles to her credit, including books for children, parents, and teachers, as well as CDs and DVDs of original music. She received an MFA from Vermont College of Fine Arts in writing for children and young adults and has traveled worldwide as an educational speaker and children's entertainer. She lives in Nashville, Tennessee, with her husband, a jazz drummer. Visit her at www.breathofangel.com.